# TWISTED

A Gay Erotic Thriller

Joey Jameson

www.chancespress.com

Twisted: A Gay Erotic Thriller

Copyright © 2014 by Joey Jameson

Published by Chances Press, LLC

www.chancespress.com

ISBN: **978-0692262931**

# Preface

"I think Hadley really likes you," I said, my eyes shying away from his penetrating stare.

"I think I like *you* better," Kyle replied.

When I looked up and finally met his face I got a flash of his blinding white teeth. The look on his face made me smile despite my attempts to hold it in.

"What's the problem anyway?" he teased through a shit-eating grin, "Do I need your brother's permission to date you, for some reason?"

"Just be careful."

He swallowed hard at the sudden change of my tone.

"What do you mean?"

"Just, be careful not to hurt him. Hadley can be a bit...strange when he's hurt."

I turned my back to Kyle as a dark cloud drifted overhead causing the sun to run fleetingly away.

"Hey, come here a sec," he coaxed, extending an arm to stop me.

The touch of his hand on my skin made me halt in my tracks straight away.

"I gotta go Kyle, just remember what I said." I took a deep breath pulled my arm free of his grasp.

"What? You're going? But-"

"Be careful," I repeated from over my shoulder, "You don't wanna make him angry."

# 1989

"Now this is just going to feel a little bit cold," the doctor warned as he smeared the cool clear gel over her bump.

As if on cue, she flinched as he made contact with her engulfed belly.

"Oh god," she muttered as her eyes immediately shot to the screen just off to the left.

"You alright, hunny?" her husband asked as he clutched her right hand in his.

She gave a small nod as both their glances focused on the distorted images on the small screen.

The doctor spread the film over the exposed abdomen and began to run the transducer gently across.

"Ok, let's have a little look."

There was silence in the room for a few moments as all eyes stared unmoving at the screen. No one even breathed as they tried desperately to make out some signs of life on the machine. The doctor moved the wand from one side of the belly to the other then back again before pausing in the center.

Both sets of eyes moved from the screen and settled in on the doctors. He squinted hard as he studied the monitor for a moment. All three were still as seconds passed by achingly slowly.

"Doctor?" her husband asked, "Is everything alright?"

The doctor broke his trance-like stare and looked from the woman to the man. A slight smile broke out on his face as he exhaled quietly through his nose.

"Mrs. Stone," he said to them both, "it seems our predictions were right."

Both man and woman continued to stare expectantly at the Doctor before them.

"Congratulations, you're having twins!"

# 2013- One of the twins

I always knew we were special. My mother always reminded us of it from as far back as I can remember. She always called us her little *blessings*, which I guess makes sense since she wasn't even supposed to be able to *have* kids in the first place. Then she goes and pops out two at the same time. Bloody doctors, can't tell their ass from their elbow most days anyway.

It's so strange too, since twins don't even run in our family. Let alone *identical* ones. I often think about how it must have been to bring two babies up together. Two mouths to feed, two appetites to suffice. Two little babies with twice as much love to give and needing twice as much attention.

Two babies that could cause twice as much trouble.

Personally, I could never do it. Especially after Dad left us. People used to see her walking down the street pushing a double pram and applaud her with sympathetic glances. 'So brave,' their looks would say without actually breathing a word.

Brave.

But what choice is a mother given when her husband walks out on her leaving her high and dry with two screaming brats hanging off her boobs.

But Mum was brave. *Is* brave. Brave enough to go it alone. Brave enough to not give up. Especially when things got really bad.

Brave. Yeah. That's exactly what she is. Poor ol' Mum.

Come to think about it, I don't really know how she's lasted all these years. I mean we weren't exactly the easiest kids to put up with growing up. If it were me, and my kids treated me like we treated her, I'd probably pull a fast one like my old man. It seemed wherever we went, bad luck seemed to follow our family.

Not just bad luck. Bad things. Things that no child should ever have to go through or deal with. No matter how hard we tried to be good, it seemed that we just couldn't avoid getting into trouble.

I can only imagine what people will say about her now once the papers get ahold of all this; their taunting whispers as she passes. *'That's her...The mother of **those** twins...'*

Maybe the lack of a good fatherly figure in our lives is where we both went wrong. I think a lot about why he left. Whenever we used to breach the subject with Mum, she'd just dismiss it as fast as she could and tell us off for something or other to get us off her back. Even at a young age I think I could tell how much it hurt her to even hear his name mentioned.

Dad. What a prick.

My shrink thinks that him leaving had, hang on let me get this right; "a negative and debilitating effect" on my brother and me. That's always a safe bet, isn't it? Blame the folks! Maybe he is the reason we're so messed up.

I wonder if that will be my brother's defense in court.

All I remember of my Dad was how much he always tried to get us to do 'boyish things', as he called them. It's so fucking sad that my only memories I have of him are him shoving a football in my direction and me putting up a stink cause I couldn't be bothered with it all. He was such a man's man. Mr. Sporty. Always down the pub, watchin' 'the game'. What the hell is 'the game' anyway? I guess in his defense, it must have been hard having not one, but **two** gay sons.

I actually read a survey once that said that identical twins are more likely to both be gay than fraternal twins. Maybe that is why he left...That time he found us both playing in Mum's closet; me in her shoes and my brother in her Sunday dress. If I could only have freeze-framed it. Hilarious. Poor sod.

Mum never once blamed us for him leaving. Still to this day she's never even brought it up. To be honest she doesn't really mention him at all these days. Except to compare us to him. She says we have his eyes…and his temper.

I hope I get to see her soon.

# The Other Twin

"Do you know where you are?"

The voice came from out of nowhere but seemed like it was all around me. With my eyes so firmly shut, each word muttered created spasms of strange neon colours to dance behind my lids. The silence that followed was deathly.

Each muscle in my body was tensed so tightly that a fire was beginning to snake its way through my veins. Somewhere in my head lay the thought that if I remained perfectly still, then I wouldn't feel. To let myself *feel* right now would be suicide, for I was sure my insides would simply cave in from the pain and no one would ever be able to hear my truth.

The long inhale I heard was a prelude to the words that would follow, and when they came they were louder than before as if spoken through a loudspeaker.

"Do you know who you are?"

Each question was more ridiculous than the last; the answer so obscenely obvious and trite that the questions did not even deserve an acknowledged response. So I remained still and unmoving. The fire in my limbs was growing hotter with each sound and my head was trying so desperately to block it out. If I were to open my eyes right now I was sure I would see that the hairs on my arms had been singed off by the pure white heat coming out of my pores. My body tightened even further, if that were possible, as if trying to fold itself away from this situation.

It was then that I noticed the beating of my heart. It was quieter than I would have expected, but I noticed it anyway. Perhaps it was *because* it was so faint that it drew my attention. After that I couldn't hear anything else. My hearing registered nothing but the slow, faint beating of my heart. In my head I counted the beats as they vibrated delicately against my chest cavity. So slow, it felt like a valley separated them.

1…2..3..4…

"You're in the hospital."

My thoughts were spurred from their trance-like state as the deep voice came once more, his words no more twinged with enquiry, but rather the cold harsh truth.

Two dark pools that were once my eyes finally revealed themselves as my head tilted upwards to face the man before me.

"Hospital?" I asked, my voice a husky whisper. "How'd I get here?"

# 1999

Mrs. Stone watched from the kitchen window, washing the dishes in the sink as Hadley pushed Everly on the swing set in the back garden. Every time Everly was pushed he let out a squeel that put a huge smile on her face.

As she rinsed each dish she let her mind wander to how lucky she felt to be blessed with two beautiful identical twin boys who loved each other so much. They were never apart. Couldn't bare to be. From as far back as she could remember they were completely and totally inseperable. They even insisted on dressing alike. She learned very early on that things for the twins had to come in pairs. If not, that's when the fits began.

Doctors said it was normal for identical twins to be so attached to each other. The boys' GP had tried to explain it as a bond that was fused between the two from having shared a womb for the first nine months of their existence! How could they not be close? But there was something that didn't seem right about this *bond*. She couldn't quite explain it. When one got a new toy, the other had to have the **same** one. When one boy went to the toilet, the other had to follow. It was even *their own* idea to keep their haircuts alike. Mrs. Stone wished that she had other friends with twins to share this burden. But alas, most of their friends didn't even have kids, let alone two of them.

She was worried about their bond at first when they began school.

As she scrubbed the dishes in the kitchen sink that day her mind was immediately brought back to that first day when the Headteacher broke the news that the boys were to be assigned to different classes. She remembered how much they both screamed and hollered when they were separated from each other. It took both her and her husband and three teachers to stop them from thrashing and lashing out. They had become so violent at the thought of being pulled apart that her husband suffered a broken nose and she a black eye, as a result.

She could still hear their screams if she shut her eyes.

Shaking her head of the memory, she tucked it away and lost herself in this happy moment of seeing her boys as they normally were; happy, together, smiling. Such a blessing they were, and so incredible how they could instantly make a rainy day that much brighter with only their smiles.

They were a very happy family.

She watched as Hadley pushed his brother carefully on the swing, both boys laughing and giggling as they played happily together. It took her a moment to notice exactly how high Everly was going. It seemed as though with each push he went higher and higher in the air to the point where his feet nearly dangled amongst the clouds. It was then that worry began to set in as any mother would tell you. Mrs. Stone knocked on the window to get her son's attention. She shouted through the double-pained glass for Hadley to slow down and ease up.

But they couldn't hear her.

She pounded harder as she saw the whole thing unravel in her mind. Why weren't they listening? He's going to fall off.

Higher and higher he went, his giggles high pitched and filling the air around them. Each push sending him closer to the clouds above.

And that's when it happened. Mrs. Stone watched the whole thing unfurl before her very eyes as Everly went sailing off into the air, the thrust from the swing making him airborne for a moment. His limbs flailed, grabbing mercilessly for anything to help him and stop him from falling. She watched helplessly as he descended at a strange angle towards the hard pavement beneath him, the swing's chains catching at full extent and returning heavily down towards where Hadley stood.

Then there was silence as Everly landed hard. His little legs connected first before giving way and his body collapsed in a heap like a sack of potatoes. As Mrs. Stone fled from her post at the kitchen counter she remembered the conversation she had had with her husband. She remembered the argument they had about how dangerous she thought that swing set was and how it should have sand beneath it. Mr. Stone dismissed the thought saying she was being paranoid. They were old enough not to fall off.

She felt like everything was moving in slow motion as she ran towards her little baby boy who now lay at an odd angle on the ground and screaming out in pain. As she rounded the corner of their house it took her a moment to place the screams that were ringing in her ear.

The sound was coming from all around her, as if Everly's screaming was echoing off the non-existent walls that surrounded them. She furrowed her brow as she got closer to her son, wondering how it could be possible. She saw the dark blood that oozed from his arm. Without a moment's hesitation she picked him up and cradled his little broken body in her arms, tears streaming down her cheeks as she attempted to calm him with her voice. She closed her eyes and prayed that he would be alright. After a moment she realised that it wasn't just Everly who was screaming and opened her eyes to investigate the source.

What she saw didn't make any sense at all.

When she opened her eyes she expected to see Hadley in the same place he had been; standing behind the swing. But when she looked he wasn't there. Instead, Hadley was on the ground, his body twisted in the same strange way as his brother. The screams she thought were only Everly's were also coming from her other son.

She was immediately furious that Hadley would be so horrible as to make fun of his brother's pain, mocking him by rolling around and faking being hurt for attention. But as she stood up, her fallen son still in her arms, she noticed the glittering dark liquid that was also leaking out of Hadley's arm. His screams didn't suffice, instead they continued ringing out into the air around them, full of anguish and fear.

As she took another step towards him she saw the impossible.

Hadley was sprawled out on the pavement in the exact same position as Everly had fallen. His arm was bent in the same exact way as his brother's and bleeding from the same spot. It was as if *he too* had fallen off the swing and landed in the same exact way as his brother.

Her head was whirring as she bent down in utter disbelief and cradled both her sons in her arms, cooing and reassuring them, trying desperately to calm them both and make everything alright...

## 2000

"Come on, it'll be fun," Hadley urged, that infectious look plastered across his smug face.

"You know we shouldn't, Hadley. What if we get caught?" Everly shot back. His palms were sweaty just thinking about it.

They were stood just outside the Headteacher's office, their voices coming out in hushed whispers so as not to alert anyone.

Hadley reached over and took his brother's left hand in his. Both boys looked down; each hand practically indistinguishable to the other's. The same strange array of freckles adorned both boys' left hands in the same circular shape; the dark spots almost too perfect to be natural.

"Everly, come on, don't be such a wuss."

He knew just how to play his brother and exactly what to say to bend him to his will. His pleading expression was enough to pull at his twins' heartstrings. Even at such a young age, both boys were mature beyond their years, especially when it came to each other. So in tune with each other's emotions, each could practically guess what the other was thinking just by looking into their eyes.

"Everly, you gotta help me out," he pleaded again, "you know this was gonna be my last chance. If Mr. Davis finds out it was me who made the mess in the boys' loo he's gonna get Mum in for sure this time. If you say it was you, he'll go easy on you, you know he will."

Everly continued to stare down at his brother's hand that squeezed his own gently.

"But why don't you- "

"Everly! This is the only way. Please."

Everly looked up and into Hadley's eyes that were glistening and about to spill over. He chewed the corner of his lip in that nervous way he always did which spoke volumes to his brother who knew it meant he was about to give in.

He took a deep breath as the Headteacher's door opened, startling both boys. Mr. Davis stood in the doorway staring down hard at the twins. He adjusted his glasses and pushed them further up onto the bridge of his nose. He continued to stare down at the identical boys in front of him and let out a long sigh before stepping back to let them in.

The twins looked into each others' eyes and exchanged a quick glance. Hadley mouthed 'thank you' to his brother as they both stepped in with heads low.

## 2001

Mrs. Stone could feel it. It wasn't glaringly obvious just yet, but deep down, if she permitted herself to think about it long enough, she knew it was true. Her boys were almost teenagers. It wasn't even that long ago that she was in her teens, which probably made it a bit worse since she didn't have to think back too far to remember what life can be like for hormone-driven teens. But she knew it was true; day by day, little by little, she was losing her control over them. And like any mother of her time, there was nothing she could do about it.

That day as she watched her little boys and their neighbour James walking along the clifftops, she felt something different in her bones. It wasn't the growing helplessness like she had been feeling for months now. No, this was something different. Something new. As their little figures grew smaller and smaller as they walked further and further away from their house, she recognised the feeling in the pit of her stomach. It was fear.

The twins had been friends with James since they first moved into their little house halfway between the seaside towns of Brighton and Peacehaven a couple of years back.

After the boys' accident on the swing set a couple of years ago, the whole town began to suspect something was up with this seemingly normal family. First the boys' father left them 'inexplicably' and then Mrs. Stone's hysterical story about how her twins could feel each other's pain. No one believed Mrs. Stone's story about what had happened with Everly and Hadley and even though no one had ever confronted her, she knew that behind her back the people of the town suspected she had something to do with her children's apparent 'accident.' Everytime she went out in public with the twins, both wearing matching casts on the same arm, she could feel the sets of eyes watching her.

*Child abuse.*

That's what everyone was thinking. That and how she must be crazy.

*Driven mad by her husband leaving, she must have taken out her fury on her poor innocent children.*

The police had been called after Everly's accident and a statement taken from Mrs. Stone. And although there wasn't enough evidence to get child services involved, it was the common belief amongst the townsfolk that poor Mrs. Stone was becoming slightly unhinged.

So not long after, Mrs. Stone decided to pack up her family and brought them as far out of Brighton as she could bear, away from prying eyes and to a part of the county where no one knew anything about them.

But unfortunately, the Stone's apparent misfortune wasn't so easily shook.

James was their next door neighbour. He was their age and their mothers quickly became friends when they moved into the quiet neighbourhood. James' father worked for the Armed Forces and was away quite often, so Mrs. Stone and James' mother were quick to bond due to the lacking adult male presence in their lives.

From the moment they all met, the boys also took to each other like fish to water. There was no denying that James was closer with Hadley, though. Growing up, Hadley was a bit more rough and tough than his twin and perhaps that was what had appealed to James more. Everly was quieter; usually prefering to have his nose in a book than to be knee deep in mud, or on the football pitch like other boys his age. And although when they all got together they resembled a younger version of the Three Musketeers, it was clear that James had a deeper appreciation for Hadley.

That aside, the three boys were so inseperable that the local children of the town had dubbed James as the third Stone child. He even looked like them; same height, same fair hair and arctic blue eyes. The resemblance between him and the twins was uncanny. If ever Mrs. Stone took all three boys out with her to town, people even mistook them for a family. Often when James would come over to theirs, he and Hadley would find a way to disappear off somewhere together, leaving poor Everly to fend for himself. They would tease him and hide from him, wrapped up in a game that only they were playing.

There was even one time that Everly came home from school with a doll that he had borrowed from a classmate of his. Hadley and James found him in his room, brushing the doll's hair and singing to it softly.

*"What the?" James had cried out, pointing his finger directly at Everly and erupting into a childish, mocking fit of laughter.*

*Everly had jumped suddenly, riddled with embarassment over being caught playing with a girls' toy.*

*"You little pansy, what are you doing playing with dolls, huh?" Hadley teased, clambering on to James' coattails.*

*Everly just stared unbelievingly at his twin, searching in his eyes for a sign that he wasn't being serious. A small shadow of doubt tinged with guilt swept across his identical features, but was gone as quickly as it had appeared. Hadley had stopped coming to his brother's aid whenever James was around; quick to latch on to whatever James was saying so as not to be left behind or cast aside.*

*James lurched forward suddenly and grabbed the doll from Everly's clutch who let go out of surprise.*

*"James, give it!" He shouted back, his voice rocky.*

*"What's that? You want your little gay doll back, do you?"*

*"Give it. It's not mine, I was just…I was just hanging on to it for someone," Everly pleaded. His eyes were turned down to the floor, too mortified to even meet their taunting gaze.*

*"It's right here, you little dweeb, come and get it."*

*James was holding the doll out in front of him, dangling it like a carrot on a stick.*

*Hadley stared back at his brother. Everly's eyes were as wide as saucers and glazed over, about to spill their contents down his flush cheeks. He could read the indecision on Hadley's face. Part of him wanted to reach out and grab the doll back to protect it from James' taunting grasp, the other was terrified of being ridiculed. He thought for a moment and just as his arm lashed out to grab at the doll, James pulled back and in one swift movement, tore the head off the doll.*

*The head came off with a soft popping sound which was followed by silence as both Stone brothers stared in awe at what had just happened. James let out a forced whooping laughter at his own stunt and turned towards Hadley expectantly. Hadley hesitated for a moment before joining in, adding to the echoing wails of laughter in the room.*

*James dropped both parts of the now dismembered doll and turned and left the room, tugging Hadley with him. Reluctantly, Hadley followed, turning his head just before leaving to inspect his brother state.*

*Everly just stared at the two boys as they disappeared through the doorway, a vacant look upon his face.*

\*\*\*

This particular day was not unlike any other. The street they lived on was set quite far back from the main road that travelled from Brighton to Peacehaven and beyond, which made it perfect for unsupervised playing. The boys would often venture out down the wide clifftop to the underside along the beach. The wall itself was quite steep and Mrs. Stone had told them time and time again that as long as they hugged the wall as much as they could and didn't venture off the pathway, then there was nothing to worry about.

Hadley was the leader today, as the three of them strode in single file down the path. He was humming something to himself more than to the other boys as they walked, a ruck sack strapped across his back. James was second in line, followed closely by Everly. James was bragging about his latest video game console to no one in particular, and as always, Everly was hanging on his every word. It seemed that lately Everly was all the more desperate for James' approval; following him around like a lost puppy dog and doing things seemingly for how it would look to James.

"Oooh, wow, that sounds so cool, James," Everly cooed from the back of their line, "you think I could come over and play it sometime?"

"Maybe," he replied, "as long as you don't bring my scores down."

You could practically hear Everly's heart sink with disappointment. His pace slowed for a moment as he mentally tried to pick himself up.

"Hey, let's go down by the jetty this time," Hadley shouted from up ahead, pointing to the elevated jetty in the water down below the cliffs.

"Oh, yeah, maybe we can go rock pooling when we get down there," came Everly's slightly over-excited voice again.

"Rock pooling's for babies," James shot back matter-of-factly.

This time Everly stopped completely and stared at the back of James' head. The other two simply kept on walking, completely oblivious to Everly's falling behind. His eyes clouded over as his whole body seemed to sag with frustration and disappointment. It seemed that lately nothing he could do or say was good enough for James and his brother. Everything he said seemed to fall upon deaf ears and every second he spent tagging along with them he felt more and more like an outsider.

All he wanted was to belong. If only there was something he could do.

The boys reached a curve in the path. To their left the path continued around a sharp corner, but straight ahead and beyond the fencing was the sloping cliff top. Some of the older children of the village used to climb down the steep cliff top to get to the beach below, far too cool and confident to take the safe route.

As they approached the fenced off cliff, James scuttled to the front of the line and with his hands on the fence peered over the edge. Below them was a sloping hill of jagged rock. Not impossible to climb down, but something that would not be recommended unless you were suited with suitable climbing gear with which to protect yourself. The twins joined him on either side and with a hand over their eyes to block out the sun, both leaned carefully as far as they could over the sloping cliff to get a better look at what lie beneath.

A boyish silence filled the air between them as they all three went a bit slack jawed, quietly contemplating what might happen if someone were to fall down. After a minute or two, James was the first to break the silence.

"Betcha I can do it."

"Do what," Hadley asked.

"Climb down, dummy."

"Don't be ridiculous James," Everly joked, nudging him with his arm.

"I'm serious," he came back, shooting Everly a challenging look, "What? You don't think I can?"

"No, no, it's not that…"

"Then what? You think I'm too chicken?"

"Cut it out guys, let's just keep going," Hadley said tugging on James' arm in the direction of the path.

"No, wait,Had. Your little bro thinks I'm too chicken to do it."

"James, wait, I never said that-"

"Yah ya did."

James was getting excited now, even standing a little taller as if his stance would help prove his point that he was daring enough to attempt the stupid stunt.

"James, look how crazy far down it is!" Hadley shouted, gesturing to the steepness of the cliff with both hands. "Don't be stupid. Let's just go already. I wanna get to the beach."

"No Hadley. I'm gonna do it."

"What?" Everly shouted in disbelief.

"It's not that far down, and it's not like I'm gonna jump or anything. You've seen me climb trees. What's the big difference?"

"I, I don't know James..." Everly's voice trailed off as his gaze travelled down to the jagged rocks below. "What if one of the rocks came loose..."

"These rocks have been here for ages, ya never heard of loose rocks before, have ya?"

Everly swallowed in response and looked towards his brother in support who was also stunned into silence as he contemplated the sudden drop off the cliff.

"James, Ev's right. It's not safe, mate.Let's just go this way. Come on," Hadley's voice had now gone quiet too, edged with uncertainty and fear.

"Forget you two little chicken-shits! I'll see you at the bottom then."

"James, come on, this isn't funny," Everly pleaded. But James just laughed it off and hoisted himself up onto the wooden enclosure.

It took him two beats before he was on the other side of the fence, his back to the open cliff below and his hands still gripping the fence in front of him. Everly stepped back, wrapping his arms around himself in a protective hug, a look of utter fear plastered across his young features.

"James, mate, come on back over, it's not too late. You got nothing to prove, mate, just come on." Hadley's voice was beginning to break too.

James turned around so that his back was to them and let go of the fence raising both fists in the air in triumph. He let out a whoop from deep down in his belly that echoed loudly off the surrounding clifftop.

He edged himself a few paces forward so that to the twins it looked like there was nothing separating him from the cliff and the icy ocean below.

"Mate, you gotta see this. The view is awesome!"

He took another small step and leaned forward, hands on his knees, inspecting the drop below and figuring out how he was going to climb down.

Hadley had had enough. He was going to have to step in and take control of the situation. He turned his head away from James for a moment to remove his ruck sack and set it against the fence. With his back to James, he reached into his bag for the mobile phone his mum had given them to use only in case of emergencies. If he could ring James' mum and tell her what he was about to do, then maybe *she* could convince her son not to be so stupid.

He couldn't have been turned around for more than ten seconds, before he heard the most earth-shattering scream ring out from behind him. It was so piercing that he was momentarily unsure as to who it was coming from. Hadley instinctually shot around as paraletic fear took control of his limbs.

As his eyes focused in and made sense of the scene in front of him, a silent 'NO' escaped from between his lips as he suddenly lunged forward with his arms outstretched.

James had disappeared from the clifftop. Everly was clutching the protective fence that separated him from the scene and leaning over the top as much as he could to see.

The shrill shriek had indeed come from James as he went over the clifftop and continued until he landed a second later, shattering against the rocky boulders below.

It was over in a flash and yet seemed to last forever as the two twins stood and surveyed and made sense of what just happened. Tears sprung from Hadley's eyes and clouded his vision as he jumped the fence and saw the small, bloody body of his dearest friend laying about ten metres below. His limbs were sprawled out at odd angles and his face was staring up at them. As the boys continued to look down, it seemed as if James' eyes were tranfixed on theirs. As wide as saucers and a look of panic forever paralysed on his face. More screams from passer-by's below echoed against the open surroundings as time sped up suddenly, and the twins were slapped back into reality.

Hadley finally caught his breath and whipped his head around to look at his brother, who continued to stare blankly at the scene below. Hadley recognised that vacant stare. He had seen it before. It wasn't sad or angry or even surprised. It was simply blank. He reached out to grab Everly and gave his arm a quick shake to force him to look at him.

He couldn't think what to ask or say to him. He simply gasped for air and opened his mouth and shook him again as if he could force words from Everly's mouth that might somehow explain what had just happened.

Everly continued to stare straight through his twin, the blank look never retreating from his face. After a third shake, this time a harder one, Everly finally opened his mouth to speak as the sudden sound of ambulance sirens pierced the calmness of their surroundings.

"He fell..."

That was all that came out of Everly's mouth but it was enough for Hadley to let go and take a step away from him. He never took his eyes off Everly, not even for a moment. Mobile phone still in hand he took another step back as if Everly had suddenly burst into flames and he had to get away from the heat.

"He fell, Hadley..." Everly repeated, his voice the epitome of calm. "He fell..."

Within moments the boys were surrounded by police and other men in uniforms, and then everything went a bit blurry.

## 2004

"Mum is gonna kill us, ya know," Everly giggled taking another long swig out of the bottle. He winced as the dark liquid slithered down his throat, burning as it coated his insides and leaving him quivering from its side effects.

He handed the bottle back to his brother who winked at him quickly before putting the bottle to his own lips and sucking back expertly.

"Don't be such a worry-wart. *Mum* ain't gonna find out, now is she?" he breathed, the scent of rum exhaling into the air around them.

They were sat on the floor of Hadley's bedroom, the late afternoon sun still weakly filtering in through the floor length poster window and illuminating the bottle's dark liquid making it appear almost amber in hue.

Hadley closed his eyes and let the alcohol work its way into his blood stream. Everly started to sway slightly. He was buzzed already after only a few swigs, but he wasn't going to let on to his brother. Hadley always had a way of making him feel inferior if he didn't play his games.

He studied his brother's face as he rested against the wall, features bathed in the setting sunlight. So identical yet so different if that were even possible. Utterly indistinguishable, but with personalities so unique. Hadley opened an eye and peered at his brother, sensing his gaze burning into him.

"What?" he asked, shutting his eye again and tilting his head back further.

Everly adjusted himself on the pillow beneath, wincing at the pins and needles that prickled his undercarriage. He reached for the bottle of rum and tilted it abruptly to his lips, missing slightly and spilling some of the booze down his top and onto the floor around him.

"Shhhhhhit," he murmured, knocking his brother out of his trance and sending him into a fit of giggles as he stared at his brother's misfortune. "Yeah, real funny, Hadley. I'm bloody covered in it."

He stood and dropped the bottle in his brother's lap as he ran for a towel, his brother's deep laughter following him down the halls and echoing off the walls around him.

"Relax Ev, Mum's not gonna be home for hours."

As Everly peeled off his soaking t-shirt and tossed it in the machine he stared out the bathroom window, suddenly mesmerised by the sunset playing out before his eyes. He had to squint for his blurry eyes to focus on the sight. Grabbing the window frame for support he laughed inwardly at himself and his clumsiness.

Hadley was right. Everly was the worrier of the two. Doomed from birth to be the sensible one, letting Hadley have all the fun yet always there to pick up the pieces when his brother fucked up.

Or take the blame completely.

Staring out at the pink sky he thought of all the times his brother had gotten him in shit in the course of their short 15 years on this planet. If it wasn't trouble at school that he was bailing him out of it was shop lifting, bullying or drinking. After the accident with James a couple of years ago, Everly became even more introverted than before. Ever the straight arrow, he seemed to have become a saint of some sort.

Of some sort.

No matter how many times he told himself that he was done covering for his other half, there always seemed to be a 'next time.'

*Bound by blood.*

The bond between the two boys grew stronger with each passing year. As the world around them changed, it was almost as if they grew closer; turning towards each other when things got tough and seeking comfort in the other when things began falling apart. After James died, their mother moved them again. That was her solution to everything; pick up, move, relocate, start over all in hopes that their family troubles wouldn't follow them. It didn't take long for people to start talking. Even though James' death had been ruled an accident, a stupid dare gone wrong, the townspeople blamed her boys. Their past had caught up with them and the rumors started. The last thing she wanted was more judgement from the people around her. Her poor boys. She would do anything to protect them from harm, but try as she might, harm and misfortune seemed to trail them wherever they went.

"My ears are burning," came Hadley's voice behind him, appearing as if on cue when he felt his brother thinking about him.

Everly felt Hadley's arms envelop his naked shoulders in a warm, soft embrace, letting his head rest on Everly's shoulder. Both boys stared out the window in silence for a few moments, each knowing what the other was thinking and not needing to say a word. Everly pulled his brother's arms around his neck tighter, appreciating their closeness despite his negative thoughts toward him. When they were near, nothing mattered but each other. Any hostility was immediately demolished by the other's proximity. They each let out a boozy sigh in unison as the last sliver of sunlight disappeared over the horizon leaving deep purple hues in its wake.

Everly kissed his brother's cheek adoringly, forcing his last disparaging thoughts to melt away. It was his way of apologising.

"Love you, geek," he teased.

"Love you too."

## 2007

"What could be so fuckin' important, Everly, what? Are you dying?" Hadley puffed as he was yanked by his brother up the stairs and into his bedroom.

As they crossed the threshold into the dimly lit room, Hadley pulled his arm free from his brother's death grip.

"Jesus, calm down wouldja?" he sneered looking down at his reddened skin from where Everly had dragged him inside. Rubbing his arm he watched expectantly as Everly turned away from him and made his way across the room, stopping to stare out the window.

Hadley waited. He knew something was up. Even though patience wasn't his greatest virtue, he knew that sometimes 'time' was what his brother needed. Especially when it involved big news, like this was bound to be. He let out a small sigh and flopped himself heavily down on the bed, coming to rest on his elbow.

Everly immediately shot him a look.

"Okay, okay, don't get your knickers in a twist," he quickly gave-in, kicking his shoes off Everly's bed so not to get it dirty. Everly was a stickler for dirt and germs; so much so that his attention to neatness was beginning to border on obsessive. As his brother's trainers hit the floor, he too sighed and turned back to the window.

A heavy silence filled the air between them, as Hadley grew increasingly bored and began picking at the skin beneath his nails. After a few moments Everly began to come around and softly turned to face his brother, arms folded tightly across his chest. To his brother he appeared almost childlike. So fragile and scared that it twisted something in Hadley's stomach filling him with the urge to practically bend over in pain.

He knew something was wrong, ever since a few weeks ago when Everly started coming home late from school saying he was at the library studying. Something had changed in him lately, as if part of him had short-circuited and his spark had been extinguished. Everybody had started to notice it; their mother, his friends…For months he had become increasingly withdrawn from everything and everyone around him. And then last week he began coming home late, having missed dinner, with a look of utter shame stricken across his beautiful dark features. Every night it was the same thing; he would head straight up to his room, avoiding eye contact and lock himself away until darkness had fallen and the rest of his family had dispersed.

Whatever it was that had been going on was about to come to a head, and Hadley could sense that it was tearing him up inside. He wasn't usually so withdrawn, certainly not from him. Their lives were mirrors of one another, and there had never existed a secret between them. Not one in eighteen years. Hadley began to get nervous as his mind went into overdrive, sensing what this was all about and growing more anxious by the second.

Seeing his struggle, Hadley was suddenly overtaken by the need to cradle his brother and rescue him from whatever was going on in his twin's head. Hoisting himself off Everly's sunken bed, he quickly crossed over to where he stood and wrapped himself protectively around his frail frame. It took only a few seconds for Everly to collapse into his brother's grip and let himself be completely supported, like a baby in his father's arms.

The two just held each other as minutes ticked by. After a while, Everly's shoulders began to quiver and Hadley felt the familiar feeling of tears moistening his top.

"Shhhh," he cooed into his brother's ear, "take it easy."

Everly began to sob softly, his tears muffled by his brother's bulk.

"I'm here, whatever it is…You can tell me."

He rubbed his back gently with one hand. Everly had lost weight over the past few months and Hadley could feel the grooves of his spine protruding almost alien-like against the skin as his hand grazed over them.

Seconds turned into minutes as the brothers stood entwined in one another's arms. The outside world had grown quiet as if it all had melted away from where they were. Hadley shifted his weight from one foot to the other, his body growing tired and restless and his impatience taking over. The love he felt for his brother was strong, but his inability to stand still for lengthy periods was beginning to surface to the point where his limbs were beginning to tremble.

He took Everly's shoulders in his hands and moved him so there was a foot of distance between them. Looking him in the eye, he tried desperately to convey a look of loving support; one that urged him to share this obviously debilitating secret.

It was then that he saw it.

*It.*

The truth.

All it took was a look into each other's eye for each to see into the other's soul. When Hadley's gaze met Everly's, words were no longer needed. The pain that Everly was feeling played across his face, distorting his beautiful eyes and forcing him to appear older than his years.

Hadley looked past his tortured stare and straight into his heart. He felt his brother's discomfort, his feelings of confusion and fear. Inside his bones he could sense the awkwardness his brother had been hiding for so many weeks and he inwardly castrated himself for not picking up on it sooner. After all, they were kindred spirits, joined in so many ways. He should have been able to tell the source of Everly's anguish. He should have been able to pick up on it sooner. How sad he had seemed.

Ashamed almost, hiding from the world and afraid to even look his brother in the eye.

Everly spoke. His voice a pained whisper that was carried away in the air the moment it left his lips. "I think I might be…"

Then he choked, squeezing his eyes together. It was then that Hadley was sure.

How could he have been so stupid?

In that moment, the same pain and confusion appeared on Hadley's face. His too, began to twist in that same pained way and without having to speak any words, he was suddenly able to portray to his brother exactly what he needed…He was able to mirror exactly what he had been hoping to see.

Tears began to prick behind their eyes simultaneously as the air in the room shifted. Heaviness began to lift and shift into relief as those *three little words* that Everly had hoped and prayed his brother would say, *that meant he wouldn't have to go through this alone*, began to manifest all around them…

*"So am I."*

Those three little words spoke volumes to Everly for they were hinged with security and comfort; relief and support.

The twins hugged each other again, each finding comfort in the closeness of the other. It was like a light had suddenly been switched on and both could finally see what the other had been hiding away in the corners of their minds for so long now.

Everything made sense now and both boys could finally rest assured that no matter how hard the road ahead was going to be, they wouldn't have to travel it alone. They held each other so tightly until their hearts began to beat as one. Each lost in the other's warm embrace and each finally finding the inner comfort that they had been craving for so long.

They were never going to feel alone again, for no matter what waited for them when this all finally came out, they would forever have each other.

# 2013- Hadley

"God, you're so fuckin' hot."

I writhed underneath his bulk, my raging hard-on pressing up against my jeans to the point of causing me to chafe inside my trousers. Before I could respond, he drove his tongue deep into my mouth again; hot and wet it explored, licking and sucking in a rhythmic manner. His hands moved up my muscular torso, finding their way under my top and running his fingers over the deep grooves of my abs. A moan escaped my lips at the sensation of his smooth palms making contact with my nipples. My mouth opened further, inviting him deeper inside me.

Lying on his sofa, I could feel how cheap it was as the rough coiled-springs drove up uncomfortably into my back causing it to arch unwillingly and force my crotch up even further against his own. He responded by driving his pelvis harder to meet me half-way, the sensation sending sparks of colourful pleasure dancing through my bloodstream.

I opened my eyes for a moment and searched his face, trying desperately in vain to remember his name.

*Dan...Darryl...Donnie...*

Didn't matter anyway, it wasn't like we were going to be friends afterwards.

I pushed him off me, forcing him to sit up and causing a look of hurt to flash across his features before quickly evaporating into lust as I lifted my black t-shirt off over my head; stopping only for a second to let him admire my sculpted chest before I started to unbuckle my shorts. I could feel his eyes roll over my naked torso; pausing at the broadness of my tanned shoulders and trickling down over my round pecs. I slipped a hand into the waist band of my denim cut-off shorts and let my eyes close as I grabbed my dick and adjusted it in the confines of my underwear. When I opened them he was practically drooling at the sight of me touching myself.

I unzipped the crotch and nodded in his direction, silently motioning for him to get naked too. He stood and clumsily tore at his shirt, letting it fall discarded to the floor. As he fumbled with his own trousers, desperate to get back to touching my skin, I stood and let my shorts and underwear fall to the ground in a pool at my feet.

He was hot. There was no denying it; similar in build to myself, same deep V definition under his abs and with just a light dusting of hair over his generously perk pectorals. The muscles in my stomach constricted as lust swept over me, and I realised just then how horny I actually was.

As he swiftly removed the last of his clothing revealing a hard-on that sliced through the air like a sword as it was released, I was on him in a flash, taking his dick in my right hand and forcing him down on his tacky old sofa. He groaned in response to my grip and laid himself back with his hands behind his head. Lowering myself down I took him into my mouth, all at once I forced the muscles in my throat to relax as I led him deep inside my mouth, trailing my wet tongue down his girth. I paused for a moment as my head relaxed further and he slid obligingly even deeper until he practically grazed my tonsils. With one hand I worked the skin around his penis in a circular motion as my tongue licked and lips sucked expertly at his head. My other hand found my own cock and worked a similar motion on myself, mirroring what I was doing to him. He arched his own back now, driving him further inside me as his hips began pumping slowly into my face. I responded by gently grazing my teeth up and down his shaft once, sending him the message to *chill the fuck out.*

He half-groaned and half-laughed as he got the hint that I was in charge.

"Fuck yeah, baby, keep doing that."

My mouth sucked harder and harder, my tongue licking and spitting as it went to town on his smooth glistening mushroom head. My own strokes became shallower as I began to feel the orgasm building inside me causing my own cock to moisten.

"Jesus, you give good head," he whispered as he took my head in his hands and knotted his fingers in my dark hair.

*I loved dirty talk. The filthier the better. The more a guy talks smut to me the fucking hornier I get.*

I groaned in response, my desire boiling up inside of me and coming out in grunts through my stuffed mouth.

I sped up my pace, my head bobbing quicker as I drilled away at his cock, sucking faster and faster, swallowing his juices every time I raised my head. I could feel his body tighten and release and when I looked up, his face and chest were flushed. I released my hand from his dick and trailed it up his stomach and then over his pecks, taking a nipple between my index finger and thumb and squeezing gently to add to the bucket of sensation that was running through his body. He reacted by stiffening even more and lifting his ass off the cushion.

"Fuuuuuuck, baby I'm gonna cum...I'm coming, I'm *coming...*"

My hand quickened on my own hard-on, desperate to cum at the same time as him. Harder and harder I worked my own cock, focusing on my own head and rubbing frantically until I was sure the friction would produce a flame.

I was coming too; I could feel my orgasm shooting up the length of my cock before spilling out into my palm. At that moment he groaned another low moan that came from deep inside his belly as he clenched and released as hot wet spunk shot into my mouth and immediately slid down my throat. I continued to suck the juices out of him as he bucked wildly beneath me, each jolt sending more sticky cum into my mouth as he orgasmed again and again, his hands back behind his head and his cock completely buried in my face. I looked up as his thrusts subsided, to see his eyes still squeezed tightly shut and his teeth biting his bottom lip. His chest was rising and falling quickly as his breathing slowly began to return to normal.

Removing his length from my mouth, I looked down at my own cloudy mess that was drizzling through my fist.

He sat up just then and lifted my head to his own. I obliged and came up into a sitting position until our heads were once again level with one another. His naughty expression scanned my own and he winked at me slightly before lowering his mouth to mine and kissing me deeply, sucking the extra cum off my lips.

When he pulled back, a smile was creeping up at the corner of his mouth, "Cheers for that," he said in a laddish voice. I smiled back quickly, a twinkle emanating in my eye before turning away in search of my clothes. He let himself fall back against the sofa and let out an exhausted and satisfied sigh.

When my head was turned away from him I couldn't help but smile. *Damn, I'm good.*

# Everly

To people walking by we must have looked like total skanks; making out in the back of a Range Rover, parked just off Brighton's seafront by the Marina, windows foggy with only the motion of the dark shadows giving away the actions inside.

It was a typical Friday night. Most guys got dinner and a movie on a date. Unfortunately I cannot be categorised under the heading of 'most guys.'

*Most guys.*

Nope. Me, I got *'treated'* to a seedy make-out session in the back of a car. A mere step up from dogging in a dark alleyway, if you ask me.

*Oh, Everly, you're such a cliché.*

The guy whose tongue was in my mouth and whose hand was creeping increasingly closer and closer up towards my crotch belonged to Matt Brewer. We had been dating a few weeks now, and still hadn't had sex.

My decision. Of course. Always was, I guess.

Don't get me wrong, I wasn't a virgin or anything…I just like to be…sure, before I let a guy into my pants. Pruddish for 2013, you say? Maybe. However, says who? Just because other gay guys my age jump into bed with anything that has a dick and a heartbeat, doesn't mean I have to follow in their grubby footsteps. In the end it was my life and I wasn't going to let anyone else, especially not some horny college stud, dictate how I should live it.

But this one *was* hot. Scorchingly so, which made it all the more difficult to wait. With messy blonde hair the same shade as my closely cropped and quiffed icy highlights, we looked damn good together. He was a few years younger than me, which was obvious by his groppy hands that pawed at me in a juvenile way whenever we were alone. Similar in height, just skimming 5'10", but slightly more built than I.

People always looked at my brother and I and envied our natural swimmer's builds; never a slave to a gym, but always liking to look good. Trim and slim, as I liked to say. I always watched what I ate and I guess it showed. I'm the complete antithesis to vain, believe you me, but if I had to say one thing that I was really proud of, it would be my flat stomach. It was just defined enough without being over the top and I will shamefully admit…I always have enjoyed showing it off.

But Matt was different. There was no denying that he was a jock, and aside from being obviously in love with his own reflection, his 'meat headed habits' and vanity were beginning to wear thin.

So there we were. The beefy college kid who wasn't even out to his family yet, and me; the calm, studious, sensible boy next door.

*Sigh.*

Sat there like deviant teenagers in the back seat of my car, I couldn't have felt any *less* sexy if I tried. Hiding away from anyone who might spot us. Ashamed to even be seen together in public for fear of what 'others' might think.

Once again his fear not mine. Let me be clear on that. I was completely and unabashedly *out*. He on the other hand…Well, let's just say he hid it quite well.

Sure he had a nice body, and we turned heads when on the rare occasion we walked down the street together, all big blue eyes and bright colour-blocked outfits…But at the end of the day, with the intelligence of a thermos and a personality to match, good looks were as far as it went.

My thoughts forced me to open my eyes for a moment and stare at the guy whose hands had somehow made their way up inside my shirt, and ask myself *if this was really where I wanted to be right now?*

The answer to that was painfully clear. As I continued to stare at this beautiful, yet ignorantly inexperienced 'Jack the Lad', something inside me made me push him away. Putting both hands on his shoulders and ignoring the hardening bump in my trousers I forced his suction-cup mouth off of mine. Matt stared back at me like a bewildered child who'd just had his toys taken away and searched my face for answers.

"What gives?"

My eyes studied his expression and with each second that passed my penis deflated further, answering every question that suddenly filled my head. His blue eyes looked so hurt as they stared back at me, shifting uncomfortably from one of mine to the other. I let out a deep sigh from the pit of my stomach and bit my bottom lip, a nervous trait of mine that apparently I did whenever I couldn't think of what to say.

Matt swallowed and lowered his eyes to his lap, adjusting himself from outside his jeans. I astained my own eyes from looking down to the size of his package, even though deep down I was just a *little* bit curious.

*Okay, a lot.*

"Everly, come on…"

But even he couldn't finish his sentence.

*He knows what's coming.*

"Matt…" I began, unsure of how I was going to even finish **my** first sentence.

I thought for a moment, my big blue eyes turning to gaze out the foggy window at the reflection of the moon on the ocean in front of us.

Water always helped me think.

"Matt, I'm sorry…I don't think this is…"

It hurt me to articulate how I was feeling. Hadley was so much better at letting guys down easily. I should take a page out of his book.

*Break-ups 101 by Hadley Stone. That cheeky git could write the book on break-ups. Well he could if he ever had a relationship last for longer than two weeks.*

"Yeah, yeah, I get it," Matt interrupted suddenly turning into a stroppy little child, "Everly you're such a fuckin' prude. I thought you'd be more like your brother," he paused for effect, his words hitting me harder than I thought they would. "If I had known you'd be such a tight wad I'd never have bothered."

And there it was. The attitude.

My eyes rolled involuntarily as the truth became painfully clear. The fact of the matter was, and what my subconscious had been telling me all along ever since I first laid eyes on this beautiful yet thick boy sat in front of me: *I was better than this.*

Looking at the guy who was crumbling from 'stud' status to 'immature little shit' before my very eyes, was making my next move very easy indeed. His attitude was giving me strength and helping me to see that I was just wasting my time with him. I was twenty-four years old and finally realising, as I sat with this groppy-little thing, that enough was enough. It was time to man-up and stop settling for guys who weren't right for me. Especially ones who didn't even have the balls to come out of the closet.

And that's when I finally spoke up for myself.

"Right. I think it's time for you to go."

Reaching past where he sat I opened the side door and let it swing wide in a less-that-subtle move.

He stared back at me and scoffed.

"What? That's it?" he boomed in a childish tone. "You're just throwing me out?"

"You know what? I guess I am."

And with that, I shoved him briskly through the open door. Matt had no time to react as my shove sent him sailing backwards, head over heals from the car, his hands reaching out aimlessly for support to cushion his fall as he landed with a thud on the rocky ground below.

"What the fuuuck-" I heard him wail in utter surprise and confusion.

But I wasted no time. I reached for the open door and pulled it shut quickly and locked it behind. Then, without even checking on him, I crawled to the driver's seat, turned the key and quickly backed out of the spot leaving poor Matt completely bothered and bewildered in a sad little heap on the ground where he landed.

Pulling out of my spot that was facing the sea, I never looked back as my car sped quickly away and into the dark night that stretched out in front of me, a small devious smile playing at the corners of my mouth. I felt happy as I stared out at the deserted road. Delighted, even. There was an empowerment that coursed through my veins when I realised that I didn't allow myself to be a doormat this time.

*I, Everly Stone, stood up for myself for once.*

The full moon above was my guide as I thought to myself that my load felt lighter already.

# Hadley- An early morning sometime later

The throbbing in my head acted as the alarm clock that I had apparently forgotten to set last night before pouring myself into bed, for as I reached for the small clock on the floor, the glowing red numbers revealed the sad truth of the matter.

*You're late shithead, get up.*

Turning over onto my side, a low gurgle escaped from deep in my belly causing me to moan in discontent as the gases in my empty stomach tossed themselves about with the liquid dinner I had consumed.

*Ugh.*

Staring back up at the ceiling, the memories of last night bubbled up to the surface and replayed themselves like a dirty movie before my eyes.

A party. Booze. Coke. Boys. Lots of gay boys. All running around all vying for a piece of Hadley Stone.

*How many did I stick it to last night?*

*Who fuckin' cares? Ya' got laid and that's all that matters.*

A satisfied smile crept up onto my full lips as I stretched my arms up before cupping my hands behind my head.

Satisfaction, indeed.

Not to toot my own horn or anything, but Hadley Stone, you do alright. Some might even say that I was hot fuckin' stuff. Life for this little lad was alright.

I let last night's events play themselves out behind my eye lids; what started out as an innocent night out with friends, led to an after party, drugs and a full blown orgy in the back room of some dude's house.

*Good times.*

Let's face the facts; guys wanted me. Badly. Fuck, even girls wanted me. All of them thinking they could *turn* me if given half a chance. I've let them have a go in the past. Why not? A blow job's a blow job, if you know what I mean. It's not that I don't find birds attractive. I love a nice set of tits, I just don't wanna stick my dick in between them if ya' get me. I don't get straight lad's fascination with pussy. Too much effort. Shit, a guy could get lost in one of them if left for too long on his own. Nah, for me it's always been about the cock. Ever since I sucked my first one at fifteen, I've been obsessed. Jesus, just thinking of one right now could get me hard. I loved everything about it; the feel, the smell, the shape, the sensation of having one in my mouth. And I was damn good with one. But that wasn't the only thing that kept the guys in this town lining up for a shag.

When I came out I quickly tuned into what guys found attractive about me. I started using these traits to my advantage; played them up so that they helped me to get noticed. I used my long lashes, big pouty lips and trim physique to bring guys to their knees. Our mum said once that we were blessed with good genes. Always bragged about how her boys had inherited all of her and our Dad's good traits, and none of the bad. The way she spoke about it was as if we were protected against bad genes. Somewhere, someone was looking out for us.

Well, usually looked out for us...

With my big, icy blue eyes and dyed jet black hair I was hard to miss and easy to pick out of a crowd. I kept in shape. Never a huge gym bunny, but always into keeping fit. I used to drag Everly down to the gym with me every now and then, but stopped once I realised what a huge cock-block he was. Too sensible and self-aware for his own good. I mean come on, the gym is the *best* place to get laid; all those jacked-up fags pumping iron in one place. It's like a candy store down there. Everly always used to bag on me when I would come back and tell him about getting blown in the locker rooms. He doesn't get how horned-up I am. Never has.

*Sensible Everly.*

Mum used to always say how I should be more like him. My witty retort was always about how the world only needs one 'Everly'. He was the sugar in life, and I was the spice. He brought the light and I brought the dark. And that's the way it always had been.

It was a brisk pounding on my door that stirred me from my narcissistic head-trip down memory lane. The person on the other end of the door didn't waste any time waiting for an invitation, instead they opened it and popped their little blonde head around the doorway; a stern look of disapproval spread across those familiar features.

My twin.

"Don't even say it." I stepped in before he could even open his plump pale lips.

He lifted a dirty blonde eyebrow at me and parted his lips as if to protest before closing them again in contempt.

I shot him a cheeky grin in hopes of having it returned to me. I could practically see his inward struggle as he fought against the almost 'paternal instinct' inside him which yearned to give me a firm telling-off for over-sleeping. He reconsidered instead as my naughty smile got through his 'sensible exterior' and he smiled back despite himself.

Rolling his eyes he disappeared behind the door once more but not before practically reading my mind and stealing the words right out of my mouth in that way that only he could do, and muttering something more to himself than to anyone else.

"You're late shithead, get up."

There he was. My other half in a nutshell.

# Everly

I sat myself down at the kitchen table, an over-sized mug of black coffee in hand, and let my mind wander as I stared out the window opposite.

*I wonder what he got up to last night. Nothing good, I can imagine.*

Hadley and I had been living together all our lives, but that's never stopped me from worrying endlessly about him. When we were eighteen, shortly after we both had come out, our mum kicked Hadley out of the house after he got arrested for possession of drugs and shoplifting. That was the only time he and I had ever lived under separate roofs…And those were very *dark* days.

Staring into the dark, syrupy liquid in front of me I let my mind wander to my dear brother. Hadley was always a bit of a loose wire; losing interest in school at an early age and slipping in with the wrong crowd. Without a dad around to ground us, forced us both to grow up very quickly. Perhaps a little too quickly. After we both came out, Hadley and I seemed to explore different paths. I threw myself into my school work, studying hard and trying to lose myself in my studies, perhaps as a way of forgetting all about the turmoil that I was feeling inside. And Hadley…

Well, Hadley *didn't*.

For years I had watched him begin to lose himself in the party scene; staying out late, drinking and doing drugs. Even though he worried me, deep down I always knew he was being responsible and that he always knew his limits. Even at his most wreckless he would always reassure me that he was okay; texting me to tell me where he was and when he would be home. In a way I felt like his surrogate father. I almost felt like it was my responsibility to keep an eye on him and make sure he was staying out of trouble.

Which is why I felt so helpless when he ran away...

When he got busted for posession of a controlled substance a while back, I think it forced him to actually step back and look at where his life was leading him...And he was never one to face the truth if it wasn't a pretty picture. At the time when mum kicked him out, she had had pretty much enough of it all. His mood swings, constantly getting into trouble. I mean how much could a mother take, I suppose? Before he disappeared Hadley took a long hard look at himself, and I don't think he liked what he saw. He didn't see himself anymore when he looked in the mirror. Even to me he started to look unrecognisable. He had changed somehow. Throughout his life when Hadley found himself in a situation that he didn't like, instead of facing it like a man, he would simply turn away.

That's why he ran.

My mum bailed him out of course, and Hadley got his wrist slapped and put on probation for a year. But that wasn't enough for Mum. She was so angry at the man he was turning out to be that she felt she had no choice but to throw him out.

I remember when he left like it was yesterday. I'll never forget the pain I felt being apart from him, like a black mass was growing in my stomach. After about three days of not hearing from him I started worrying. I tried calling and calling, but his mobile would go straight to voicemail. For six very, very long days he was completely off my radar. I didn't know what to do. My mind was imagining all sorts of horrible things. I kept picturing him alone in a gutter somewhere, strung out of his ass or worse...It was so unlike him to just completely disappear like that. We had literally never been apart for longer than a night in our entire lives, which is why I felt so lost and alone without him near.

When I realised that he wasn't going to come back or make contact on his own I tried tracking down all his friends in desperate attempts to find out where he was or at least if he was ok. No one seemed to be able to help. No one had seen him, or at least weren't giving anything up if they had. I became almost feral searching everywhere for him; skipping school to patrol the streets, I even put up signs around town to try and track down his whereabouts. Nothing. Mum even got the police involved. When she realised what she had done, she became overwrought with guilt at having driven one of her boys away. I could barely look at her. In my mind, she was the one responsible for all this. I needed someone to blame and couldn't see past her part in this whole nightmare. If she hadn't flipped on him, then he would still be here. Safe. With me.

On the seventh night Hadley was away, I woke up in the middle of the night after having the worst nightmare. I had dreamt that we had received a call from the police and that they had found him barely alive somewhere a few towns over. I had shot up in bed, quivering and crying into my pillow. It was then that something inside me told me to get up and go look outside. I can't explain it, but something woke me up from a deep sleep, got me out of bed and forced me downstairs.

I remember feeling like I was sleep walking or something, legs moving on their own and without my permission. I crept downstairs as if in a trance and stopped when I was facing our front door. My arms covered in goose bumps, I knew there was something I had to see waiting for me on the other side of that door. I reached carefully for the knob and turned it in a swift movement and let it swing open on its own.

What I saw as my eyes adjusted to the darkness outside almost brought me to my knees. There, waiting for me on the other side of the door...was Hadley. A hunched dark shadowy figure, identical to my own in every way, scared and quivering in the cool night air.

*Hadley.*

He had come back to me. He was safe. He was home.

We took a step towards each other at the exact same moment and crumbled into each other's arms. There we stood, holding each other for dear life; the week's events melting away into this moment. Bright white relief flooded my body as all the worry I had felt vanished as we embraced. I'm sure we were both holding our breath as we held each other like long-lost relatives who had been separated for years.

To us that's how long it felt. Seven long days of not knowing and fearing the worst. It was over.

From that day on, Hadley and I had never been apart. Our mother had accepted him back into the house, desperate to have him home and back under her watchful eye. Hadley decided to turn himself around. I knew that he had been through hell and back those seven days he was away. Every night I laid down to bed I swear I could feel the torment he was feeling; the fear, the anguish, the feeling of failure that plagued him. That feeling that he had let *me* down.

We never spoke about where he was that week or what he had gotten up to. We didn't need to. We simply moved on. He was home. From that day we made a silent pact to never keep the other in the dark again.

After all, we were twins, and in it together.

# Hadley

Dragging my hung-over ass from my bed I forced myself into the toilet and stared at my reflection in the mirror. I ruffled my black hair and rubbed my cheeks to get some colour back into them.

*Jesus, I can't believe I have to pretend to be a grown-up today.*

I could hear Everly in the other room bustling and busying himself in the kitchen, probably feeling smug with himself after having woken me up. Sometimes I thought he found a secret pleasure in feeling like he was better than me. I could practically predict word for word the conversation we were about to have when I joined him in the kitchen. I would get a stern telling-off for partying way too hard and some "Everly-style-life-advice" on how to turn myself around. I would make fun of him for being such a twat, and he would shout at me for being such a flake.

But hostility never lasted between us. We knew each other too well.

You know that question some people ask about who you would like to have with you if you were ever stranded on a deserted island in the middle of nowhere? Well, if I were unlucky enough to have shipwrecked somewhere and found myself with one other person in the whole world…I would hope it were Everly.

Everly was like the angel on my shoulder; my conscience, my savior. Call it cliché for a twin to be so fond and reliant on his other half, but in our case this cliché seems particularly true.

I don't think I was always so fond of him though. There was a time there when he was actually the last person I'd want to see waiting for me when I got home at night. I think he reminded me of all the things that I would never be. But looking back and trying to explain why I felt the way I did, it's now a bit clearer how he was merely an outlet for all the anger I was feeling towards myself at the time.

I always think about how our lives took such a shift after we both came out to each other and the world. Mine seemed to spiral into shittsville, where as his seemed...to get better.

As I said, it wasn't always easy to accept him. This is gonna sound retardedly selfish and very-up-my-own-ass, but for a while there I actually resented him. Growing up we couldn't have been more different. Everyone seemed to take an easy shine to Everly. No wonder, I mean let's face it he's practically a Golden Boy. Blonde, smart, clean-cut and always presentable...the boy almost shimmered in the sunlight for Chrissake. I guess I always felt like the black sheep when I was next to him, even though our bodies were identical, there was a great difference between us when you looked us in the eye. Once when Mum was pissed at me, she said that she thought Everly had a glimmer, but when she looked at me, all she saw was darkness.

That definitely stung.

Over the years those differences have begun to fade away and the twinkle in my eye has returned to mirror the one in his. I'm not kidding myself in thinking that I've got it all together and everything figured out, but I'm getting there.

I don't think it was until after the whole shitty situation with me and Mum that I started appreciating him again. I guess you could say that I sorta lost it there for a while. My own fault. Like any other teen I just didn't know where I stood for a few years there. I don't envy the teens of today.

Fuck. Poor lot. They've got it bad.

If only someone had stood there, looked me in the eye and forced me to listen to what was right for me, maybe I wouldn't have gone down the road I did. Not that I woulda listened, though. You know what it's like when you're young and stupid. I think my mistake was surrounding myself with people who didn't really care about *me*. Maybe if I had of hung out with Everly's crowd more, then I wouldn't be as fucked up as I am now!

Oh well. We are who we are, as they say.

# Everly

The heavy footsteps above my head spoke volumes as to his mood. *Lethargic. Moody.*

Without saying a word, they acted as a forshadowing to the conversation we were about to have. He would drag his sorry-self downstairs and plunk himself down in the chair across from me, his expression silently demanding a caffeine fix to help remove him from his funk.

I had heard him saunter in last night as I always did. I think whenever he goes out for the night I turn into a watchful mum; always falling asleep with one eye open and my ear forever listening out for his return. Try as I might to switch it off, I always end up giving in to it.

*For his sake.*

At least that's how my head sees it.

Hadley and I had moved into a split-level flat of our own almost two years ago now. Mum had insisted on cutting the cord, so to speak, in an attempt to get us more independent and less reliant on her help. You'd think a couple of twenty-something's would **want** to branch out and get away from their mother's protective ways…But what can I say, we're a couple of 'mumma's boys.'

We decided we couldn't imagine living outside of Brighton and found a little cosy flat just up from the seafront and not too far from Mum's Kemptown house. To be honest we lucked out. The rent was affordable, and it was close to the restaurant where Hadley busked tables and the bakery where I worked. The flat was in a quiet part of town but still rife with Brighton's cosmopolitan vibe and villagey-feel. I loved our little home and looking around at the beatifully decorated walls, I was filled with a warm, safe, homey-feeling.

Hadley, on the otherhand, was a messy flatmate. Early on we agreed that as long as he kept his mess confined to his own room, then I wouldn't complain. Every now and then it seemed to trickle out into the rest of the flat, which was when I turned into the nag that I so desperately tried to keep hidden from the world.

All in all, life with my little shithead of a brother was pretty good.

Thinking back again to last night, it was almost half past four in the morning when I heard his key in the lock. Whatever he was up to wasn't really any of my business. *That* I stopped caring about years ago. Hadley was his own man and I was through with trying to change him.

The creaking floor boards on the stairs prompted me to push my chair back and go over to the cupboard to pull down his favourite mug.

It was a gorgeous, early Autumn day outside. As I poured the hot black liquid into his oversized ceramic mug I couldn't help but admire the vivid colours out the window. It was early September and the leaves had just started to change. A dull breeze shook them and made them dangle fragilely from their branches. A mother and her child passed by outside, both bundled up with wooly jumpers to shield themselves from the shifting temperatures.

I turned just in time to see 'his Lordship' appear in the doorway. He paused momentarily, slumping against the doorframe and shooting me an all-telling glance which morphed into one of his sly smiles, which I knew meant he got lucky last night.

"Fuck me, you missed a party last night Ev."

Hadley shifted his weight and as predicted, eased himself into one of our kitchen chairs, resting his chin in his hands and letting out a deep grisly sigh.

"Good times, I'm guessing? Don't you have to work today?" I asked him, extending the cup of strong, steaming coffee to him.

"Cheers," he shrugged at me in that dismissive way he always did when he was trying to avoid talking about something.

I turned back towards the kitchen sink and silently urged him to go on with his sordid tale. As much as his particular lifestyle wasn't for me, I couldn't deny my curiosity.

"Seriously Ev, there was this bloke there last night who was all over my shit."

"Your *shit?*"

"Oh mate, you have no idea. Second I walk into the party he was on me like a rash," he joshed slugging back the thick liquid, "didn't bother me though, was kinda hot."

"And did he have a name?" I teased.

"Who gives a shit? To be honest he was a bit naff after a while, talking random shit all night, finally had to stick my dick in his mouth just to shut him up!"

I choked out a laugh. This was Hadley to a T. Honest, crass and completely in your face. I turned to face him once more, crossing my arms over my chest and taking him in. He was staring off into space, probably reliving last nights 'sex-capade' as he sipped his morning 'Jo'. He looked so cool and confident as he sat there before me. Freshly fucked and loving revelling in it in front of me.

I sighed as I wished for a second that I could be more like him.

Reading my thoughts he lifted his icy blue gaze to me and a smile cracked across his lips.

"What?"

I considered telling him off for being such a slag but quickly reconsidered and returned to the pile of dirty dishes in front of me. Sometimes it just wasn't worth it.

A moment's silence passed between us, the only noise the clanging of the dishes and Hadley's slurping at the table.

"So…You know Mum's going to be back in Brighton sometime today, right?" I implored changing the subject entirely.

Without turning around I could hear Hadley set his mug down on the table.

"Yeah, and…" he said, sounding somewhat annoyed at my implication.

"…And well, I'm not being funny, but you still…" I paused, "you still haven't sorted it really, have you?"

"Mate, I told you to leave it with me," he shot back defensively.

"Well Hadley, it's been weeks now."

"And I told you I'd bloody sort it, ok?"

I could tell by his tone that this wasn't going to end well if I kept pushing.

Our Mum had been away on business for the past three weeks, which was long enough for Hadley to borrow her car, without her permission I might add, and end up denting the front bonnet and smashing off the passenger rear view mirror one night when he'd had a little too much to drink. I gave him a severe tongue lashing and told him that I wasn't going to help cover his ass this time around. He'd made his bed and now it was time to face up for his stupidity.

If this had of been a few years ago then I would have taken a bullet for him, but enough was enough.

I went back to scrubbing the dirty plates, somewhat vigurously, and decided to let him fester in his cruelty. It must have worked, because a moment later he was up and at my side. Hadley put his hands lightly on my shoulders, his way of calming me and asserting his dominance at the same time. It was a truly patronising move on his part, but it usually worked.

The feeling of his hands on me made me feel instantly more relaxed. He had a way of making me feel reassured despite whatever I was feeling at the time.

"Come on now, don't be like that," he cooed into my ear nuzzling me in that way that made me squeemish. I jerked him away in disgust, which was exactly the reaction he was gunning for and made him erupt in a jerkish laugh.

"Hadley," I began, my back instantly up again, "you're such a-"

But I couldn't think of a word to finish my sentence. Instead I just sighed and went back to my dishes, recognising a losing battle when I saw one.

"Listen, I know I fucked up, but believe me I'll sort the bloody car...Stop worrying, k?"

There he went again. His tone so full of promise and assurance. I was powerless to fight back.

"Besides, I think you're bringing this up to distract me from the *real* issue at hand here."

"And what *real issue* might you be referring to?"

"The issue of *tonight* my dear boy."

"Tonight?"

"Don't pretend like you don't remember..." his voice trailed off giving me a second to catch up with his train of thought.

Truth was, he was right and I knew exactly what he was talking about.

"I don't know what you're talking about." I dismissed curtly.

"Fuck off, you don't!"

I didn't say anything. As always Hadley had seen through my clever distraction technique; whenever I wanted the spotlight off of me, I would instantly turn on the guilt and shine it directly on him and his latest failure. I knew he was smart enough to get the car sorted before our mum got back from her trip, hell he had enough dodgy types on his speed dial to call in a favor of the automobile sort whenever he needed one, so I wasn't worried. Truth of the matter was, I was silently hoping he would have forgotten by now about tonight. But that would have been too good to be true: Hadley had gotten us on the guest list for a new club that was opening tonight in town. Said it was pegged as being the 'hottest club in all of Brighton' and if we weren't there tonight at the opening then it would be social suicide...In his eyes obviously, not mine. Hadley knew clubbing wasn't my thing, but he said he had wanted to do this for me in lieu of our birthday that was coming up next week.

Personally I saw right through his gesture and knew he wasn't doing this for me in the slightest. He had probably only invited me in the first instance because his other friends couldn't make it.

Giving up my fake façade I decided to acknowledge him. "I don't think I can, Hadley."

"A-a-a-a, don't even think of bailing mate, I can see right through you," he tutted, leaning against the kitchen counter and crossing his arms over his chest.

"Hadley, why do you even want me to come with you in the first place? You know I'm just going to get there and then instantly want to leave, and then-"

"-And then nothing, you little shit! Come on, you promised! Besides we've been on the guestlist for weeks, and you don't even wanna know what I had to do to sort that in the bloody first place!"

He was right; I didn't want to know how he managed it.

"Oh Hadley, you know it's not my thing..."

"Listen Ev, it's gonna be huge. Monumental. A night to remember. Plus, I told you it was my birthday present to you!"

"You mean your birthday present to *yourself?*"

"Don't be so cheeky, you little bitch!" he said through a cheshire cat grin.

"But-"

"But nothing. Seriously Ev, you'd think I was dragging you to a fuckin' funeral. It's one night."

I sighed again. Something I had been doing a lot lately.

"You never know, you might actually have a good time."

"Doubt it," I groaned, knowing I'd been defeated.

"Hey, just think, you might actually meet someone."

I looked at him to see if he was actually serious. He widened his eyes as if to say 'why not?'

"Seriously?"

"What?"

"You know full well that I'm never going to meet anyone in a club."

He uncrossed his arms and rested his hands on his hips.

"Well aren't we Mister Hypocritical all of a sudden."

"What's that supposed to mean?"

"It means that you're being a little bitch who's knockin' something before he's even tried it."

"I am not!"

"You so are, Everly. I know you, so don't even try and pretend otherwise. You're coming tonight and that's *that*."

And with that he pushed himself off the counter and moved towards the doorway. I turned to follow him with my eyes.

"But Hadley, I…"

"Be ready by nine, we'll head to the Black Dove for cocktails beforehand," he shouted dismissively now from down the corridor.

I sighed once again knowing I had no choice in the matter. As I turned back to look once again out the front window and onto the street I had to smile despite myself. The more I thought about it, the more my feelings towards tonight started to change.

Deep down there was a little part of me that hoped Hadley was right. Maybe I would have a good time tonight, seeing as I wasn't being given much of a choice.

The sun was shining strongly on my face now as I leaned closer to the window and up at the steely blue sky above. It seemed the Universe was telling me to go out and let my hair down a bit.

I guess I did deserve a little break, didn't I?

# Hadley

I pulled open the doors to my walk-in wardrobe and mentally put together an outfit for tonight's festivities. I was thinking slutty-chic ; tight leather trousers, shirt unbuttoned practically to the waist, no underwear.

No point in going all out if you're not going to go all out, I always say.

Tonight was going to be insanity. I had heard about this new club opening up months ago now, and have been counting down the days ever since. A mate of mine was working the door and had oh-so-graciously hooked me up with VIP tickets to the opening in exchange for some oh-so-special cocaine that I had a link to.

As I rifled through the pile of clothes that lay on the floor of the wardrobe before me, I could hear Everly riffling around downstairs. No doubt he'd be shitting himself about tonight.

*Poor thing. He needs a good night out, not to mention a good ol' fucking while he's at it.*

He barely spoke about what happened with the closet case he had been 'secretely seeing,' and I didn't ask. The way he'd been sulking around the flat over the past few days was enough of a sign that things had fizzled out. Tonight he needed to just let go a little. Forget about his responsibilities and let me take care of everything.

I mean, what else are brothers for?

## Everly

Hadley was right. I did need a good night out. Sometimes I forget that I'm only twenty-four, and if it weren't for him I'd probably have become an old spinster way before my time.

*I hate when he's right.*

As I stood at the kitchen sink, peering out the window at the life that was passing me by, I decided then and there that tonight I would let myself go a little. I shuddered slightly just then as if a cold gust had just swept through the room. Swallowing hard, I hoped it wasn't a foreshadowing of an impending doom that was approaching tonight.

\*\*\*

Nine PM on the nose, and Hadley was nowhere to be found. I had just finished getting ready and already felt that my outfit was making a mockery of me. I had decided on a black denim button-down top with studded collar and a pair of spray-on skinny jeans and boots. As I stood in front of the bathroom mirror, desperately trying to decide on whether a bow-tie would be over the top or complementary, I could feel myself begin to waver.

*I would love nothing more than to climb into my pyjamas and sit on the sofa with a book and a glass of Pino Grigio.*

No. Stop it. That was enough. I didn't have to work till later tomorrow, and I was going out tonight to shake things up for once and that was that. I just needed to get myself out of my own head…and into Hadley's. But where the hell was he? He said he was headed out for the afternoon but to be ready by nine sharp.

I looked at my watch. Three minutes past nine. Sighing, I inwardly castrated myself for the hundredth time today for being such a square.

*It's only early still. He'll be here, so just relax before you get yourself all in a tizzy.*

Straightening up I reached for the black satin bow-tie that I had found in Hadley's closet and wrapped it around my neck. Taking one more look at myself in the mirror I gave myself a cheeky wink.

All modesty and nerves aside, I didn't look half bad.

*Well done me.*

# Hadley

I was late. I just knew Ev would be pissing himself wondering where I was. It had taken me longer than I had thought to take care of Mum's car. A guy I knew who owned his own garage owed me a favour and said he could fix the busted mirror and bonnet in a flash. As I pulled the Volvo into Mum's drive and shut off the engine, I contemplated ringing my control-freak of a brother to let him know I'd be there to pick him up soon but reconsidered.

*Let him sweat it out.*

Chuckling to myself I got out of the car and began the quick walk back to our flat.

Butterflies fluttered away in my stomach as I thought about the club tonight. It was going to be epic. It was about time Ev let me take him out and show him a good time. Poor sod needs a bit of a break. Sensible Everly. Always the good boy.

I slipped my hand into my pocket and felt around reassuringly for the small plastic baggie containing tonight's party favors. Convincing Everly to partake would be a bit of a challenge, but one that I was up for.

*This oughta loosen him up.*

\*\*\*

As anticipated, Everly gave me quite the verbal tongue-lashing when I opened the front door. But all was forgiven with a flash of my award-winning, shit-eating grin and a promise to buy the first round when we got there.

Being that I was running fashionably late, we skipped the pre-club cocktails and headed straight for the venue. The club was directly on the seafront, opposite the string of hotels facing Southward. Under

Brighton's promenade lay enough clubs and pubs to suit anything you fancy. If you were into techno, then 'Digital' was the one to hit. If it was more of a gay-poppy night you were after, then you went to 'Revenge'. But if you wanted house music, you went to 'Nitro' which was exactly where we were headed.

When the taxi pulled up outside the front of the club, I could feel Everly tense up beside me. Paying the driver, I followed his gaze to the enormous queue of people lined up outside and down the entire length of the building. He swallowed hard like he was passing a hard candy, and I put my hand on his and squeezed.

"Hey, hey," I whispered to him, "Relax…It's just a party."

He met my eyes and I could feel him loosen up slightly already as my calming twin-fluence washed over him.

"Thada boy, now come on. We've got a dance floor to hit."

No matter where Everly and I went together, heads turned. I'm not being cocky or nothin', but there's no denying the fact that we're fit looking lads. And when you multiply our good looks by two, well, let's just say we get a few lingering looks when we walk down the street.

Tonight was no exception. As we approached the queue I linked my arm in Everly's; a slightly overt gesture, with a tiny hint of homoeroticism.As expected, the sight of us approaching, arms entwined sent some tongues wagging. We looked *good*. I had decided on complementing Everly's look for the night and dressed up a bit more than I normally would have. My black velvet smoking jacket and open necked satin shirt contrasted nicely with my tight leather-look trousers.

As we got closer to the front of the queue I could feel the eyes of the other clubbers upon us. Their stares washed over us both taking in the sight of these gorgeous identical twins walking towards them, dressed to the nines and touching eachother just enough to suggest the most taboo of thoughts. Without even making eye contact I could hear their thoughts as we sashayed past.

*Are they?*

*I think they are.*

*Oh my God. Hot.*

*Sexy.*

*I wonder if they make out sometimes?*

Our minds obviously thinking the same thing, Ev and I turned our head at the same time to see our suspicions confirmed; jaws slightly slack and eyes wide, taking us in from head to toe. Everly squeezed my hand tighter, a sign of his teetering anxiety levels. I took his hand in mine and with my thumb gently stroked his palm; my never-fail trick to put him at ease. Instantly I could feel him relax further as he took a deep breath and turned to face the doorman who was also staring at us, a look of disbelief mixed with arousal splashed across his face.

Once face to face we stopped and both flashed him our sexiest 'come hither' look. One that I coined, and my copycat brother caught onto quickly enough when he realised how easily it got me what I wanted. Everly may come off all innocent and shit, but boy knew how to get what he wanted, believe you me. The doorman swallowed hard as he involuntarily let his eyes trail over us, lingering just a little too long and bordering on perverse.

"We're on the list," I breathed, both of us not taking our eyes off his.

He was silent for a moment as his brain processed the situation. He gave his head a quick shake as he remembered where he was.

"Uh," he stuttered, "names?"

"The Stone brothers," Everly piped up unexpectedly.

The doorman's eyes shifted from me to Everly then back to me again as he reached dumbly behind him for his list. After a quick glance he swallowed again before stepping aside and unfastening the red velvet rope that acted almost as a moat to the club.

"Have a good night gentlemen."

We obliged and walked through the doorway, stealing one final glance behind us at the queueing clubbers who were now slightly more pissed off than before. I tossed them a wink of my eye which was greeted with bitchy moans before disappearing into the darkness of the club.

# Everly

Once inside, the club was like an assault on your senses. The air was thick and dark except for the flashing rainbow-coloured lights that beamed down on the crowd from above the DJ booth. The throbbing of the base was so intense I could feel it reverberate inside me with each step I took. I slowed my pace as my eyes adjusted to the sudden darkness inside.

I was still holding Hadley's hand as he led me blindly into the club. It was crowded inside. Hundreds of faceless people danced and moved before me like shadows in time with the music. The décor was complete kitsch, from the old 60s pin-up girl paintings hung from every inch of space on the acid green painted walls, to the opium den-like furniture. The tables were low to the ground and placed inside little nooks carved out of the walls which obviously served as VIP areas. The barstaff wore butler uniforms and carried wide, round trays on flexed fingertips, balancing brightly-coloured drinks almost like acrobats. Looking around, I took note that the music didn't at all match the look of the club and I almost expected to hear jazz playing from a live band off in the corner instead of the thumping house that was beating its way out of the speakers in the room.

As Hadley pulled me towards the brightly lit bar I noticed that all the cocktail glasses were lit-up making them seem to almost move of their own accord as they contrasted with the dark shadowy figures that held them. There didn't seem to be a pint glass or beer bottle in sight. Instead everyone seemed to be sipping out of tall flutes or glow in the dark martini glasses.

"What do you want?" he screamed at me to be heard from over the pounding music.

"WHAT?" I yelled back, only half registering his voice.

"To drink? What do you want?"

"What are you having?" I couldn't begin to think of what I might want to drink, even though I knew that booze was exactly what I needed.

Hadley didn't answer, which was never a good sign, instead he just flashed me his best shit-eating grin, for the tenth time today,and yanked me further towards the glowing bar.

As we approached, the crowd of people seemed to spread its wings creating the perfect path leading us to our drinks. Upon seeing us approach, the bartender's eyes seemed to gravitate towards us leaving behind whatever or whoever he was attending to. Hadley leaned in as he came closer and whispered something in his ear that I couldn't hear over the roar of the speakers. I took the time to scan the room further, slowly getting used to my surroundings and starting to relax into it more and more by the second. Maybe it was the constant 'sizing you up' stares that made me so anxious in situations like these, or maybe it was simply my OCD that reared its ugly head whenever I submerged myself in social situations to that felt out of my league.

Whatever the reason, I was here now and as much as I would never admit it for fear of being socially castrated forever, I was proud of myself for making the effort.

*Maybe it wouldn't be such a bad night afterall.*

Hadley's subtle nudge made me spin back around towards the bartender whose sultry gaze was firmly locked on my brother. In between the two of them stood two neon-lit martini glasses containing the same cloudy elixir.

"Ev, this is Tom," he said grinning cheekily in the direction of the bartender.

I lifted my eyebrows in response, taking the martini glass and turning away while allowing myself an eye roll behind his back. A moment later Hadley joined me, resting his back against the counter.

"Cheers to a fuckin' great night," he jeered clinking his glass into mine.

"I turn my back for two seconds and already you've secured yourself a hook-up for tonight?" I teased, taking a sip of my drink as Hadley tossed back most of his in one go.

*Mmm, a cosmo. He knows me well.*

The bitter sweetness slid down my throat a little too easily, and I followed my demure sip with a heartier one now that I knew what I was drinking. The alcohol immediately began its loosening effect and I instantly felt more at ease.

Hadley just shrugged and finished off his drink, settling it on the bar behind him without turning his head from the dancefloor.

"Cheeky git," I muttered under my breath, a smile beginning to creep up upon my face. I took a page out of his book and tilted the glass back, quickly finishing off our first round. I studied Hadley's face for a moment, before taking in his stature. There was no denying the fact that he oozed confidence. His laid back stance and flippant attitude made him seem rebellious and carefree. Even as we stood there at the bar, out of immediate eyesight of the others in the club, it was as if he commanded the attention of those passing by without even trying. People couldn't help but let their gaze linger every so slightly too long over him as they went by. Besides his handsome features, (our handsome features) Hadley had something else going for him, as if he gave off some sort of scent that drew you in and forced you to stare. And he just ate it up, a smug little shadow of a smile flashing over his perfect mouth every time it happened. He'd deny taking any notice at all, but I knew better.

*I wish I could be as nonchalant as him.*

Although looking at him was like looking into a mirror, at the same time we couldn't be more different. Genetically identical, yet opposites in every other way. I looked down at the way I was holding myself; stiff, rigid and full of nervous energy. How easily I could fade into the crowd if I let myself. All my life it'd been this way; always willing to stand back so that Hadley could shine and lap up all the attention. It was he who was the more theatrical one of us. It was in his nature to be at the center of it all, while I seemed to prefer slinking away into the background. For whatever the reason, I felt safer when the focus was on someone else. But that wasn't the reason why we were here tonight…To disappear into the shadows. People came to places like this to *be* noticed. Night clubs were built to allow fantasies to come true. As I stared into the neon lights shining down on us and breathed in the heavy smell of intoxication, I started to see the appeal of it all; the thrill of acting out and letting go a bit.

*That's why you're here Everly.*

I could hear Hadley's voice ringing in my ears, begging me to relax. Maybe it was time to get out of my head and start living a little. No one knew me here and chances are I would never see them again. Tonight I could be someone else. Perhaps the way I had been feeling lately was a sign that it was time for me to stop playing the opening act to Hadley's main show.

I mean after all, *what did he have that I didn't?*

His eyes must have been able to hear my thoughts for he shifted them in my direction, a grin breaking out on his face.

"What?"

I didn't have to say anything. Instead I just turned around and winked in the bartender's direction. He responded immediately and sashayed over, much to the disdain of the other clubbers waiting to be served.

"Two more," I shouted, feeling a renewed rush of confidence all of a sudden.

"Thada boy," Hadley congratulated, turning around and resting both arms on the bar. "See?"

"See, what?"

"I knew this is what you needed."

"What do you mean?"

"I mean, THIS." He motioned with his hands to the space around us. "You needed to get the fuck out of the house, mate!"

As much as I hated to admit it, he was right. He could see how tightly wound I had become over the past few months. How I wasn't letting myself have any downtime. I hadn't had a decent relationship in what felt like ages and I was beginning to tire of carrying so much weight and baggage on my shoulders. If I didn't allow myself to unwind then I could see myself begin to crumble.

The bartender was back within seconds with another two glowing glasses. Hadley didn't waste any time reaching for one and knocking it back with an elegant toss of his head, all the while his eyes studying me, challenging me without saying anything at all.

He widened his stare as if to say *'go on then hot shot.'* He didn't think I would rise, I could tell. Accepting his challenge I turned to the bartender and flashed him my best attempt at a flirty smile before taking the drink and tossing it back in the same nonchalant way.

*There.*

He grinned at me, sticking his tongue out in my direction. "Rock n' roll, baby!"

Hadley dropped a note on the bar and grabbed my hand, pulling me away from the slack-jawed bartender before I could utter another word.

"Lesson number one for tonight…Leave them wanting more," he shouted over the music as he led me into the lion's den.

We made our way onto the dance floor and in moments were surrounded by the other clubbers. Completely immersed in the crowd, it felt as if we had been swallowed up and were now deep within the belly of the beast. In the center of the throng of faceless people the air was thicker; hot and laced with the sweet smell of sweat and aftershave. As we started to dance I began to feel anonymous amongst the people around me. No one was staring anymore. In fact most people's eyes were closed or focused straight ahead on the DJ in the booth overlooking us. In the air there was no judgement. No one was sizing you up or there to make you feel uncomfortable. Everyone was moving so uniquely; some with the sharpness of experience, while others simply moved from side to side with their hands stretched above their heads as if reaching for something unattainable dangling in the air. It was then that I let myself go…I started to move. I didn't imitate anyone, I just closed my eyes and let the music take over.

The alcohol that was running through my veins combined with the thudding base of the music was making me feel more alive than I had in weeks. As the people around me danced to the beat, I felt myself begin to drift away almost as if I were losing control of my limbs. If I closed my eyes I could pretend I was someone else. Someone free who lived in the moment. Someone more confident who didn't constantly worry about what others were thinking. It was so freeing to have a clear mind with only one focus. My head seemed to open up and with every stamp of my feet I was able to shake off a worry and leave it on the dancefloor. I felt lighter than air as the music seemed to carry away my insecurities leaving me feeling refreshed and alert.

The sudden heat of a hand on my forearm forced me to open my eyes and focus. It took me a second to realise it belonged to Hadley. He had stopped dancing and through the blinding strobe lights I could just barely make out a smile on his face. Staring at me I could see him giggle quietly to himself. I suddenly felt self-conscious and stopped dancing.

"What?" I shouted into his ear, "Do I look stupid?"

"Are you kidding?" he shouted back, leaning in close so I could feel his breath against my ear, "You look incredible."

I pulled back to see if he was being serious and was instantly at ease when I took in the sincerity of his stare.

"Come with me for a second."

"But we just-"

"Just come on, trust me."

It was never comforting when he uttered those words.

***

When we got to the toilets, the queue was about thirty people deep. Hadley sighed and got on his tiptoes to get a better look at the hold-up. Without hesitation, he took my hand and began to bypass the queue.

"What are you-" I began before being silently hushed by his wide-eyed look that said '*shut up and follow me.*'

"Sorry, sorry guys, got a *puker* here! Emergency folks, stand clear!"

People started to clear a path as Hadley took no prisoners in dragging me inside. Once inside and around the corner the toilets were surprisingly posh looking. Wall to wall mirrored stalls surrounded a circular shaped sink/water fountain in the center with numerous taps all ejaculating water into a large basin. In the center of the room above the sink hung an enormous chandelier, with a huge spotlight above our heads shining directly onto it. The effect showered the room with hundreds of twinkling irridescent shards of light. Off to the side, as if hidden from view, another DJ was spinning beautiful chilled house music as if inviting people to get comfortable in the loo's and stay a while.

Once again I was torn from my trance by the feeling of Hadley's hand on my arm tugging me towards an open toilet door. Before I could protest and question exactly what my brother had up his sleeve, he was sliding the lock to the cubicle shut behind me and digging his hand into his trouser pocket.

"Hadley, what are you…"

It took a moment for my eyes to adjust the sudden darkness inside the toilet, and a moment further to focus on what he was holding out in his palm. I had to lean in closer to get a better look.

"Hadley, I…" I stuttered upon seeing the small clear baggie in his hand. I knew exactly what the generous amount of white powder was that bulged inside and I could feel my heart begin to race and a sudden wave of nausea wash over me at the implication.

When I lifted my eyes up to his, it was as if his stare had darkened. His smile wasn't warm and inviting anymore, instead it seemed almost feral in the shadows of the toilet.

"You looked so amazing out there."

"Thanks, but I-"

"No but's."

After silencing me with a finger to his lips, he turned towards the toilet and opened the little baggie and began emptying some onto the top of the tank.

"It's just a little something to help you get even more into the groove."

His hushed tone was like liquid velvet. That same voice he always used when trying to get what he wants.

"Don't worry, I'm here with you. I won't let anything happen to you, k? I promise." He turned back towards me and his eyes were instantly warmer, as if he could heat and cool them on demand.

I didn't know if it was the two cocktails I had just downed, or the intoxication of the club itself, but I was letting his words work their magic on me. For some reason, when they came from Hadley I couldn't help but believe him and feel safe putting myself in his care. He cracked a slow burning smile as he realised I was letting him in.

"Rock and roll," he whispered through gritted teeth as he pulled a note out of his back pocket and rolled it up tightly. I leaned my head to get a better look at his technique as he placed the rolled up bill into his right nostril and plugged his left with his index finger from the other hand. He inhaled deeply with a quick sweeping motion of the bill across the toilet tank. His head shot up and he inhaled a second time, tilting his head back and staring up at the ceiling.

"Damn," he whispered, wiping his nose with the pad of his thumb. "Your turn."

*What the hell am I doing?*

I hesitated. My arms were tightly at my sides and my hands had balled themselves into knotted fists. The courage and the carefree feelings I had just felt were quickly disintegrating, and I could sense the familiar feelings of awkwardness and fear begin to creep back up into my throat. Hadley must have been able to read my expression because he instinctually put both hands on my shoulders. The heat from his palms had a calming effect on my body and I took a deep breath as my worried eyes searched his for reassurance.

"Hey, hey, hey, I'm here…What did I just tell you, yah?" His liquid tone was back again, and this time I closed my eyes and focused on his voice. "Just a little, k? I'm not going anywhere…I'm so proud of you, remember? You need this."

I opened my eyes and forced another deep breath down into my lungs.

"Ready?" he inched me towards the toilet.

*Come on Everly…Live a little.*

I nodded and took the rolled up bank note from his hand.

"Awesome," he cooed, obviously very happy with himself that I had let his bad influence win over my rational side for once. "Right, stick this up one of your nostrils and plug the other with your other hand. Let out all the air in your chest and when you're ready, stick the note at the end of the line and just inhale as quick as you can and snort it all up."

"Are you sure? This seems like a lot."

"It's only a little line, trust me. You'll be fine."

I nodded again and with the bill in my nose, swipped it clean across the surface, snorting the white powder up in one go. I lifted my head and gritted my teeth as I sniffed hard again, pinching the skin at the bridge of my nose in an attempt to counteract the burning sensation that quickly followed. Opening one eyelid, I saw Everly staring back at me with the same dark expression as before, an eerie smile twisting his beautiful features.

I let out a deep breath and straightened up. I could feel the sharp powdery taste of chemical as it seemed to drip from my nasal cavity all the way down my throat. The taste almost made me gag, which Hadley picked up on immediately.

"Let it happen…It's the drip, it's the best part."

Closing my eyes, I obeyed and stilled myself for a moment as I let the drug do what it intended to do. As moments passed, I could almost feel it begin to settle inside of me. I imagined it sliding through my veins, igniting the pleasure principles as it went. I knew enough about cocaine already and had researched it in the past, mainly as a precaution in case I ever had to phone an ambulance on my brother so I knew what it did. I peered out under my long lashes and looked Hadley in the eye and imagined what he was thinking, realising quickly that the thoughts running through his head in no way mirrored those in mine. He looked so alive and beaming, whereas I was positive I must look haggard and messy in comparaison.

Shutting my eyes again, flashes of the drugs biosynthesis danced before the inside of my lids.

*You are such a nerd, Everly Stone.*

I knew Hadley still did coke after all these years, and I had taken it upon myself to learn as much about the drug as possible so at least one of us would be educated on how to be cautious around it. As each second passed, the geek inside of me  listed the effects as they hit me one by one. I could practically feel my serotonin reuptake being inhibited as an intense euphoria grabbed hold of me, tightening my chest like a vice. I saw the chemical compounds listed in my head like a grocery list and as I scanned through it I felt myself begin to shiver uncontrollably realising what I had just voluntarily put in my body.

Never did I think that I would be here, locked in a bathroom stall voluntarily doing what I had always tried to prevent my brother from doing. As much as I tried not to, I couldn't help but feel like a bit of a martyr.

When Hadley touched me again, his skin on my skin felt warm and more fantastic than ever before. My lids shot open and I could sense the sudden wideness of my eyes. I took another deep breath, and let the oxygen infuse me even further until the point where I smiled at the intense pleasure that was seeping into my bones. I was giving in, despite all the rational thoughts in my head telling me to fight it, it was a losing battle. The devil and angel on my shoulders were duking it out to the point where their voices in my ears began to deafen me.

Hadley returned my smile then in the best way he knew how, which once again seemed to aenesthetise me with its hypnotic appeal.

"*Now*, let's go *fucking dance.*"

# Hadley

*This was good coke. Fucking hell.*

My man had come through for me again. I looked back at Ev as I dragged him back to the dancefloor, much more obediently this time I must admit, and couldn't believe the smile plastered across his face.

*Well done Ev, you fucking did it!*

I knew he just needed to let go for once. Always the sensible one, taking care of everyone except for himself. I knew if I could actually get him out of the house for once and into *my* world, he'd have a little taste and finally let loose a bit. I mean, what are brothers for anyway, right?

I knew deep down that tomorrow he'd probably wake up and feel like shit and hate me for letting him get into this crap. But seeing him happy like this, dancing with not a bloody care in the world, this made me happy.

When we got back to our little niche in the center of the crowded dancefloor, I reached into my back pocket and took out my mobile.

"Come here," I shouted at him with an outstretched arm. He didn't hesitate and immediately came in for a cuddle and focused on the mobile in my hand. "Say cheeeeeeese."

We positioned ourselves, cheek to cheek and stared up at the back of my phone for the world's cheesiest selfie. I snapped a picture of us; the flash momentarily blinding as we both blinked hard as spots filled our vision. I wanted to have photographic proof of how fucking cool my brother can actually be when he takes the tampon out of his vagina and actually lives a little.

I couldn't stop staring at him. With his arms above his head and his eyes down to the ground, he moved to the sound of the cracking bass with more ease and rhythm than I had ever seen him. As the sound of the music began a sharp crescendo that swept across the crowd like a tsunami, everyone let out loud whoops of approval. I looked up at where the DJ stood in his pedestal above the crowd, a fist pumping hard into the air like he was trying to burst an invisible balloon above his head. The energy in the room was electric. Everly was completely lost in the music. When he lifted his head again, his eyes were lightly closed and he was letting the beat rule his movements.

I leaned my head in and took his in between my hands. "This is the hottest you've ever looked, Ev."

He didn't respond, but instead wrapped his arms around me and hugged me hard.

"I love you so much, mate," he screamed.

I couldn't help but giggle as I took in the surrealism of the night so far. I knew it was going to be an epic night, but I didn't expect this from Ev. Inside I could feel a faint pang of guilt seep into my gut as I hoped he wouldn't regret tonight and instead just go with it. As we danced side by side now, I couldn't help but think what our lives would be like if Everly and I were more alike. Partners in crime, each as much a toxic influence on the other.

People always said the fact that we were so different was what made us so strong. He, always there to balance me out when I got out of hand, and I always there to…Well, there to shake things up, I suppose. I couldn't help but frown at the realisation of my true part in our lives.

*Was I always going to be like this?*

I was knocked out of my own thoughts by a sharp push from someone behind me. Spinning around, my face a mask of sudden fury, I was greeted with a sight that I hadn't expected. Everly felt me turn sharply and mimicked my immediate response, stopping as quick as I did upon seeing the apparent 'pusher'.

Both of us were momentarily stunned by what we saw.

# Everly

I could feel the bass in my bones. It was as if the sound had become a part of me. My ears were no longer the only orifice from which to experience the music, instead the notes seemed to almost seep into my pores as if by osmosis. Every inch of my skin tingled and I'm sure if I were to look down, the hairs would be standing at complete attention. My feet began to feel lighter as they pounded into the floor, as if they were preparing to take flight and lift me above the crowd so I could look down onto them from up high.

I reached to grip Hadley's arm for sudden support and to relay to him how happy I was at that moment. But before I could grab hold, out of the corner of my eye I saw him whirl around suddenly, the movement swift and born out of anger. Turning as quickly as he had in the same direction, I'm sure my mouth dangled open when I laid eyes on the person standing just behind us…

## Hadley

It was the way he was standing that caught my eye at first; so tall and sure of himself, almost as if he literally were God's gift to gay men. And as the thumping strobe lights above us illuminated his face, I almost began to think that he was.

# Everly

He was just about as tall as us. Dark hair, with a face dusted lightly with perfectly grown in facial hair that signalled a few days worth of growth.

Immediately I thought it suited him.

He wore a tight-fitting red t-shirt that hugged his chest in all the right places, showing off what appeared to be rock hard, round pecks. My eyes drifted down his body of their own accord and stopped at the outline of his round nipples, which despite the incredibly heavy heat of the club were surprisingly erect.

He cleared his throat suddenly, which forced my gaze back up to his face. I squinted in the darkness to make out his features.

"Sorry about that," I think he said, although I couldn't be sure over the roar of the speakers.

"Don't worry about it," Hadley replied, his initial fury quickly stricken and replaced with his usual familiar look of demure sexiness. He leaned in to say something else to him that I couldn't hear, putting his hand gently on his bicep. I took the moment to study his face a bit closer. His hair was swept back in a casual quiff off his smooth forehead. His eyebrows were thick and masculine and even in the shadowy darkness of the club, I could make out the warm brown hue of his eyes. His cute nose was almost button-shaped which made my stomach flutter, and his lips were plump and moist, curled up into a sort of half-smile. His shoulders shook slightly as he laughed softly at whatever sweet-nothings Hadley had just whispered in his ear.

Hadley leant back beside me and entwined his arm in mine.

"This is Everly," he motioned, resting his head on my shoulder protectively.

"I'm Kyle," he said extending a hand in my direction in a tone that was at once manly and boyish despite his impressive frame.

I wasn't sure of how to react. I met his hand with my own and opened up my mouth to speak, but nothing came out. His grip was firm and I tried my best to shake it back with a bit of force to mirror his confidence, but found myself caught up in the deep pools of his eyes.

He chuckled to himself, obviously amused at my apparent muteness.

"You'll have to excuse my brother; he's the shier one of us."

Hadley's condescending tone woke me up and I pinched his forearm hard sending him reeling away from me.

"Ow!" he screeched releasing me from his grip.

I took the moment to recover quickly and turned on a smile, flashing my teeth in Kyle's direction.

"You'll have to excuse **my** brother, he's the sluttier one of us," I shot back with a wry smile in Hadley's direction.

Kyle laughed again and returned my smile.

*Oh my god, he's cute.*

"Wow, I don't think I've ever actually met *identical* twins before," he said, his eyes darting up and down Hadley quickly before returning to rest on me.

"Oh really?" Hadley said, desperate to get the attention back to him. He ran a hand through his black hair, displaying a flexed bicep in a very unmodest attempt to get him to stare.

Unfortunately Kyle bit, and I saw his eyes trail over Hadley's muscular arm and his gaze begin to smoulder slightly at the sight.

"I guess it's my lucky night…" Kyle said biting his bottom lip slightly. His tone was quieter as if I wasn't meant to hear what he said.

I straightened up a bit, the pleasure in my veins beginning to wain slightly.

*You're no match for Hadley.*

My eyes narrowed at the sight of my brother, my twin, begin to turn on the charm and flirt his little bum off with the beautiful stranger who stood in front of us. I quickly began to feel out of place as Hadley took Kyle's arm and turned him slightly more towards him and away from me. I stood there watching them for a moment too long as that oh-sofamiliar feeling of awkwardness took over, and I suddenly felt like I didn't belong there.

I took a step away from the scene being played out in front of me and contemplated my next move. Looking around the room, everything now seemed almost unfamiliar, as if I was looking at it for the first time all night. The lights seemed somewhat dimmer and the people even more faceless than before.

I felt sick. Claustrophobic, even. Immediately craving the comfort of my bed and the familiarity of home. My feet moved me another step away from Hadley who now had his arms around the beautiful stranger and whose head was leaning in closer to his face. My stomach churned and gurgled as a foul taste rose up my throat and stung my taste buds.

I was just about to turn and walk away when Hadley's eyes shifted to meet mine. He tilted his head towards me slightly, just enough for me to see the smallest smile creep up onto his lips before he turned again and pressed them against Kyle's.

I'm sure I flinched as he kissed him right there in front of me. Hungrily his lips moved against Kyle's, opening further to invite his tongue into his mouth.

That's when I turned and headed for the exit door.

# Hadley

The taxi ride home was brutal. Lucky me scored a chatty fuckin' cab driver who wanted nothing more than to regale me with stories of his daughter's recent bloody graduation the whole fuckin' ride home. It was all I could do to not do a 'ride and ditch' just to teach him a lesson. I mean, come on; dude gets in a cab at five AM from a club, do you think he's gonna be up for a bloody chin wag?

When I saw our building coming up on the right, I scanned the North facing wall for our flat, hoping to see Ev's light still on. But the entire wall of our small building was in complete darkness. My stomach sank a bit as the car came to a stop and I paid the man.

*He's gonna be so pissed I bailed on him. After all the convincing I had to do, and I go fuck it all up for us.*

I must have lost Ev at some point in the night. The last time I remember seeing him was just before I hooked up with…What was his name, again? Kevin…Karl…

*Fuck.*

I wracked my brain for his name as I approached our front door and fumbled drunkenly for my keys. I could almost hear Everly's voice in my head as he began his inevitable scolding and telling-off rant. He'd throw words like *responsibility, respect* and *family* into the mix and top it all off with a whopping of *disappointment.* I hated when he got all high and mighty on my ass.

*Kirk? No…*

I could feel my legs sway as I tried once, twice and three times to get that bloody key in the slot. On the fourth try I took hold of the door frame for support as the coke and booze continued their toxic dance inside my belly, forcing my eyes to go in and out of focus.

Finally, the bloody key worked its magic and our front door released itself open. I had to shield my eyes from the fluorescent brightness of the communal hallway. Bleery-eyed, I made my way up the two flights of stairs to our flat. The feeling of guilt and dread beginning to overflow inside me more and more with each step I took...

# Everly

I was still wide-awake when I heard Hadley fumble his way inside the flat. The feeling I felt when he finally dragged his ass home was two fold; part of me was relieved he was home safe, as I always was when he went out, and another part of me was furious at having been ditched.

I had been sat stewing ever since I stepped in our front door, staring at my phone and willing in vain for Hadley to ring. If only he had at least rang to check that I was okay, or that I got home safely...I would have been able to fall asleep.

But alas, he didn't call. I guess I never really expected him to. Mum would say that I was only setting myself up for disappointment by hoping he'd do something he was never going to do. Hadley wasn't the type to call and check-in. Never was and probably never would be. Mum seems to have come to terms with that long ago, but for some reason I still hung on to the hope that one day he would wake up and start thinking of other people's feelings for once over his own.

I'll probably always be waiting for that day.

\*\*\*

The next morning I awoke with a throbbing numbness in my head. It wasn't the worse hang-over I'd ever had, but it certainly wasn't the tamest. As I rolled over and let my feet gently touch the cold floor beneath my bed, I immediately felt the smallest seed of guilt begin to manifest itself in my gut. My head began to catch up with my body and started to relapse into the events of last night. I squeezed my eyes shut in an effort to will the guilt away. I knew exactly what it wanted. It wanted me to feel bad for last night. It wanted me to wallow in the fact that I had allowed myself to be influenced by Hadley's peer pressure and succombed to his will. But as I sat there on the edge of my bed, feet dangling just inches above the floor and head slightly throbbing, I realised there was no point in feeling sorry for myself.

*What's done is done.*

I knew myself well enough to be able to predict how I would feel about things this morning. I *should* be beating myself up internally about how I should never have done what I did, and how I regretted the whole night and how I should have listened to that little voice inside that told me to just stay at home with pyjamas and a dvd...

But as my eyes cracked open slightly and veered towards the sunshine filtering in through my open window something inside me seemed to click and begin to drain the threatening guilt from the pit of my stomach. The cool breeze that fluttered my curtains, reached my face and I closed my eyes to let the breeze work its sweeping motion over me, taking with it the guilt and leaving instead a feeling of tranquility. I inhaled the sweet outdoorsy scent of Autumn leaves that was slowly drifting through the window, and immediately felt more at ease.

*Why sit here and feel bad about myself? I'm only twenty-four, afterall! So I have one wild night in my early twenties, is that so wrong?*

My mind began to replay the events of last night and I couldn't help but smile despite my inner conflict. Letting go, actually felt good. I was always in control of things in my life, and for once it felt almost liberating to be able to relinquish it, even if only for a night. I allowed my face to crack into a smile and I wrapped my arms tightly around my chest, giving myself a warm hug of acknowledgement, before finally stepping out of bed.

I caught a glimpse of myself in the full-length mirror along the wall and nearly let out a gasp.

*You look like crap.*

Running a hand through my icy blonde mop, I took in the time.

*11.50*

Just enough time for a quick shower before work. If I hurry...

# Hadley

I could hear him start to move around in his room next door, and I rolled over onto my back to get a better look at the ceiling. Staring at the ceiling always helped me to think. I thought about that guy. Kyle, was his name. I remembered it as soon as I opened my eyes.

*Kyle. Fuck, he was sexy.*

Hooking up with guys was nothing crazy unusual for me when I went out. To be honest, *not* hooking up with guys was unusual for me when I went out. But this one didn't turn out exactly as I had hoped.

I remember when I first turned around last night at the club, fists already balled, ready to give the guy who pushed me a piece of my mind…That was when I saw him…My fists had relaxed almost immediately. Damn, he was hot. No denying that. Totally my type too; tall, dark, muscular, tattoos. And a club kid, which is right up my alley. I didn't waste any time sticking my tongue down his throat; givin' him a little taste of what Hadley Stone has to offer. He was such a great kisser. Even as I lay here I could still taste his mouth. His lips were some of the biggest I've ever made out with. Big, soft and tasted of cherries.

I closed my eyes and let my mind wander back to last night. My right hand began to creep under the sheets and started playing with my dick, just gently rubbing at first as I thought about having him here with me. Naked. His lips on mine again. Kissing him last night, I knew straight away I was going to fuck him. I always know when I kiss someone for the first time whether they'll make it with me or not. And he was a sure thing…

*Only it didn't happen…*

When I pulled away from him last night and saw that Ev was gone, it totally ruined my groove. I could picture Everly's lecture already, and I hadn't even left the club yet. I looked around for him, but I was too coked up at the time to care enough to go looking for him. Especially with this guy's tongue licking my ear. He must have felt me pull away slightly and followed my eyes around the room.

"Something wrong?" he had asked.

"My brother…I think he split."

I had squinted in the darkness of the club to get a better look, but it was no use. He'd gone. I turned back to Kyle, but the moment had abruptly ended.

"Sorry…I just…"

"Nah, it's all good. I get it," he let out in a slightly hurt-sounding tone, "You want me to help you look?"

And then he did. We looked all over the club; toilets, chill area, smoking area outside. We even went down to the beach, climbing blindly over the pebbles, the pounding of the waves our only guide.

Everly always came to the beach to think…

I called out a couple of times. Tried his mobile again for the hundredth time and still got nothing. That's when this sexy stranger invited me to sit.

Yup, to *sit*. Not to climb on top of him. Not to blow him there on the rocks.

Just to sit. And talk.

I was sure he was fucking with me, but as he took my hand and gently pulled me to a seating position, I realised he was actually serious.

My coke and booze fueled body that wanted to dance, or fuck, or at least move, was fighting with my head who was shouting at me to just fucking *sit* already before this guy disappears for good. Since he had to be some sort of drug-fueled figment of my imagination, cause there was no way he was for real!

But he was.

As I sat there next to him, staring out at the dimly-lit sea before us, I felt an unfamiliar calmness sweep through me. I peered at him out of the corner of my eye and saw that he too was staring out into the water. I couldn't quite explain the feeling I was feeling, sitting there next to him, our legs just gently touching. It was as if I had swallowed a bunch of actual butterflies and they were going ape-shit inside my stomach. I could almost hear my heart beating inside my chest. Thudding away and obviously excited by what was going on.

"I love the sea at night," he breathed quietly, "don't you?"

"Uhh," I stammered, slightly unsure how to answer such a question that had absolutely no undertone. "Yeah, I, it's beautiful?" My words came out more as a question than a statement.

Kyle chuckled softly to himself and cocked his head towards me, bending his legs and resting his arms on his knees.

"Don't you ever come down here at night?" he asked surprised.

Truth was, I didn't. I didn't really come down to the beach at all. This was totally more an Everly thing to do; come down to the sea with a date and just peer out into the waves. Thinking. The butterflies were still working away at my gut to the point where my hands were beginning to shake. I started panicking at the thought that I might actually disappoint this guy who was sitting next to me if I didn't pretend to be exactly who he was hoping I was.

I shuddered as I realised that perhaps I shouldn't be here, doing this with this guy. Everly was obviously pissed at me, but maybe not for the reason I was thinking he was. Maybe he was upset cause I got in there first with this bloke. I thought back to the look on his face when he too turned around to see him staring at us. I had seen that look in Everly's eyes before. That dumb struck look. He did seem quite taken with him when he started to speak.

*I am such a shit.*

I suddenly felt very uncomfortable and started to wriggle where I sat, as if I couldn't get comfortable.

"You alright?"

I looked into his eyes and was caught by how the light from the moon made the brown hue in them almost glow.

"Did I say something?" his voice trailed off. I continued to stare into those beautiful eyes, momentarily mute as I took in how beautiful his face actually was. His dark brows were furrowed causing a slight crease to form inbetween them above the bridge of his nose. His lips seemed almost fuller when he wasn't smiling and I noticed that his ears stuck out, just slightly more than they should, giving his face a boyish cuteness to complement his very manly physique. When I didn't move he took it as his chance and lifted an arm to cup my cheek in his hand. The soft pad of his thumb grazed my bottom lip ever so gently before he used his hand to pull my face into his. I closed my eyes, knowing what was about to happen was going to add to the guilt I felt tomorrow, but let him press his lips to mine anyways. His kiss was so gentle. His tongue parted my mouth and worked away softly at my own. I could taste his sweet breath as our heads kneeded into eachother, tilting slightly in opposite directions to allow the other to hungrily lap away. He pulled me in further still, grinding his face into my own, his tongue beginning to kiss and prod a little more feverishly as our temperatures rose and our bodies started to ache and wain. I could feel my own hands find his torso and work their way down to the bottom of his t-shirt, calling out to feel the touch of his skin.

It was then that I pulled away slightly. He sensed my reluctance and allowed his hand to drop back to the ground, releasing me of his clutch. I didn't want to open my eyes, for fear of the expression staring back at me. I was sure he would take it as rejection, even though it was anything but.

But as I peeled my lids open, there was a boyish, side-ways smile across his face. His light dusting of facial hair gave him a more manly shadow.

"I'm, I'm sorry," I was nothing but stutters now.

"Don't be, I get it…"

"I'm sorry, really, I just should probably be-"

"-Getting back, I know. Your brother."

"He doesn't usually come out clubbing, so I'm a little worried where he might have gone."

"I understand. Really. I think it's sweet that you care so much."

I allowed myself a little laugh as I realised that I was letting him think something of me that wasn't at all near to the truth. He was wrong; I wasn't the type to be so worried about someone else…And yet I didn't correct him. Something inside me liked the fact that he thought I was something I wasn't. Maybe I *wanted* to be something that I wasn't.

"Listen, do you think I could, maybe, possibly…" he began.

He was looking at me from under his long lashes in a cheeky, naughty way, willing me to finish his sentence. I obliged, smiling at his charm.

"Ring me sometime?"

"I'd love to!" he said, straightening up and allowing a full blown grin to take over his face, obviously pleased with himself.

He pulled out his phone, and I dictated my number to him. I actually had to concentrate so as *not* to give him a fake number as I was accustomed to doing so many times in the past. If he were anybody else, I would have completely lost interest in him the second I realised he wasn't just interested in me for a quick fuck, and then gone and given him a fake number just to satisfy him and get him off my back. I couldn't quite put my finger on it exactly, but something inside of me was urging me forward and telling me to give it a go. Everly was a disappearing memory already as I found myself so completely lost in this moment that I was dreading its end.

When Kyle's head was down I took a chance and stared at him like a retard, studying the side of his face, the colour of his hair and the curve of his jaw line. All in case I never got to see them again, I was suddenly desperate to remember him and this moment exactly as it was in case it all turned out to be a dream…

But it certainly wasn't a dream…

The second I woke up this morning, he was the first thing I thought of. His lips. His chocolatey smooth eyes. The roughness of his facial hair against my skin. It was then that I realised I had a full blown hard-on that was pitching a tent beneath my thin sheet. I squeezed obligingly, the sensation of wrapping my hand around my own meat sending ripples of pleasure up and down my hung-over body. I let my thoughts wander further and imagined his breath on my face as he jerked me off in my bed, studying my expression as his hand brought me closer and closer to coming.

*Delicious way to start my day…*

# Everly

My shower helped me to feel half-way normal again. I had let the water run super hot before stepping inside so as to burn away my sins from the night before. And as I walked the brisk early Autumn walk through the twisted side streets to work, my skin still felt warmed.

Work was at the Angel Food Bakery, and after fours years of being employed I was recently awarded the elusive title of manager to my little team of six bakers. The bakery was my little haven; it was the one place in my life where I could come and feel in complete control. The staff were respectful and compliant, the customers were always kind, and we were truly like a little family.

And don't even get me started on the cupcakes.

I had always loved to bake. Cakes, cookies, scones, didn't matter! It truly was my ambition to one day own a little bakery, such as this one, that I could call mine. Angel Food felt like mine, but deep down I think I would always know that even if I were to one day miraculously come up with the money to make an offer on the business itself, it would always be someone else's venture that I was just lucky enough to take over.

No, when I was ready to own my own shop, everything would be one hundred percent authentic Everly Stone. I could already envision it; from the counter tops, to the wall décor, to the name: '*Slice of Heaven*'.

Mum was behind me all the way, always had been. She was so proud of my drive and motivation to be successful. Perhaps even more so since my twin seemed to have none whatsoever. Hadley and I couldn't be more different in that way. He was more than happy just doing shit job after shit job, simply to pay the rent. He never seemed to have any ambition beyond making a bit of cash to satisfy his many vices.

Where as I always knew I wanted to be a business owner. After secondary school I had taken a business management course at the local college and came out top of my class. My lecturors told me I had a very keen business savy and that with my solid approach, would go far in that world. And at the ripe old age of twenty-four, I doubt many people could call themselves 'manager' of a place they love so much.

When I opened the door to the shop, the waft of sugary sweetness that greeted you on arrival was enough to make your mouth-water. I stopped for a split-second and allowed my eyes to blink shut and appreciate for a moment before continuing my path behind the counter.

Katie, my newest and youngest employee, was the only one on staff so far and greeted me with a smile that quickly turned into a frown as she took in my appearance.

"Oh my, Everly, are you alright?" she asked making a face like she had just bitten into a lemon.

"Bloody hell," I shot back putting down my sling bag and giving her a playful slap on the arm, "is it that bad?"

She quickly straightened up at the realisation that she may have really hurt my feelings. "No, no, no, I mean…You just look a little…Tired, that's all."

"Yah, yah," I began reaching for my apron that was hanging on the other side of the stock room door.

"Fun night then, I'm guessing?"

"To a degree."

"To a degree, eh? And what degree would that be, exactly?" she inquired, leaning up against the counter and crossing her arms.

"Well, it was fun. Sort of. Until…"

"Until, what? Let me guess, until you actually had *fun?*" she jeered, accentuating the word.

"No, thank you very much. I had fun…It was fun, until, well until I met this guy…" my voice trailed off.

The look on Katie's face was priceless, speaking volumes without muttering a word. I took the wideness of her eyes as a sign that she wanted me to go on.

"Don't get too excited, I mean nothing...happened."

She instantly relaxed, disappointment flashing across her dainty features.

"How come?" she asked, jutting out her lower lip in mock dismay.

"Well..."

"Let me guess," she interrupted, putting up a hand to silence me, "Hadley got there first."

My eyes lowered themselves to the ground and I busied my hands with tying my apron behind my back.

"Honestly, that boy." Katie steeled herself away from me shaking her head as she turned back to the job she had started before I came in. "How did I know that was going to happen."

Whenever people put Hadley down, I instantly felt the need to defend him, even when I knew they were right.

"Wait a minute, wait a minute don't get ahead of yourself, he's not all to blame."

"Oh, really?" she challenged putting a hand on her hip. "How so?"

"Well he...I mean, I didn't..."

"You chickened out, didn't you?"

I started picking my nails as I always did when I got nervous.

"Honestly then Everly, I think it's time you grew a pair. I can't blame the guy for swooping in and stealing him as I imagine you were trying to play it cool, as you always do, and probably missed your opportunity in the first place."

I knew she was right. Hearing it from someone who wasn't in your own head made the reality seem all the harsher.

"Am I right?"

I whispered an acknowledged response under my breath and more to the floor than to Katie.

"I'm sorry, I didn't catch that."

When I looked up her expression had softened and I could see that she was on my side despite the tone of her response.

"Oh Everly Stone, what am I going to do with you."

I let her words swirl about in my head as I punched my log-in details into the till and let out a sigh from deep inside my belly that expressed my inner-frustrations more than winging ever could.

Outside the shop, the throngs of passer-by's in the Lanes, Brighton's infamous shopping entanglement of sidestreets, continued to parade up and down the narrow passage-ways, the sounds of nonchalant laughter echoing across the walls as they disappeared out of view. I watched as faceless Brightonians went about their merry way, unbeknownst to the inner-plight that I felt deep in my gut. Katie was right. I did let a good opportunity pass me by and I couldn't blame Hadley for getting in there first. Afterall, all's fair in love and war, as they say. Why should it be any different for brothers?

At the end of the day Hadley had something I didn't. Confidence. It didn't matter that on the outside we were mirror images of each other. On the inside we couldn't be more different. The fact of the matter was that I cared what people thought, where as Hadley couldn't be bothered. I thought before I acted, where as Hadley jumped in head first, so when the chips were down I missed out and my other half came out on top. Every time.

Shaking my head in a vain attempt to bring myself back down to earth I steered my thoughts towards the day ahead.

\*\*\*

To say the day dragged by would be an understatement. In fact I'm sure I fell asleep standing up at a few different occasions. My mobile that was securely tucked away in my tight denim jeans tickled me incessantly as it vibrated every few minutes throughout the day. I didn't need to look at it to know that it was Hadley. By half three when I dared to venture a peek I saw that there were thirty three missed calls. All from the same number.

Hadley never left voice mails. He always stood by the notion that with caller ID, seeing his name pop up on your screen was enough of a message to say 'ring me the fuck back' without the necessary obligatory words.

To be honest I wasn't even really that upset with him. Although what he did was inherantly asshole-ish, a big part of me knew that it was my fault for not standing up and going after what I wanted. Such was life, though. Opportunities present themselves, and it's up to you to grab them before someone else did.

But I liked making him stew in his guilt.

Hadley rarely felt guilty about anything he did. Except for when it came to me. I was his Achiles heal and I could make him bathe in his self-loathing by doing the thing he hated the most in the whole world; give him the silent treatment. He couldn't bare to know that I was angry with him. Drove him nuts.

*Which is why I took so much pleasure from it.*

By about quarter to five I was contemplating closing shop early. We were dreadfully slow and the sudden turn of the weather was keeping customers at bay. The skies had opened up about mid-afternoon and hadn't stopped chucking it down ever since. As I stood at the window, I surveyed the 'river' that was running down the pathway outside the shop. People scuttled by, clutching anything they could over their heads to shield themselves from the offending rain.

You could always tell the Foreigners from the true Brits. Brits were always prepared for whatever shit Mother Nature would throw at us. Most never left the house without at least a few layers on, just in case there was a sudden freakish hot-spell that struck, as well as sunglasses and an umbrella. The people who passed by today all looked naively unprepared for what meteorological surprises the day might bring. I couldn't help but giggle.

I turned away from the sights outside the shop window and flung a tea towel over my shoulder and crossed the empty shop towards the counter. Katie had left an hour ago after I sent her home due to the dwindling clientele and the worsening weather, and I had busied myself with odd jobs while counting down the minutes till it was closing time.

Sighing and leaning against the back counter I found myself dreaming of my bed and longing to wrap myself up in my thick duvet and hibernate till morning.

The sound of the door opening stirred me once more from the blissful images in my head and I spun round to see who it was that was interrupting my peaceful state.

I had to squint just then to allow my eyes to focus on what they thought they were seeing as sheer disbelief and panic quickly washed over me.

*No…It couldn't be.*

A guy stepped into the shop, a navy blue hooded rain coat covering him from the offending weather. As he stepped inside he paused to remove the hood from his head revealing a thick mop of dark brown hair, expertly coiffed into the perfect quiff like he'd literally rolled out of bed. His eyes scanned the room as he shook the excess raindrops from his dark blue coat and a sideways smile crept slowly up his face as he looked towards me.

It was him. Kyle, from the club.

I immediately felt as if I were about three feet tall and could feel my palms begin to sweat and almost slip from the counter on which they were resting as my brain assessed the situation.

*What is he doing here?*

His smile widened as his eyes trailed me up and down quickly, obviously making the link between last nights event and the shop.

"Well it is my lucky weekend after all," he said pointing his finger in my direction as he approached the counter casually, "You!"

I swallowed hard, wanting to run and hide but knowing that there was no escape.

*Pull it together Ev.*

I decided to play it as coyly as I could, thinking how Hadley would handle something like this. Straightening up, I lifted my chin and returned his smile, pushing myself off the counter to meet him half way.

*"You,"* I shot back nodding my head in his direction as if to acknowledge I half remembered who he was. "Don't I know you from *somewhere?"* I joked, my fake pondering melting quickly away into a huge grin.

He nodded flirtatiously, or at least in a way that I assumed was flirtatiously, his grin wider than ever and showing off a set of blinding white teeth.

*I love a nice smile.*

But before I could say anything else, what could only be described as a puzzled look swept quickly across his face as he narrowed his eyes, as if he was considering something in his head. I could sense the question forming on his lips that he was too nervous to ask and decided to come to his rescue.

"Everly, not Hadley," I assured him.

His expression immediately relaxed and his smile returned. I did a little dance inside when I realised he seemed actually relieved it was me and not 'my other half'.

"I'm surprised you remember me at all actually," he said, gathering himself.

"Oh really, and why's that?"

"Well, you disappeared so quickly after we were introduced," he said a bit more seriously, a note of concern in his tone, "I was worried I'd said something wrong."

"Well I don't usually stay around to watch my brother make out with his conquests right in front of me." I joked, half-seriously so that he got a hint of how hurt I was but so that I still had the upper hand.

"Conquests?" he asked with genuine surprise.

I just blinked at him and tilted my head slightly, challenging him almost.

He tilted his head to mirror mine, like a dog waiting for a command. His eyes narrowed as he took in the situation, awkwardness growing in the air between us. "Do you mean," he paused lifting his pointing finger again, "you think I…" he pointed to me then back to himself again before shaking his head. "Did your brother *say something?*"

To give him credit he did sound genuinely concerned and curious as to what he thought I knew.

"Did he *need* to say something?"

Kyle let out a slow laugh, awkwardness turning to embarassment.

"Actually after you split, we spent the rest of the night looking for **you.**"

Now it was my turn to stop and contemplate the situation. "Really?"

*Play it cool Ev.*

I stood still for about a moment too long and when I looked up into Kyle's eyes he was studying my expression, waiting for me to speak.

*Maybe nothing happened with him and Hadley. Maybe that's what he was ringing to tell me. Could it be that my slut bag of a brother actually held back and thought about someone else but himself for a change?*

My studious look melted away quickly as I realised how stupid I must look, completely lost in my own thoughts. I shook my head in an effort to clear it and stood up straighter still, laughing inwardly at my social awkwardness.

"I'm sorry, let's start over," I said sheepishly, "How can I help you?"

"Kyle," he said pointedly with a hand on his chest.

"I remember. Everly."

"Everly," he repeated as if testing the word out on his tongue to see how it tasted. "I love it."

"Thanks, that makes one of us."

"Aww, no, it suits you. Wear it proudly."

I stiffled a giggle, "yeah, Mum was going through her Harlequin Romance phase, I guess."

We both laughed as I wiped my sweaty palms on my apron. His smile returned as our eyes met again. His were such a deep brown. I immediately remembered how I felt last night when I first looked into them; chocolately and smooth. In the light of day he seemed a bit taller than I remembered, and he had shaved since last night revealing baby soft, slightly tanned skin. His hair was the same dark shade of brown that I remembered and even beneath his boxy rain coat I could see the outline of his impressive frame.

*He definitely works out.*

He took in my appearance which I'm sure looked ridiculous compared to the suaveness of last night's outfit of choice.

"Nice apron by the way," he joked to which my hand instinctually shot out to slap his shoulder in a slightly over-the-top flirtatious move.

"Shut up!" I joked back, immediately regretting losing my calm composure.

"Hey, easy there!" he lifted his own hand to rub where I had hit him, faking hurt. "So have you worked here long, then?" he asked, ignoring my question as his eyes moved slowly over the cakes in the display case.

I studied his expression to try and determine if he was for real and did in fact just stumble in off the street in search of his sugar fix, or if he had an alterior motive. Stiffling a laugh, I decided to just go with it.

"Umm, yeah, actually I'm the manager here."

"Really?" his eyes shot up to meet mine.

I nodded, squeezing my lips together and allowing them to curl up into a proud, tight smile.

"That's cool, I'm surprised I've never seen you here before, I love it in here. I'm here all the time."

I stopped following him along the display case and put a hand on my hip. It was time to call him on his bullshit. He stopped as well and peered up at me over his nose, like a little boy who'd just been caught telling the biggest, fattest lie. His glib expression cracked into the biggest shit-eating grin I'd ever seen as he realised he'd been caught out.

We both laughed a slightly nervous laugh and I looked down at the floor, full of nervous energy all of a sudden.

"Alright, alright, you got me."

I couldn't help but smile up at him, despite his blatant lie about coming into the shop.

"I saw you."

I urged him to go on, hand still firmly on hip.

"-Through the window as I was passing by. Stopped me in my tracks."

His expression suddenly went quite serious as his smile faded away and the irises of his eyes grew until they smoldered the most deliciously warm shade. I swallowed as the air in the room seemed to be vacuumed away leaving nothing but the heavy scent of pheromones in its place. I could feel my face begin to flush as his eyes seemed to take in every inch of my face. He must have caught wind of my sudden self-awareness for he shook his head slightly and blinked a few times as if to clear his thoughts and bring him back down to earth.

"Sorry."

He seemed so different from the cocky boy from last night who got with my brother. Here, in my shop, on my territory he almost gave off an air of innocence and inexperience.

"Don't be," I spoke, my voice coming out just above a whisper, "I'm glad you came by."

I wrung my hands and wiped them on my apron again, "I mean it's nice to see you again."

He smiled a relieved smile, glad that I wasn't angry at him. His stare was so genuine and full of hope that I found myself thinking how anyone could ever be angry at that face. His eyes were exactly the same as I remember. So warm and inviting. When I looked into them I could imagine myself getting lost in them. They were almost hypnotic, and they reminded me of the softness of velvet.

A moment of silence passed between us as we both just stood there appreciating this meeting. Even though it was only the second time I had even seen him, there was something so familiar about being around him, almost as if we had met before somehow. I let my eyes swim over his frame and found myself suddenly overcome with a desire to touch his skin. The smoothness of his wide neck that led down to his masculine, round shoulders. I imagined the veins in his biceps and remembered the shape of his chest.

*I wonder if he's hairy or smooth.*

In my head a picture was forming, like the pieces of a jigsaw. My brain put them together and just as quickly I could feel myself begin to stiffen in my jeans. I shifted my weight from one foot to the other in an attempt to sway my wayward thoughts. His face cracked as if being able to read my thoughts, and I suddenly wondered how long I had been staring.

"Right, so what's tasty?"

"I'm sorry?" I asked, momentarily taken aback.

"The cakes. What's tasty?"

"Oh, right, the cakes," I stuttered, "ummm, I recommend the strawberry velvet. It's to die for."

"To die for, eh?" he repeated, his tongue darting out of his mouth quickly to moisten his lips. "Well that sounds too good to pass up."

My eyes searched his face for the true meaning behind his words as his expression turned serious once more.

"Uh, strawberry velvet it is." I tore myself away from his hypnotic glance and grabbed the tongs and a take-away box to wrap it up in. "Oh, uh, are you planning on eating here or taking-away?" I asked mid-packing.

"Oh I'd love to eat here," he said, the words tumbling out of his mouth a little too casually, "but it looks like you're about to close-up shop for the night."

His glibness caught me off guard again and I was momentarily lost for words as I searched for the appropriate flirty response, before coming up empty. He saw the effect he was having on me and mercifully saved me from myself.

"It's ok, I'll have it to go. Thanks."

I tucked the cake away in the little box and fastened the lid shut carefully so as not to crush the beautifully swirled crimson icing on top.

"How much do I owe you?"

Sliding the box towards him on the counter with both hands, "on the house."

"No, I couldn't possibly. It looks amazing. Really, how much?"

Shaking my head I squeezed my lips tightly together in a smile showing that I wasn't going to let up.

"Well, thank you. Really. That's amazing."

Now it was his turn to be embarassed. "How can I repay you?"

His every sentence made me blush further until I was sure my face must have resembled the colour of the strawberry velvet cake.

"Do you think maybe I could…"

I could feel my pulse quicken when I realised the intention of his words.

"...Call you sometime?"

Inside I was jumping for joy, but my face told a different story. I immediately thought to Hadley and of the unwritten code that existed between friends and, even moreso, brothers. The smile disintegrated on my face and I could feel the muscles begin to pull my lips down into a slight frown. Disappointment washed through me as I began to think that this might be the last time I ever saw this beautiful stranger.

"I...I don't know."

"Come on, I can't walk out of here a double winner and not at least give something in return!"

"Double winner?" I repeated back to him.

"Yeah; I get a free cake and get to see you all in one go. Double winner!" He suddenly seemed like such a jock, speaking out about scoring the winning goal in a football match. I found my smile creeping back at the adorableness of his face.

"Alright, now you're just not being fair."

He tilted his head, not understanding what I meant.

"I mean, you and my...Last night, you and Hadley..." I wasn't sure how to finish my sentence. I stood there, my eyes focusing on the tiled-floor beneath me, silently urging him to go on and save me from having to say the words.

"Hey, I told you, nothing *happened.*"

I wanted nothing more than to believe him and give him my number. But something stopped me.

*Brotherly intuition.*

"I don't know...I just wouldn't feel right."

As the words left my mouth they seemed to take all my strength with them.

He sighed in response to my shut down and narrowed his eyes as he studied the validity of what I said.

"Well then here. I'm not backing down without a fight." And with that he reached over the counter and took the pen that was by the till and began scribbling something on a napkin from the dispenser.

"In case you change your mind," he said mid-scribble, "here's *my* number." He finished and held the napkin out in the air between us. I took it and glanced down on the numbers scrawled out on the serviette before returning my eyes back to his face. "I just wouldn't want this to be the last time I ever got to see you again."

With those words the butterflies in my stomach returned to their ballistic fluttering and I felt almost weak at the sound.

*Damn him.*

Kyle turned on his heal and strode confidently towards the door, cupcake in hand. As he opened the door to the shop, he half-turned quickly and shot me a warm-toothy smile that was the nail in my coffin.

*He had me.*

And just like that, he was gone leaving me embalmed in my thoughts of lust and confusion.

# Hadley

It had been a few days now since I took Ev to the club for our upcoming birthdays. Although he says he has forgiven me for what happened, there's still something a bit off with him. I can't quite put my finger on it. Normally I'm pretty down with this sort of thing. Twin-tuition, as they call it or some bullshit like that. But this time he's got me stumped.

The other thing that's got me even more fucked up is how I've been feeling lately. Something's definitely up and it's driving me mad. Ever since the night at the club, and this is so not me normally, I've literally not been able to stop thinking about that guy I hooked up with.

If this were any other bloke I'd be so far past it by now that I would have probably already had another couple fellas by this point. But this one is different. I can tell. I can tell because I've got that weird feeling in my stomach when I try to go to sleep, like when you feel hungry all the time and no matter how much you eat you can't seem to fill up. That's literally how I feel 24/7.

I can tell this guy is different cause he makes me think of my Ex, Charlie. Charlie was the only guy who ever *got* me.

That feels like another lifetime ago now. Charlie was the only ex I ever had who made me want to be a better person. Or maybe just a different person. I guess it doesn't matter now anymore.

Anyway, maybe I'm feeling like this because nothing happened with 'club boy,' as I've deemed him. Maybe my inner-whore is challenging me to see if in round two, I can actually get into his pants. I don't know. I tried mentioning it to Everly this morning over our usual coffee, but he just got all weird and changed the subject.

That afternoon I was sitting in my room, fresh out of the shower and wearing nothing but a pair of Calvin Klein white briefs. I was looking at myself in the full-length mirror that lay up against the far wall in my bedroom examining my body; looking at the curve of my ass and admiring the slightness of my waist and how it contrasted so nicely with the bulk of my pecs.

Call me a narcissist, but as my eyes inspected the reflection in the mirror I knew I looked *goooood.*

I slid my thumbs under the waistband of the briefs and let it snap against my taught stomach.

*Shit, mate.*

Something about CK briefs that always makes me feel confident. I always wore them when I had something big coming up, they were like my power pants. And if I was in fact going to take this plunge and do what I was thinking I might do, then it was certainly a case for my 'power pants.' I lowered myself down onto my bed, stared at my phone and tried to find the energy to psyche myself up for what I was going to do

Inside I was feeling what could only be described as 'butterflies', although if you tell anyone that I mentioned having 'butterflies' than I'll deny it to the grave. I held my hand out in front of my face and watched as it trembled slightly like a leaf about to fall off a tree in Autumn.

*Jesus, Hadley get a grip.*

I took a deep breath and shut my eyes, trying to work up enough courage.

*You are such a pansy; just fucking do it already.*

Unlocking the phone, I quickly scrolled through my contacts for *his* number and selected it from the list. Within seconds it started ringing and I literally felt my heart leap up into my throat.

*I feel like such a chick. Get ahold of yourself, mate.*

After a couple of rings he picked up.

"Hello?" came the voice on the other end of the line, even hotter than I remember.

"Hi, Kyle? It's Hadley…"

***

"I never thought I'd hear from you."

"Really? Why's that?" I asked him.

We were sitting across from one another in a bar called Vodka Revolution just up from the seafront. His choice not mine. I wouldn't normally choose such an obvious place for a first date. If that was in fact what this was. The jury was still out. It was a rather large space for such a pub with about a dozen or so little tables scattered across the room. When you entered your eyes were immediately drawn to the enormous, brightly-lit letters on the far wall that spelled out 'VODKA' as if to advertise their main selling elixir as if to clarify to anyone who may not have gotten the hint based on the bars actual name. The rest of the lighting inside was fairly dim, casting just the perfect amount of shadow for an intimate get-together such as this.

But my eyes were transfixed not on the décor of the bar, but instead on the man in front of me.

Kyle. Club boy. He looked so good. Even better without my cocaine goggles on. His dark brown hair was done up into the same casual quiff that I remembered, with the sides closely cropped to just above his ear.

*I loved the feeling of closely cut hair; made me want to run my fingers through it…*

He wore a white crew neck shirt with long sleeves that seemed to hug him in all the right places. As I let my eyes drift over his body I found it hard to imagine him looking bad in anything. He had one of those figures that designers loved to dress; masculine, broad, one that would fill a suit perfectly.

As we sat there chewing the fat, he drinking a pint of cider and me a vodka soda, it was his mouth that was hypnotising me the most. His lips were so full and perfectly shaped that if he was a chick, I'd accuse him of having collagen injections. When he spoke I caught him moistening them occasionally with the running of a wet tongue over them.

Needless to say the sight was making me rock hard.

I had gone for a casual look too; dark blue skinny jeans, boots and a tight black button-down shirt to complement my black hair. It seemed mission was accomplished for as we sat down at the booth in the bar and I took off my denim coat, I caught him checking out my physique in a less than obvious manoever.

*Cha-ching.*

I almost forgot he was speaking and had to steal my wayward thoughts back to the now.

"It's just that when you left, I couldn't quite read you…" his voice trailed off, obviously trying to bait me into complementing him somehow.

"Couldn't quite read me?"

He chuckled. I wasn't making this easy for him.

"Yeah, you just split so quickly. I thought I might have said something wrong."

"No, you didn't say anything. It was my-"

"-Brother. Yeah, I remember."

"Yeah."

"How was he anyway?" he asked quite sincerely.

"Fine, yeah, Ev's weird like that. He held a grudge for like five minutes; then we were fine."

"Twins. I can't imagine him being angry at you for long."

I tilted my head inquisitively.

"I mean, you're identical twins. You shared the same placenta!"

I rolled my eyes slightly. "Yeah, tell me about it."

"You two not close?"

"Actually, we're probably *too* close."

"Really? How's that?"

"To be honest I'm just as much to blame as he is; for years we sort of fed into the whole 'twin' thing. You know, dressing alike, never being apart."

"You ever pretend to be the other one, you know, to fuck with someone?"

I immediately flashed back to that time in school outside the headteacher's office and let out a short guffaw.

"Once. When we were younger."

"Oh? Do tell," he urged sitting forward in his seat.

"Christ. We were like ten years old. I can't even remember what the reason was, but we were in trouble at school for something or other."

"Really?"

"Mmhmm, actually I should be more clear; I was in trouble at school for something or other. Stupid kid stuff, probably. Anyway. Due to the fact that this was a regular thing for me, and I had probably run out of 'get out of jail free cards' by this point, Ev agreed to cover for me."

"Uh oh, this doesn't sound like it went down well."

"Oh, now I remember. I had been caught putting some firecracker or something down the toilet, and I begged Everly to say it was him who did it and not me. I was literally this close to exclusion and I knew that if he didn't take the wrap for me I would be fucked," I said motioning with my hands.

Kyle sucked air through clenched teeth as if to say how shitty that sounded.

"I know, right. Anyway, he agreed and was excluded from school for a week. Mum literally almost castrated him. See, the 'good kid' always gets it worse than 'the naughty one'."

"Ahh, so *you're* the naughty one," he jeered rhetorically, following his statement with a chuckle.

I looked at him sideways as if to say 'fuck off'.

"Wait a minute, wait a minute," he said putting a hand up for emphasis, "Surely people could tell you apart, somehow?"

"To be honest, when we were younger Ev and I kinda played into it. Still kind of do."

"Why's that?"

I shrugged as I thought about it.

"Dunno, really. I mean, it's kind of like what you said; we literally came from the same zygote. He's like my other half, and it took a long time before I saw us as different people. I don't feel right if he's not near by."

I was staring at a spot on the table now, my words sinking in and making me reflect on what I had actually just said. Sometimes Everly and I's closeness scared me. Like I wonder what I would actually do if he wasn't around and how I would cope.

Kyle sat back in his seat, his hands joined together on the table. I could feel his eyes on me and after a moment he reached out a hand and placed it on top of mine reassuringly. I looked up into his dark brown eyes and couldn't help cracking a smile.

"I'm sorry, I don't know where that came from."

"No, I'm sorry. I shouldn't have brought it up."

"It's cool," I shyly turned my eyes down to our hands. "Besides our different hair colours and obvious senses of style," I paused for effect to which he grinned madly, "there are subtle differences."

"Oh?"

"We're so alike we even have the same pattern of freckles on our right hand, but aside from that Everly's got this crazy shaped birth mark on his lower back. Looks like a triangle. It's weird."

Kyle just stared at me.

"And I'm sure he'd love me telling you all this."

It was my turn to laugh at my own overshare.

There was then a moment of silence as we both sipped our drinks. Me, tossing it back whereas he sipped his demurely. It was a nice silence; comfortable, like we had been sharing them for years. I could feel his eyes flickering over me, perhaps trying to read what I was thinking or maybe just taking the opportunity to check me out.

Either way I wasn't opposed.

After another minute or so he broke the silence.

"Did Everly tell you I ran into him?"

His words hit me like a sudden slap to the face. I stopped and stared hard at him, digesting what he had just said and immediately suspicious.

"Sorry?" I asked, hoping I had misheard him.

Kyle swallowed, his jaw tensing slightly, "um, yeah, at his work. The other day when I was in the Lanes."

"Oh, really?"

"Yeah, can't believe he's the manager; that's cool."

"Have a bit of a sweet tooth, do ya?" I cooed to him, sitting forward on my bench and locking my eyes on his in the most forwardly-flirtatious way possible. Inside I was beginning to think this conversation had strayed too far towards Everly and become less about *us*. I needed to get his focus back on me.

Kyle laughed and looked away, feeling my advances and easing into them.

"Yeah, I guess you could say that."

"No, Everly never mentioned he saw you."

"Oh," he said quietly, his lips still forming the word even after they'd let it go. Something flashed across his expression.

*Disappointment, maybe?*

I quickly dismissed the look and propelled myself forward into fifth gear.

"Anyway. What do you say we get outta here?"

\*\*\*

I suggested a walk down by the beach, although I think my intentions were pretty clear and that walking was the last thing on my mind as we left the bar.

After three cocktails each we were both quite buzzed which was apparent from our slightly quickened speech and slightly slower pace. As we reached Brighton beach's rocky terrain, walking got progressively more challenging.

I looked over to Kyle and caught him looking back at me. He quickly turned away embarassed, his eyes focusing again quickly on the stones below his feet.

"Thanks for tonight, by the way," he said in a boyish tone.

"What do you mean?"

"Thanks for ringing."

"I almost didn't."

*What's with me? I am not usually this forthcoming.*

"Really? How come?" He asked, his boyish manner becoming almost hurt.

"I mean, I told you…I'm not usually *this* guy."

"And what do you mean by 'this guy'?"

I windmilled my arms for emphasis, "*This!* I don't normally do any of this; dates, walks along the water."

He laughed a quiet laugh that was more understanding and appreciative than mocking.

"Well than I'm honored."

"Honored?"

"Yeah, honored. That you chose me to be your first."

I turned to look at his face and caught sight of his rediculously huge grin plastered across his smug features.

"Shut the fuck up," I jokingly slapped his arm to which he feigned hurt once more.

By now we were plenty far from the beach traffic and with the setting sun in the sky to the West of us, we were bathed almost completely in shadow. Looking up towards the promenade, it felt like we were a million miles from anyone. Normally there would usually be at least a couple speckled couples down here, enjoying the sights and watching the sun as it disappeared beyond the buildings, but tonight we were eerily alone.

Kyle stopped walking for a moment and put both his hands on my shoulders. Looking him in the eye, I saw for the first time that he was slightly taller than me. His face looked even sexier in the dimness of the inky sky. He stared back at me for what felt like ages, his eyes scanning my face and taking in my appearance. I returned his seeking gaze and allowed myself the chance to really look at him without feeling at all self-conscious.

His jaw line was speckled with the lightest sprinkling of dark hairs, obviously freshly grown since this morning. His cheek bones were quite pronounced making him seem almost 'all-American' and boy-next-doorish. His grip on my shoulders was making me weak as the heat from his palms penetrated my denim coat and I was suddenly over-taken with the urge to feel his skin on my skin.

I broke our trance and looked around us once more, scanning our surroundings for anyone that might object to what I *hoped* was going to happen. He sensed what I was doing and also cast his eyes around before returning them to mine. His hands slid down from my shoulders and I waited for his face to dip to mine. Searching my memories I tried desperately to recall what it felt like to kiss him; to have his lips on mine.

Luckily I didn't have to think for too long.

Kyle quickly ducked his head down the few inches to reach my lips and gently touched his mouth to mine. The feeling was like fire as we connected skin on skin.

I moaned against him as his tongue passed through my lips and into my mouth, feverishly pressing against my own. Within seconds I was nothing but sensation. My head was spinning as I slowly took in what was happening; when I realised how much I had beenwanting this and how delicious it felt to finally have it.

I let my head fall back, exposing my neck to him who took it as his cue to begin to work on it. Wet butterfly kisses covered my throat and traced the contours of my collar bone making my moans deepen as my skin became alive at the sensation of his stubble scraping against it. I dropped my arms limply at my sides as Kyle sank slowly to his knees, his hands trailing behind and worshipping at my chest as he travelled down my body.

Hungrily he lifted my shirt and let his tongue marvel all over my abs. The feeling of his wet mouth licking the deep groves of my stomach made my knees buckle. I could already tell his tongue was experienced as it lapped over my six-pack and traced the trail of fine, dark hairs that disappeared down into my jeans.

"Fuck, I want you so badly," I moaned into the cool night air.

Kyle responded by quickening his pace and began unbuckling my belt. As he worked away at it clumsily, desire causing him to struggle, I quickly unbuttoned my shirt and peeled it off my muscular shoulders. Kyle paused and looked up at my naked chest and forgot about my belt,lifting himself enough off the ground to wrap his lips around my right nipple. I called out suddenly as the feeling of his tongue massaging my nipple made it rise and harden.

I could feel the outline of his cock pressing up against my thigh as he lost himself in the definition of my pecs. I pulled my shoulders back and down towards my hips, giving him the full show by forcing my pecs even further into his mouth. His tongue lapped furiously at my chest, leaving the skin hot and wet as it passed over. My hands got in the game and quickly lifted and clawed at Kyle's white long-sleeved top, desperately trying to tear it off so my eyes could finally feast themselves on his body.

Both of us were moaning so loudly I couldn't tell who was making what sound. He pulled back for a moment and helped me remove his top. My mouth dropped as he pulled his shirt off over his head. He too stopped for a moment, letting his shirt fall to the pebbly beach at our feet. His pectorals were like two, perfectly formed dinner plates, complemented by two dark round nipples. In the light from the newly-risen moon, the deep colour of his smooth, tanned skin shone almost golden in the shadows. His arms were defined without being overtly veiny or freakishly muscled, and my eyes stopped to study his arm-sleeve tattoo before settling on his tiny waist and washboard stomach. His chest rose and fell with every sharp intake of breath he took, a signal that if he didn't pounce soon he might lose it right here in his jeans.

He lifted his right hand and wrapped it around the back of my head, pulling me in hard for a kiss. We collided so hard I was sure he cut my lip, but I didn't care. I was so overcome with a need to have him that I quickly finished what he had started with my belt and with his tongue still in my mouth, sucking on my own, I let my jeans fall to the ground and kicked my boots off in the process.

He pulled away for a second to mirror my actions. Then pausing again to take in the situation, we both looked around once again. Within seconds we were naked except for our underwear. His legs were well defined, compared to my slightly skinnier ones, and covered with dark, masculine curly hairs that trailed from his thighs right down to his ankles.

*This is so hot.*

There we were. Like teenagers making out on the beach, only we were going to fuck. Right here. Right now. In plain sight of anyone who dared to walk by or just happen to find themselves on the beach tonight. The thrill of getting caught was making me shiver and shake. All I knew was that I wanted to fuck him so badly at this point and audience or no audience, it was gonna happen.

I trailed my eyes down to his dark pair of underwear and the generous bulge that was buried inside. I reached out my hand and started rubbing at it, keeping my eyes focused on his to gauge his reaction. He closed his eyes, letting them roll back inside his head as I massaged his dick through the soft cotton of his boxer briefs.

"Yessss," he breathed, sucking air in through clenched teeth. He reached out and massaged my bare shoulders and his mouth found mine once more. Our heads twisted and turned, hungrily trying to devour the other as much as possible as my hand continued its expert worshipping of his stick.

He was almost at the breaking point and I didn't want him to cum just yet. I stopped as I felt the head begin to moisten beneath my hand.

He opened his eyes and stared at me now, imploringly. Completely in sync, we both bent and removed our underwear in a quick movement. The gentle material struggling over the length of our cocks. It was the sexiest reveal I think I had ever had.

I couldn't believe what was about to happen. Here, on the rocky Brighton beach, with the chance that anyone could see us at any moment.

We studied each other's expressions, searching for answers to the unasked question on both our minds. Kyle spoke first.

"Do you have one?"

I nodded before quickly reaching down to my trouser pocket and fishing out what he was asking for. My hands connected with the square condom I always carried in case of emergency and sticking the corner in my mouth, quickly tore the package open.

"I want you to fuck me…" Kyle breathed once more.

*The magic words.*

I took his shoulders, spun him around so his back was to me and pushed him to the ground. He called out as his bare knees made contact with the pebble bed at his feet. I stood over him and placed the condom on the tip of my cock and unrolled it all the way down my long shaft.

*This was going to be quick and rough.*

I took a second to appreciate the sight of Kyle on all fours, his beautiful perky ass sticking up in the air. All the muscles in his smooth tanned back were flexed simultaneously as if he was completely tensed and psyching himself up for the inevitable penetration that was going to happen. I stroked my cock, getting it used to the feeling of the having the foreskin jerked back and forth. The moist latex of the condom glistened in the moonlight and the masked head was engorged and ready to start pummeling.

"Ahh Hadley, do it, I want it so badly…"

That was my cue. He was primed and ready. I got down on my knees, my shaft like a sword cutting through the air, sticking out at a perfect 90 degree angle to my body. I felt so powerful and free at that moment, as the cool late evening breeze licked my naked body. The sound of the gentle lapping waves that were only a few feet away and threatening to soak us at any moment soothed my nerves.

I approached his ass, and with two fingers slid them down the crack between his cheeks. He flinched at the sensation and craned his neck around to see what I was doing. His eyes were tightly gripped shut, and I whispered for him to relax, running my other hand up and down his back in reassurance. I tossed my head back to remove a piece of my fallen hair from my eyes and let my two fingers find his aching hole.

His ass was moist and sweaty and bare except for a light dusting of natural hairs in his crack leading to his ball sack. I pulled my hand back and spat in my palm; the closest thing to lubricant we were going to find down on the beach. I quickly placed my moistened palm to his ass and lathered it the best I could and then roughly shoved my first two fingers inside of him. The muscles in his sphincter were tight and constricted and he let out a muffled cry that was a mix of pain and pleasure as my digits moved past the initial opening and felt their way around his warm interior. With every turn and twist of my fingers his whole body reacted; tensing and then releasing, slowly getting used to the feeling of having something foreign shoved up inside him. I curled and then uncurled both fingers, searching for his g-spot, and then pounded him with them in and then almost all the way out, mimicking the action my dick was about to take. He arched his back and relaxed further like a cat in heat, allowing my fingers to enter him deeper. He was working with me now, trying to open himself up as much as possible to deepen the sensation that only fingers could produce. They spread his hole wide, right up to the knuckle, as I continued burying them inside him like I was searching for something I had lost.

When I felt he was ready, I withdrew and used the sticky sweetness to wet my sheathed cock further. I looked down at it; twitching and throbbing with anticipation. Kyle's right hand had found his own penis and was beginning to move up and down his shaft, furthering his pleasure and associating being fucked with something pleasing and less invasive.

"You ready?" I breathed through clenched teeth.

He nodded his consent as I wasted no time in lining my cock head up with his hole. The head eased its way in smoothly, slipping inside with no tension. I paused, feeling his sphincter react and tighten.

"Let it happen…Let it happen," was all I could moan as I let my head tilt back to stare up at the stars. I closed my eyes so that I could experience every sensation without distraction.

"Ahhhh," Kyle moaned, signaling his pleasure as he gave himself over to me.

My hips took their cue and slowly pulsed themselves forwards, burying my dick in his ass.

*Fuck, he's so tight.*

"You ok?"

"Yeah, just go easy."

"Not a chance," I mouthed with a devilish grin. I thrusted my hips forward another few inches and let my right arm slide up Kyle's naked back. I didn't care who saw us now. I wouldn't have cared if the police had shown up at that exact moment. I was gonna fuck the shit outta him and nobody was gonna stop us.

Another thrust and I felt my ball sack slap against his ass, and yet I thrusted again, desperately trying to deepen myself inside him. And again, and again. He cried out each time, the sheer girth of me inside him sending him further and further to orgasm. I let out a deep inhuman moan from inside my belly as I pulled out and began fucking him in a more rhythmic manner. In and out, in and out, deeper and deeper I went inside him.

"Yah, fuck me Hadley, *fuck me…*"

His voice echoed around us but was instantly drowned out by the sound of the waves, the tide becoming increasingly violent, almost mimicking our actions.

Harder and harder I drove myself up inside him. It was raw. Carnivorous. I wanted him so badly. The feeling of the stoney pebbles beneath our bare flesh, driving up and cutting at our skin as I pounded the shit out of him. There was something so unbelievably hot about seeing this 'American-jockey-type' on all fours, completely at my mercy, surrendering to me as I fucked him on the beach. I looked down and saw his right hand was quickening its jerking motion on his own penis. The other hand's knuckles were white as he gripped the rocks beneath for support.

"Keep going, I'm close."

"Me too," I assured him. And I was. I wanted so desperately to rip off the condom and cum inside him, but even I found a slither of rational thought that told me that probably wasn't the best idea.

I don't think I'd ever been this hard. It was almost as if my cock grew with every thrust I made. I bent over him, my body beginning to buckle until my nipples were grazing his back. He was taking the brunt of both of our weight as I surrendered even more to him, the change in position allowing my cock to slide even further up inside.

He howled now at the sensation of the tip of my dick massaging his prostate.

*"Jesus, fuck, Hadley, I'm coming,"* he screamed out.

I thrusted again, and again and again, until I could feel my own juices begin their journey and start to explode from inside me.

*"I'm coming too, oh fuck, oh fuuuuuck."*

And with a final thrust I came, I came the hardest I think I had ever come. Thrust after thrust, our bodies bucking together, my lips kissing and biting at the skin at the nape of his neck as I exploded my sweet sticky mess inside the condom. Kyle exploded cum all over his hand, his body stiffening and bucking beneath me. He kept jerking himself up and down, up and down, emptying every last drop of his load into his hand and onto the rocks below, his cloudy cum splattering all around us.

And then we were still.

I wasn't sure how much time had passed before either of us moved, and to be honest I didn't care. Our bodies were slick with perspiration, and our chests heaved as our breathing slowly returned to normal. Both of us sucked air in through clenched teeth, exasperated and drunk and spent. I was still inside him, my cock showing no signs of deflating. He let go of himself and repositioned both his hands on the ground to better support our weight. I put my hands on his hard hips to lift myself off him and pulled out slowly.

He winced at the feeling of me withdrawing, and I did it slowly to further the excrutiating feeling of leaving his body.

The sky was pitchblack now. We both peered around to see if we had gained an audience throughout our show, but to my surprise we were seemingly still alone. In the distance I could hear music playing and the sound of muffled laughter up on the promenade. I squinted further but couldn't make out anything in the distance.

Kyle sat back on his bottom and turned himself around to look at me better. I was hypnotised by every move he made and how every muscle in his body seemed to flex and respond simultaneously as he eased himself around. I noticed for the first time that his pubic hair was neatly trimmed and even as his cock began to go down I was impressed by the size and shape. The skin was smooth around it and the head was plump and moist with his cum.

He smiled up at me his million dollar smile, nothing but pearly white perfectly straight teeth. I smiled back briefly, my bedroom eyes lazy and probably glazed over. I ran a hand through my black surfer quiff locks before resting both on my thighs. My breath was slowly returning to normal and the cool breeze against my naked skin felt icier than before. I opened my mouth to speak, my voice coming out a raspy whisper.

"Fancy a dip?"

# Everly

I told myself to go to bed. I knew what was going to happen if I didn't. And sure enough, I was right. I didn't go to bed after Hadley left for his date. Instead I did exactly what I tried so hard not to do.

I stayed up. Or better yet, I *waited* up.

Even worse than waiting up, was waiting up **and** obsessing over what they might be doing. Which is exactly what I did. Everytime our old Grandfather clock that was stood in the entrance hall of our flat chimed a new hour, I grew more and more weary. My thoughts ran rampant, thinking the worse, of course. How could I not; my brother was out on a date with a guy who try as I may to deny and forget, I had developed feelings for.

How did this happen? How did I allow myself to go down this road? Fact of the matter was Hadley got there first. Hadley might as well have peed all over him to mark his territory, for like always, Hadley beat me to the punch. Who am I kidding, I never had a chance anyway.

But it's so bizarre because Hadley and I are never attracted to the same kind of guy. Thank God, I mean talk about competition, right? Two guys who look exactly the same save their hair colour, how can one compete with the other especially when one of them is a big ho who always gets what he wants?

If Hadley and I attracted the same sort of bloke, I probably would never have even lost my virginity in the first place, since they would always choose him over me. How couldn't they? He was up in their face, flirty, sexy, confident. And there was I; shy, nervous, book-worm…I never stood a chance.

So why has this even happened? I should have seen that Hadley was interested and then just backed off. But it wasn't like I went out searching for this guy afterwards. It was *he* who came into *my* shop. **He** found **me**, not the other way around. So therefore, I can't be blamed, right?

*Then why did I feel so guilty all the time now?*

Mum was always telling us growing up, not to deny the heart what it wants. She was an eternal optimist and over the years she had begun to rub off on me. Hadley was more a realist; seeing things at face-value and never a dreamer. Whereas I seemed to have taken after dear ol' mum. And unfortunately, being so positive sometimes only built me up to be let down. I couldn't help but feel that this might be one of those times.

*I can't believe he gave me his number and then is now on a date with my twin.*

The more I thought about it, as I lay there on the sofa watching the minutes pass by, I started to think about what kind of a guy does that? To be honest it's not something that's ever happened before. Probably because guys aren't normally that stupid to try and play both twins at once. If it were me on the date and Hadley who was second fiddle, then you can bet he'd have something to say about it.

But it wasn't Hadley who was second fiddle. He was the first string and I was the stupid one who was getting strung along and currently left at home alone while the other half had all the fun.

*Everly, you are just going to get hurt.*

The rational side of me was saying to forget all about him and just pull out now before I got anymore involved. But life is never that easy, is it?

I could see where this was going. I could anticipate how it would end, and as the clock struck one AM, things looked bleaker than I had imagined.

\*\*\*

The next morning Hadley was up and gone to work at the restaurant before I had even stirred. I awoke to sun streaming in through my bedroom window and a house filled with silence. It took me a few moments to realise what was going on until after I tiptoed to outside Hadley's bedroom door and confirmed my suspicions.

*I'm alone.*

As much as I would never admit it out loud, if Hadley had brought his 'date' home last night I probably would have died. I listened with an ear pressed up against his door for a moment longer, straining my ear to hear even the smallest sound from inside the room. But there was nothing. Thank God.

It was my day off and I suddenly felt like I didn't know what to do with myself. Sauntering down to the kitchen I saw that Hadley had made coffee and left me some. Not much, mind you, but at least he left some.

*How considerate.*

I poured the steaming black liquid into my favourite oversized mug and sipped slowly, the caffeine filtering its way into my bloodstream and forcing me alert. I was tired. Full of shame and tired. I couldn't believe I had waited up last night for him to come in, silently praying that it had gone badly and that they had agreed to never see each other again. But judging by the time I passed out in what was still an empty house, Hadley had probably scored.

*Sigh.*

\*\*\*

Regardless of the fact that it was my day off, I still always found a reason to pop-in to my work. Probably the control-freak in me that needed to know what was happening all the time; a trait that was lovingly passed down to me from my mother's side of the family, no doubt. As I walked through the busy streets of town towards the bustly-labyrinth of connected posh side-streets that was the Lanes shopping district, I checked my phone.

*Still nothing.*

Either he's quite busy at work or he's avoiding telling me about his night. I hoped it was the former, as keeping quiet about his conquests wasn't really Hadley's style. In fact I was more surprised that he *didn't* wake me up last night by pouncing on top of me like some drunk and deranged version of Tigger from Winnie the Pooh to regale me with every sordid detail of his evening.

*Whether I wanted to hear about it or not.*

A pang which could only be described as deep seeded jealousy had begun to sow itself through my stomach. I was jealous. Insanely, so. The more I tried to push the idea of Kyle from my mind, the more he seemed to worm his way in. It seemed ridiculous that I was this pent up over a guy who I had barely met and knew nothing about, however it was also 'classic Everly' to fall so hard and so fast. A look at my previous track record would confirm that. I shuddered as I thought about Matt Brewer; my most recent train wreck-closet-case-college guy I threw out of my car. Even he had left his mark on me after our first or second date. I sighed again as I crossed the road with the bakery in sight.

I was a classic case of 'wears his heart-on-his-sleeve'. Just waiting and waiting for the right guy to come around and pick it up and take care of it forever. I inwardly castrated myself for even allowing myself to think that maybe this Kyle character might be interested. And then I remembered that his number was burning a hole in my phone, so to speak. All I knew was that there was no way I would ever or could ever ring him. Certainly not after he went on a date with my brother. He sealed that deal when he agreed to see Hadley. Nothing I did wrong. Not like I waited on it too long till he lost interest, like I had been notorious for doing in the past. Hadley got there first. End of.

*But then why didn't I just delete his number from my phone?*

My thoughts were still on Kyle as I crossed the threshold into the shop. Inside it was busier than I was expecting with nearly every table occupied except for a couple of stools which overlooked the main storefront window. It was Katie and Wendy, my newest employee, who were working today and both gave me an all-knowing nod of their heads as I appeared inside.

"How did I know you'd show up here on your day off?" came Katie's cheeky tone from behind the counter. She wasn't even looking my way as she counted out change for the customer standing in front of her. She handed them some coins and a take-away cupcake with a smile before turning towards me, the guilty offender to her right.

"Yeah, yeah, well you know me too well it seems."

"Seriously, are you checking up on us or something, cause you know I got this, right Wendy?"

Wendy looked up seemingly surprised to hear her name suddenly. "Umm, yes…To whatever you were saying."

I smiled despite her and held my hands up as a surrendering motion. "Hey, I know, and believe me when I say that I trust you both implicitly."

"Then what is it? And don't even think about coming behind here, cause today this is an 'Everly-free' zone," she used her index finger in a circular motion to demonstrate her ruling of the store.

"Just literally passing by. Honest. Came by to see if you-"

"-Needed any help?" she interrupted me, raising an impatient eyebrow.

*Damn.*

"No, not at all," I recounted, desperately trying to think of an excuse as to why I was there. "I just wanted to see if you needed any more ingredients from the shop around the corner. Flour? Sugar, maybe?"

Katie and Wendy both looked at me with disbelieving looks on their faces.

"Alright, alright, I can tell when I'm not wanted," I admitted, letting my eyes do a quick sweep of the store to make sure things looked more or less in order, "and my phone is always on. So feel free to call if you need anything. Anything."

"Yeah, yeah, now would you get out of here already. Go enjoy your day off."

I rolled my eyes at being dismissed so uncordially and held up my phone in one hand and pointed at it with the other. Both girls waved me goodbye as I turned and walked back out into the busy street.

The sun was high up in the midday sky and even in the early Autumn month, I could still feel the rays begin to beat down upon me. Sighing, I racked my brain for what to do today. I checked my phone, more out of habit than anything else, before deciding on a take-away lunch on the beach.

\*\*\*

There was always a spot on the long stretch of Brighton beach that I tended to gravitate towards. It was the place that Mum used to bring us to when we were younger, just a little bit past the old West pier that burned down in 1975. It was a quieter bit of the beach, where the tourists and day-trippers tended not to go, but still had a beautiful view of the relic that was the burned down pier as well as the new Palace Pier.

Being by the beach always had a calming effect on me. It was where I came when I needed to think, or make a big decision, or simply when the outside world got a bit too much for me. Hadley always made fun of me and my 'hippy-ways' as he called them. But the ocean never let me down, and truthfully, as stupid as it may sound, it was always there for me.

I settled down in my favourite spot, with my take-away Starbucks sandwich and steaming hot coffee and breathed in the salty freshness. Instantly I felt satisfied, calm and full again. Another deep breath and I seemed to exhale all the negativity I had been feeling and felt lighter and more positive.

*Why was I wasting so much time thinking about someone who wasn't thinking about me? Don't I deserve better? Don't I deserve to want someone who wants me just as badly?*

I opened up my sandwich wrapper and peeled it back exposing the roasted vegetable panini inside, and took a big bite. I closed my eyes and appreciated the feeling of the warm sun on my skin. It was days like this that made all the Brits come out of their hiding spaces, desperate to lap up the last few remaining rays of the fading summer sunshine.

Just as I was about to take another bite, a shadow moved in front of my sun causing everything to darken in front of my closed eye lids. Instinctually I opened them.

"Hey!" I shouted without thinking. Sure enough a dark figure stood directly in my eye line, completely blocking the sun like a human eclipse.

"Everly?" came the voice. It was deep and masculine with just a twinge of gay. The muscles in my stomach tightened instantly as I realised who it was that was standing in front of me. "No way, what are the odds?"

I squinted again, not believing my ears and hoping to get a better look at who it was. He bent down quickly causing the sun to assault my unprepared eyes. "Sorry, my bad."

Sure enough, I was right.

*Kyle.*

I stopped chewing. Thank God for my sunglasses, which shielded him from seeing the dumbfounded look in my eyes. What were the odds that of all people to run into on the beach, in the middle of the day...

"How are you?" He asked, sensing that either I had gone mute or didn't recognise him. "How weird that I ran into you again."

I swallowed and took another moment to gather my wits, unsure of how to proceed.

*What is he doing here?*

"Umm, hi," I stuttered, my voice coming out full of nerves.

"Hi," he shot back. He was kneeling down now in a squatting position. He wore a simple plaid button-down shirt, open at the neck a little too much giving anyone who'd venture a look a peek at his man-cleavage, and faded jeans. I clocked his pair of Ray Ban wayfarer sunglasses, which only served to add to his laid-back sexy look. His hair had that fresh-just-rolled-out-of-bed look that I'd never been able to pull off and that made me insanely jealous at how easy people like him made it look.

I suddenly felt like I might be drooling and straightened up further, tucking my sandwich away and gulping a swig of blazing hot coffee which burned my tongue and made me flinch.

"Oh, careful there, easy," he joked, a beautiful toothy smile cracking on his full lips.

"What are you doing here?" I asked, a little too accusatory.

"Well hello to you, too," he shot back faking hurt.

"Sorry," I collected myself, "I mean, 'hi'."

"Hi."

We both smiled at each other awkwardly before erupting into small laughs that were rife with pending nervous energy.

"Are you sure you're not stalking me?" I said to him, slowly easing into the conversation.

He laughed again, that College-guy laugh that had probably gotten him laid a million times before.

"Hey, I'm innocent! I'm just on my lunch break and thought I'd take a quick stroll down on the beach. And for the record, you're in *my spot*," he said pointing to the ground on which I sat.

"*Your* spot?" I guffawed at him. I removed my sunglasses to get a better look at him.

"This is my territory, my flat's just up behind the Hilton hotel."

"Really? I mean, wow, I never knew that."

He tilted his head in that adorable, puppy dog way, "how would you?"

I looked away, unsure of how to answer.

"May I?" he asked, pointing to the spot next to me. I nodded and scooted over, scooping up my Starbucksbag.

"Keep eating, don't stop on my account."

I carefully took another bite, suddenly self-conscious that I was the only one stuffing my face of the two of us.

"I've already eaten, but thanks anyway," he mused sarcastically. I shot him a look over the top of my sunglasses.

"So...How are you?" I asked, my tone full of inuendo. It occurred to me that I still hadn't heard from Hadley in regards to how his date went, and now I was going to get the full story from the other party!

"I'm good thanks," he said glibly, obviously waiting for me to inquire further.

*My, he's cheeky.*

"Did you have a good time last night?"

He stared at me for a moment, trying to decipher my cryptic tone. He bent his legs and rested his forearms on his knees and picked up a stone and began fiddling with it in his hands.

"Have you spoken to Hadley today?"

"No. Have *you?*"

He shook his head and removed his Ray Ban's and rested them up on top of his head.

"Yeah, it was fun, but..."

"...But, what?"

A grin appeared on his lips and he suddenly looked kind of uncomfortable.

"But I...I found myself thinking the whole night that maybe..."

My heart started to thud like a snair drum inside my chest. He stole a glance up at me from under his long lashes.

"I started thinking that maybe I was out with the wrong brother."

That was it. I could instantly feel my insides begin to melt. My face blushed an odd shade of crimson that it did when I got nervous and I couldn't help the corners of my mouth from lifting up into a shy smile despite my efforts to play it cool and remain nonchalant.

"Oh you did, did you?"

*Go on Everly, flirt a little.*

"Mmhmm," he mumbled, returning his stare to the rocks.

"Aaaaaand, did you happen to mention this to your *date?*" I drawled imploringly.

He snickered, his shoulders hunching a bit as if admitting defeat.

"Not yet, but I was thinking of it."

I swallowed hard and set my sandwich down on the carrier bag beside me. I straightened up, brushing my hands on my jeans. I started thinking about Hadley and how excited he was about this date.

Hadley. My twin brother who never got excited about any guy, was actually *nervous* to go out on a date for once in his life. And there I was, shamefully flirting away with the object of his affection completely unbeknownst to him. This was certainly breaking some sort of ethical code, I was sure of it. The butterflies that had dusted off their wings and begun their ritual ballistic fanning inside my stomach were beginning to fade and die off as I came back down to earth a bit and realised that what I was doing was wrong.

"Kyle, I…."

But I didn't know how to say it. Probably because I didn't *want* to say it. I knew I should, but something inside of me stopped me short and caused me to lose my will.

"I know, I know," he said coming to my rescue, "this is probably not the best time to say this to you."

I shook my head and looked away from his beautiful brown and intoxicating stare. If I allowed myself to continue to look into his eyes, I was sure the little will and self-restraint I had would certainly leave me.

"It's just…Hadley is my brother, obviously, and I just don't…"

He was nodding. His silence drew me in once more and I suddenly felt locked in his stare. I caught glimpse of his face and his eyes; warm and inviting like something so familiar and comforting from my childhood. I started to feel slightly light-headed as I swam around in them, weightless and giddy and suddenly not in control of my own body.

He was looking at my mouth and his lips were parted ever so slightly as if he were about to say something but then thought again and stopped himself. I began to tremble as his hand reached out and cupped my left cheek. My insides continued to liquify even quicker now that his hand was touching me. The skin of his palm was warm and smooth, and I allowed my eyes to shut briefly to relish the sensation. When I opened them a moment later his smile had faded and he appeared more serious.

Hungry, almost.

His head moved towards me, his eyes clouding over and closing as his lips began to descend upon my own. My head was shouting out for him to stop but my body had other things in mind. My eyes closed as he got closer and suddenly all the sounds around us silenced themselves and it was only us two in the world.

Then he kissed me.

He planted his moist, full lips on mine and pressed them gently against my mouth. The feeling was so sweet and familiar and made every muscle in my body tense. My stomach lurched and I could feel myself begin to instantly harden in my jeans. It was as if a light had been switched on inside my body and all my organs were responding at once, alert and alive and stunned into ecstasy.

He didn't pull back like I thought he might, instead he persevered, opening his mouth and parting my lips with his tongue. It was wet and warm as it passed through my opening and lapped itself gently against my own. I let out a soft moan as he kissed me again, gently but with feverish intent. His hand was still on my cheek and slowly moved to cradle my head, his fingers twisting themselves in my blonde hair. I returned his kiss, slightly harder this time but still full of tenderness. The feeling of his mouth on me made me wonder what it would feel like to be in other places as well.

I was hard now, my shaft pressing up against the rough confines of my trousers. I pushed my hands off the rocks behind me and lifted my right hand to his own face, gently caressing his lightly stubbled jawline. He moaned back at me, signalling his approval.

Then as quickly as it had begun, Kyle pulled away. The feeling of his mouth pulling away was like being splashed with cold water. Sobering and reeling. I opened my eyes and saw his pained expression, full of confusion and frustration and desire. He looked down at the ground and I did the same, shame quickly replacing the lust I had just been consumed with and forcing me back to reality.

We were both out of breath, as if the whole experience, brief as it may have been, had sucked all the energy from our bodies. Or perhaps it was the pulling away that had drained us completely.

"I'm sorry…" he said, still looking down at the ground, "I'm so sorry…"

I cleared my throat and pulled away, turning my head to look at the sea and replacing my sunglasses over my eyes.

"I'm sorry too."

"No, really. I shouldn't have…"

"It's my fault too. This wasn't a good idea."

"I know. I just…I just couldn't help myself."

I looked at him just then, studying his face and trying to read the validity of his words. He looked so sincere, so genuine that my heart sank even further.

"You're so…sweet, Everly."

My face was on fire again, awash with emotion and so unsure of how I was feelng at the same time.

"I think you're sweet too, Kyle."

He smiled back at me, his eyes focusing on my lips again before being pulled North to look me in the eye .

"I better go."

"Yeah, I better be getting…" my voice trailed off.

"I'm sorry. Again. I should be going."

I nodded in agreement wiping at my mouth and taking a quick look around the beach.

And with that he stood and with a tiny wave of his hand disappeared off down the beach as quickly as he had arrived, leaving me full of doubt and self-loathing.

# Hadley

The next night I could still taste Kyle on my lips, and when I closed my eyes I could imagine myself inside him. As I lay in bed I thought about how it felt when I stuck my fingers in him and the noises he made as I worked him out. I stiffened at the thought beneath my sheets and let a hand slither down my naked body and stroke my hardening cock.

*Damn he was good.*

I cupped my balls with my other hand and put pressure on the area inbetween my ass and my sack.

*Fuck, that feels good.*

He was so hot. Fucking him was so heavy and rough that I still had stones in my shoes when I went to work this morning. I thought about him all day today; every table I served, every customer who came into the restaurant, I wished they were him. I imagined him showing up and me meeting him in the men's room for a quick repeat of last night on the beach.

I even had to escape quickly during a slow period to go rub one off in the loo's cause I was rockin' a semi for about an hour. Customers were starting to stare at the bulge in their server's shorts.

I started jerking harder now as I lay back, one arm stretched over head and my hand resting under my pillow the other working its magic beneath the sheets.

*Fuck, what I wouldn't give to have him here with me now. I'd suck his cock so hard that he'd be stiff till next week.*

Then suddenly I stopped. My eyes shot open and stared straight up at the ceiling as a cold, harsh realisation set in.

*What am I thinking? Am I really still thinking about this guy...*

Normally after I'd scored with a guy, that was it. Move along! Next, please! Don't let the door smack your bare ass as I throw you out of it!

*What was happening to me?*

There I was. The next night after a great fuck, and I was still hanging on to it. Still thinking about him, wishing he were here so we could have a repeat performance, instead of being out on the lash and looking for my next pull.

*I'm fucking turning into Everly.*

This is what a little bitch would do after a date; sit here, thinking about what happened, and if he'd call, and if I'd ever see him again. This was so not me. I should have moved on by now. That was practically my motto; never look back.

Something had changed. I could feel it. That same feeling in the pit of my stomach had returned and there was no denying it, I was still thinking about Kyle. I had been all day, and to be perfectly honest…I was looking forward to seeing him again. I thought back to the last time a guy had such an effect on me.

*Charlie.*

That felt like a million years ago. I never wanted to feel like that again. It had been rough. Way too hard and I swore I would never go down that road again.

And yet here I was. At the beginning of it. Staring it straight in the face and already beginning to feel powerless against it. I liked him. I really liked him.

Part of me was thinking about what's the worst that could happen, while another part of me knew that nothing good could come from these feelings…

# Everly

I wasn't sure how much time had passed since Kyle disappeared down the beach. My ass felt like it had become a part of the pebbles and that if I didn't move soon my body would become a permanent fixture right there where I sat, like some sort of commemorative statue for a public figure. I watched as Kyle shrank more and more in the distance, leaving my lips hot and my insides churning with guilt.

*What am I doing?*

This wasn't me. I'm not *that guy*. And yet I didn't try and stop him when he kissed me. I didn't push him away and remind him of my brother who he had just been on a date with. The devil on my shoulder was telling me not to worry and that he and Hadley had only been on one date. It wasn't like they were engaged or anything. And besides, it was *Hadley* we were talking about. Let's face it; he's a bit of a man-slut and I bet he's already moved on to whomever would be his next conquest.

But the angel on my shoulder was shaking his head at me in distaste, whispering condemning words of shame and regret. He was warning me of the kind of guy that Kyle was shaping up to be; a two-timer. The sort of guy who says he'll call and then never does. The kind of man who tries to get with both brothers at the same time. A player.

As I sat there on the beach, my gaze turned towards the rolling waves before me, I suddenly realised my life was turning into some sort of shitty gay soap opera. Never one to listen to my darker side I decided to stop wallowing and take hold of the situation that was quickly unravelling before my very eyes.

Shaking myself off, I stood, grabbed my litter and strode off purposefully down the beach. Ever the masochist, I allowed the tiny seed of guilt to manifest itself in my stomach. I welcomed it, urging the pain to course through me as I walked, knowing that if I let it take over it would stop me from allowing something like this to happen again.

I thought of Hadley as I began the walk back to our house. He did seem to be into this guy; why else would he initiate the date in the first place? He had his chance to sleep with him that first night they met at the club, and if Kyle was telling the truth that nothing happened that night then maybe this would be different for Hadley this time around.

My thoughts slid away from me as I considered the last actual relationship that Hadley had and a slow worming shiver worked its way through my core. I travelled back in time in my mind, to those many years ago when things took a turn for the worst for our family. Memories of the guy who almost broke up our little family crept their way into my head. I could actually feel my teeth begin to chatter as my mouth formed *his* name on my lips.

*Charlie...*

# 2008

Hadley had been dating Charlie for nearly six months. When they were together nothing else mattered. It was as if the world around them didn't exist when they were side by side, which was pretty much all the time these days. Charlie was his first true love and Hadley would do anything to make him happy.

The two met through mutual friends and hit it off instantly. It wasn't long before Hadley had introduced Charlie to Everly and his mum and vice versa. Charlie was an only child though, and his father had also left his mother when Charlie was still a child; which was another detail that the two had bonded over. At only nineteen years old, the two found solace in each other's company in a time when they should have been out having life experiences and travelling the world. But both boys only had eyes for the other, which left little time for anyone else.

And that included Everly.

Everly was still the shier of the two twins, made even more of an introvert by the fact that he had also just came out of the closet and had still yet to meet anyone. Hadley, on the other hand seemed to have the boys flocking to him from all angles. Charlie just happened to be the lucky one chosen of the bunch.

In truth, Charlie seemed to be better suited for shy, quiet Everly, than for hyper, extrovertly-out-spoken Hadley. Charlie was naturally fair-haired with an equally almost turquoise stare as the twins. Pale skinned and only moderately built, he was still unequivocally handsome in a very traditional way. But for whatever the reason, he seemed to have latched himself onto Hadley, and they were seemingly very much in love.

Charlie was always at the Stone house. His mother worked late
hours and didn't approve of Charlie having guests over, especially boys,
when she wasn't home. So this meant that the Stone residence had
quickly become their own semi-private little love nest. They had had sex
quite early on in the relationship, probably due to Hadley's influence,
both boys giving up their virginity for the other. When Charlie would
come over, the two would often quickly proceed up to Hadley's
bedroom, lock the door and not emerge for hours, if at all. This made
Everly beyond curious. He would harass Hadley for details about their
sex life. What it felt like; what they did together; how it all worked; to
which Hadley would gush all the gory details including who did what
and who put what where, whether Everly wanted to hear them or not.

Often Hadley would catch Everly staring at the two of them as they
cuddled on the sofa, a look of longing upon his face. But when
confronted, Everly would surely deny everything with a look of fake-
disgust on his face. But he was jealous, there was no denying it. Everly
wanted what Hadley seemed to get so easily, but with his nose always in
a book and his trim figure hidden beneath over-sized clothes, it was no
surprise that Everly went unnoticed.

A few months passed and as summer approached, things between
Hadley and Charlie seemed to change somewhat. They had been
together for almost a year when from seemingly out of nowhere, Charlie
began making more excuses about missing dates and often going out
with his other friends and leaving Hadley at home. At first it seemed
innocent enough and Hadley put it down to Charlie simply wanting
more time with his own mates. But as the incidences became
increasingly more frequent, paranoia began to manifest itself and
suspicions arose.

Weeks passed and Hadley began to feel more and more distant from
him. And then one night when the two were together and lying in bed,
alone in the house with Everly and his mother out at the cinema, Charlie

even dismissed Hadley's sexual advances saying that he was tired and incidentally not in the 'mood'. As Hadley lay there in bed, staring at the ceiling as his seemingly 'perfect' boyfriend snored quietly next to him, his mind began to wonder and he gave in to the realisation that he was losing Charlie.

The next day while Everly was in town doing the food shopping on his own, he swore that he saw Charlie sitting in a coffee shop, across from a rather attractive-looking stranger. Upon closer inspection, Everly was surprised to see that it was indeed Charlie sitting with a mystery lad, and by the look of the two together and their body language as seen from outside through the shop window, Everly couldn't help but suspect that the two were more than friends. Everly quickly snapped a picture on his mobile of the two canoodlers as proof to expose to his twin.

Upon showing it to his brother, Hadley was stunned into silence. He stared at it for what felt like hours, the wheels in his brain working and churning as they tried to make sense of what this small grainy photo meant. The more he stared at it the more his expression hardened. His brows furrowed and his eyes clouded over, darkening to almost a shade of navy. Everly watched as his twin's jaw clenched and the veins in his neck protruded causing his whole frame to shake slightly as emotions overcame him. He seemed to change somewhat, the colour draining from his face as if a switch was flicked somewhere inside his head causing him to appear cold and lifeless.

He never spoke about the photo to his brother. He simply turned his head to hide his tear-stained eyes and left the room. Everly wasn't sure what he was feeling as he watched his brother leave through the door to their house, taking nothing with him but a set of keys. He was angry *for* his brother. The same reaction that Hadley had just displayed was beginning to manifest itself inside of Evelry. He stared at the photo on his mobile and imagined what the two had been talking about.

*How dare he go behind my brother's back,* he thought to himself.

He thought of poor Hadley and the betrayal he must have been feeling. He was angry at Charlie for being so hurtful to someone he loved and yet still couldn't believe that Charlie could do something so terrible if indeed the photo was proof of him cheating. It was the same Charlie that Everly had grown so fond of. The same guy who Everly had watched from afar and admired and respected. The more he thought about him, the more the same rage mixed with hurt surged deep down in his belly. At once the same tenseness seemed to take over his own body as did Hadley's, making him quiver and shake violently as a result.

It wasn't the first time the boys' 'twinship' had caused them to feel each other's pain, and it certainly wouldn't be the last. When one seemed to experience deep seeded displeasure, the same was mirrored in the other. The downside to when the link between the two boys acted up like this was that as their past suggested, bad things usually happened.

Charlie was in fact seeing someone else; he had been for some time now. He said it just sort of 'happened'. Hadley confronted him at his house, the picture in hand having been sent to his own mobile and a look of utter devastation twisting his beautiful features. He screamed words of love and anguish at his boyfriend, who took them with a blank look upon his face. He didn't deny anything, nor did he offer up any sort of explanation. He simply said he was sorry, with nothing but vacancy in his eyes.

It was this vacancy that stirred something in Hadley and morphed his feelings of betrayal into something a bit more sinister. Perhaps if Charlie had apologised more profusely and hung on to what they had a little bit more, then Hadley wouldn't have been so distraught. But he didn't. He didn't fight for them or cry or even act the least bit upset. Instead he seemed to let go; releasing his hold on Hadley and metaphorically signing his own fate.

Charlie's affair was with a boy a couple of years older than him named Dale. Hadley knew who he was; he was from the same town and in fact his mother played Bridge with Mrs. Stone every week at the local parish church. He came from a good family and was studying law at Brighton University. He was a good boy.

*Was* being the key word.

It seems that Charlie's fate was to be as unhappy as he had made Hadley, for after that day, the object of Charlie's affair vanished, as if into thin air, never to be seen again...

Word spread quickly and a police investigation was opened to attempt to figure out what had happened to this young man. All that is known, still to this day is that Dale, the object of Charlie's affection, went to work at noon the day of his disappearance, but never came home that night. No body was ever found although the boy's family, and Charlie, all suspect foul play.

The case remains unsolved.

Hadley took the brunt of the blame. Charlie went on to later tell police that when Hadley left his house after confronting him, it was as if he had turned into someone else. In his statement he described Hadley as angry, furious even, hell bent on revenge for having been betrayed like this. Said he left in such a state that Charlie was frightened for his own life, shouting threats that if he couldn't have him then no one would.

When Hadley was questioned he denied everything; he admitted confronting Charlie with evidence that he had cheated, but that he had calmed down once he got home, and that was that. When asked if anyone could verify his wherabouts that evening it was Everly who came forward, confirming every word of his brother's story and saying that Hadley had been home with him for the remainder of the day.

With no body ever found, there was nothing to charge Hadley with. He got off with a restraining order, put into place by Charlie, stating that he could not come within a hundred metre radius of Charlie ever again. The whole town was divided. Another hideously distressing act, seemingly brought on by the Stone family.

No one knows what happened that afternoon after Hadley left Charlie's house, except that Dale disappeared, and two hearts were broken. Hadley swore he was innocent and although nothing was ever proven in regards to what happened, people never looked at the Stone family the same again. Because of Hadley, the whole family seemed to be cast aside from the town they once loved and blamed for things that one of them wouldn't confess to. To everyone else, Hadley was the only possible explanation for what happened to Dale, and even his own mother had her doubts as to her son's innocence.

From that day onwards, Hadley changed once again; he became withdrawn, darker even. he dyed his hair black, changed the way he dressed. He became increasingly distant from everyone including his own family. There was no denying he was rebelling and he ended up dismissing his friends and all the things he used to enjoy. Even Everly felt that he was slipping away for a while. But what people didn't realise at the time was that Hadley was hurting. Beneath the tough exterior that he faked to those around him, inside, he was bleeding. A broken heart caused him to push everything away, including anything and anyone who reminded him of Charlie. To himself he swore he would never get close to another man again and would only see them as objects that he could play with.

He was alone. And remained that way until now…

## 2013- Everly

The next morning I sat down at the breakfast table, sipped a cup of coffee and waited for Hadley to get up. As I sipped, the coffee only added to the buzzing that was going on inside my head. I had barely slept last night; tossing and turning and thinking of nothing but that kiss.

*That kiss…*

I felt guilty and angry and happy and excited, all at the same time. Stilling myself, I tried desperately to choose an emotion but came up with nothing, as if my brain had suddenly developed ADHD over night and refused to settle.

Of one thing I was certain; in the period of a week, my life had gone a complete 180. Shy, meek little Everly was starting to transform into, well, Hadley.

This whole situation was something Hadley would do. This was exactly how Hadley would behave; sneaking around behind other people's backs, playing with fire and only thinking of himself. It made me angry to think how quickly I'd fallen down the rabbit hole the moment a cute guy paid me any sort of attention.

But that was just it. He *was* paying attention to *me*. He was kissing *me*. Maybe that meant something. Perhaps that meant that he was meant for me, and not Hadley.

*But how do I approach this with him?*

I thought back to Charlie and the last time Hadley had become involved romantically with a guy. I thought about how upset he got when he got hurt and how quickly he seemed to *turn* when he was betrayed.

A noise from upstairs stirred me out of my own head and nearly made me drop my cup of coffee all over myself.

*He's up.*

Within moments, after a few seconds of shuffling around on the stairs, Hadley appeared from the hallway, yawning and scratching at his unruly mop of black hair that even though slept in looked remarkably fashionably styled.

"Alright?" he asked me in a voice drenched with sleep.

I nodded in his direction, sitting forward in my chair and cupping the hot drink in both hands on the table. I waited as he fiddled and fussed about in the cupboard for a mug and poured himself a generous amount of black coffee. He never added anything to it, generally prefering it as strong and bitter as possible, whereas I needed to sweeten mine slightly with a lump or two of sugar.

He swivelled in my general direction and I could feel his eyes on me, studying me as if he knew I had done something wrong. I opened my mouth to speak and then reconsidered, my eyes never leaving the cup in front of me. After another second of agonising silence I took the plunge.

"I feel like I haven't spoken to you in days."

"Mmm," he mumbled taking a sip of his drink.

"How was your date?" I ventured nervously testing the waters.

Hadley pushed himself off from the counter and started busying himself with a bowl and some cereal. "Yeah, it was good. Actually, it was really good," he said with his back towards me.

"Oh?"

He snickered. "Yeah, he's pretty cool."

I nodded suddenly aware that he wasn't going to volunteer much information unless I prodded him for it. "What did you guys do?"

"Umm, drinks, you know…Whatever."

"I see…Listen, I-"

"You never told me you ran into him," he said turning towards me, his words came out more as an accusatory statement than a question. I blinked in his direction and tilted my head, stalling as I thought about what to say.

"Uhhh, really? When was this?"

Hadley's eyes narrowed and his mouth thinned into a hard set line. "He said he came into your shop. Before our date."

"Oh, of course. Yes, he did. That day it was chucking it down. Yes, sorry. He came in and I gave him a cake."

He nodded his head slowly in my direction, his eyes much wider now as he tried to decipher my tone. I was acting my ass off, desperate not to give away too much until I was ready to take the heat. I was feeling the waters to see how much he knew. Or suspected.

"That was nice of you..." his voice trailed off as he turned back around to finish making his food.

I rolled my eyes at the scene that had unfolded between us. I felt ridiculous acting like this in front of him but every time I tried to open up something inside stopped me. The more I considered it, the more I realised that it was fear that was keeping me mute.

"Well, he's a nice guy..." I ventured again, feeling like I was walking out on a limb all of a sudden. "Listen, Hadley, I wanted to t-"

"-I really like him, Everly," Hadley interrupted.

He rarely used my full name, unless he was angry at me for something. The sound of it as it escaped from his lips almost made me jump back at the bluntness of his words.

I didn't know what to say. I could only stare at him in disbelief and I suddenly felt like he was able to see the huge scarlet 'A' that was etched across my chest. My heart sank deep into my chest and I was sure my expression reflected how pained I felt.

"I really do.Remember that."

His face was so stern as he picked up his bowl and mug of coffee and strode purposefully from the room leaving me to stew with my guilt.

\*\*\*

Hadley left soon after our talk and went to work at the restaurant leaving me to pick up the pieces of what had just happened. I hurried myself to get ready for work and left earlier than I needed to just so I wouldn't be alone with my thoughts for longer than I needed to be.

As I walked briskly along the seafront towards the bakery, Hadley's words resonated through me.

*"I like him Everly. I really do…"*

It had been so long since he'd been this way about anybody. How could I pursue anything with Kyle now that I knew how he really felt?

Thankfully I had work to busy myself with today otherwise I wasn't sure what I would do with my idle hands. It was colder today, the early Autumn air taking a turn for the worst despite the bright sunshine in the clear skies. I clutched my cardigan tighter around me to shield myself from the brisk temperatures and kept my head tucked down towards the ground.

As I turned the twisty alleys of the Lanes shopping district and my shop came into view, something else stopped me dead in my tracks, forcing me still like a deer caught in headlights.

There, stood outside the shop main entrance, with one leg bent at the knee and his foot resting against the brick wall behind him, was Kyle. Panic rose in my throat as my eyes rested on his beautiful face. He was typing something into his phone and looking around him at the faces of the people passing by. I took a few steps closer to him and he caught sight of me approaching. His face lit up instantly. Seeing him look so nonchalant as he stood there waiting for who I presumed to be myself, only made me more nervous. A thousand thoughts ran through my head as we inched our ways closer to each other. His smile must have been contagious for as we drew nearer and I got a whiff of the sweet citrusy scent of his aftershave, I couldn't help but return it despite my nerves.

As much as I tried to deny it to the best of my abilities, I was happy to see him.

When we were only about two feet in front of each other we both stopped. I looked to the ground in a half attempt to hide my shy grin from him which would only give away how excited I was to see him here. I could feel his eyes on me, so self-assured and probably eating up every inch of how shy I had instantly become in his presence. He loved how on edge he made me and how I stiffened like a board when he was near. I shook slightly with anticipation of what he might say.

"Hey," came his voice, masculine and deep with the slightest hint of allure.

"Hi," I returned shyly.

"How are you?" He put a finger under my chin to tilt it upwards so he could see my face. The movement was slight but incredibly domineering and dare I say it, *beyond sexy*.

"I'm good, I guess," I paused, "what are you doing here?"

"I needed to see you."

"But, why? I thought…"

"Yes, exactly. *You* thought. I, on the other hand feel differently."

His tone was as domineering as him even being here suggested. I felt minuscule as I stood in front of him, like I was there to receive punishment for some wrong doing of some sort and could do nothing but receive whatever he was there to give me.

"Take a walk with me."

What should have been a question, came out as an order and before I knew it he was leading me back down the alley from which I had just come, his arm on my bicep but quickly slinking down to my hand which he gently took in his own.

I melted just a little bit more at the feeling of my hand in his…

\*\*\*

"I think Hadley really likes you," I said, my eyes shying away from his penetrating stare.

"I think I like *you* better," Kyle replied.

When I looked up and finally met his face I got a flash of his blinding white teeth. The look on his face made me smile despite my attempts to hold it in. I looked away quickly, afraid that he'd see too deep into my soul if I studied him any further.

We had wondered down the Lanes to a bench in the sun and were sitting side by side, my eyes permanently glued to the ground at my feet while he relaxed casually on the bench, an arm resting on his right thigh while the other stretched out behind my back.

"What's the problem anyway," he teased through a shit-eating grin, "Do I need your brother's permission to date you, for some reason?"

"Just be careful."

He swallowed hard at the sudden change of my tone.

"What do you mean?"

"Just, be careful not to hurt him. Hadley can be a bit...strange when he's hurt."

I turned my back to Kyle and stood as a dark cloud drifted overhead causing the sun to run fleetingly away.

"Hey, come here a sec," he coaxed, extending an arm to stop me.

The touch of his hand on my skin made me halt in my tracks straight away.

"I gotta go Kyle, just remember what I said." I took a deep breath and pulled my arm free of his grasp.

"What? You're going? But-"

"Be careful," I repeated from over my shoulder, "You don't wanna make him angry."

# Hadley

Our birthdays were in exactly two days and even though Ev didn't know it yet, I was gonna throw us a massive party at our place to celebrate it. Not 'get-thrown-out-by-our-landlord'-big, but still big enough for those invited to remember it.

If I'd spilled the beans to him he'd just whinge and complain that our place wasn't big enough and that I should have consulted him first and blah, blah, blah. It was always better this way when it came to breaking news to my brother. Yeah, he'd bust my balls for a while but in the end he'd thank me for taking the reins and planning something fun.

Things were set already. The keg was ordered and those lucky enough to get an invite had already been notified. Only thing left to do now was figure out what to wear.

After our run-in yesterday morning, I had kept my distance from Everly; something I had gotten very good at doing as of late. I could tell that there was something between Ev and Kyle. Something about the way Ev started mumbling and stuttering whenever I mentioned his name. I mean, even after our date the other night I came home only to find him asleep on the sofa, obviously waiting up for me.

He was jealous. Always was when I scored with a guy or whenever they chose me over him. If you asked him he'd blame me for being too outspoken and for always swooping in there and taking them from under his nose like they're baby birds and I'm some sort of fucking vulture. Everly doesn't know what he wants when it comes to blokes, whereas I do.

*Well at least I do now.*

If he wants to sit there and cry or mope like a little bitch cause he let his insecurities get in the way of him pulling a guy again, then let him. I'm done feeling guilty about it.

My mobile beeped from across the room. Stretching and pulling myself up from the bed, I crossed the room to see who it was. When my eyes saw it was a text from Kyle I couldn't help but light up.

*"Thanks for the invite sexy, I'll be there."*

I tossed myself back down on the bed and stared up at the ceiling, already getting a stiffie just thinking of the birthday sex I was sure to get tomorrow night.

*Oh yes, this was going to be a birthday to remember.*

# Everly

Hadley thinks I don't know about his little soiree he's planning tomorrow night. He does this every year; plans a big hoo-haa, invites everyone and their dog and then complains when the cops get called or when I force him to clean up all the mess. I'll bitch about it for about a week afterwards when something gets broken and he'll find some way of turning things back around and blaming me for being too uptight.

We know each other so well it's like being an old married couple for crying out loud. Call it 'twin-tuition' but I can almost always predict his next move even before he puts pen to paper, so to speak.

He must think I'm pretty stupid and have no idea what he's planning this year. But I took the bloody phone call from the keg rental place the other day confirming the date and time for delivery. That's the beauty of being an identical twin; taking each other's phone calls to catch the other out!

*I just hope to God he doesn't invite Kyle along. I don't know what I'd do if he were in my house…*

# Hadley- The night of the party

*Just an intimate gathering of fifty or so of my favourite people.*

The music was loud and the party was banging, if you know what I mean. The three kegs I had rented arrived just in time before the first guests  and my friend Jason brought his old school decks which he was currently stood behind, mixing beats compiled especially for the occasion. Drinks of all sorts were flowing from the round table in the corner of the lounge that was littered with a bunch of different bottles to suit all preferences of poison; vodka, gin, and of course my favourite, Champagne from the finest distilleries in France. A few of my lovely ladies from the restaurant had brought balloons filled with helium, which as I surveyed the back garden area of the house, were now being huffed by some of the local kids we had gone to school with. I had made a huge banner printed for the party which read 'Happy Fucking Birthday Stone Boys' and had it hung from the rafters in the lounge, so it was the first thing you saw when you came in the room. There were a few bowls of assorted nibbles scattered around the room; most of which remained untouched as people were seemingly more interested in swallowing pills or snorting powder than they were in swallowing food. The lights were low in the house, providing enough dim lighting for my esteemed guests to indulge in whatever sort of nastiness and naughtiness they deemed fit for the occasion.

As I strode slowly across the lounge, stopping for a quick shake on the make-shift dance floor that had formed in front of the DJ, I swilled the dregs of what was left of my first bottle of Moët, straight from the bottle of course.

*Who can be bothered with glasses when you're at a party?*

I closed my eyes as I moved to the music for a moment, random hands running across my back as I danced, hugging me and shouting gestures of 'thanks' and 'great party' and all that shit.

I was drunk. Proper messy already, and I couldn't give a shit. My champagne buzz was making me feel electric and as I opened my eyes I saw that things around me were moving slightly slower than they should.

"Hey Birthday slut!" came a voice from behind me. Turning slowly, my eyes fell upon Nick, a bloke from the restaurant and a couple of his mates all crowded around a side table against the far wall of the lounge. "Come over here a sec, I got something for ya."

Nick was a pretty far out guy normally. Good guy to work with and an even better drug dealer when you needed one. Unfortunately he was straight, but would sometimes take head over payment for his supplied services if ever you were running a bit low on funds. He was the best sort of straight guy; not homophobic in the least and never opposed to a bit of old-fashioned flirting. He'd indulge me once in a while when I joked about wanting to get him in the sack. Who could blame me, he was hot; a muscle jock with tattooed arms and a huge cock which he loved to accentuate with tight jeans and normally no underwear. As I approached he pulled me in for a hug, wrapping his muscular arms around my torso and squeezing me tightly. His pelvis was pressed up against my own so hard that I could feel the outline of his dick through his jeans. He was pretty hard already and as I looked down at Ev's shabby-chic coffee side-table I saw why. Laid out neatly on the table were about a dozen fat white lines of delicious-looking coke. I could smell the metallic-aspiriny scent from there without even bending down and immediately felt a twinge inside my own pants.

"Birthday boy," he growled a little too sexually for a quasi-straight dude, "my man, for you, an offering." Nick held out a straw and as I took it he led my free hand south and pressed it up against his jeans, giving me a feel of how hard he was. "Let's make this a proper party!"

I opened my eyes wide at his sexual advance and thought to myself that this must be some good shit for him to be coming on that strong. Bending down I didn't hesitate; lining the straw up at the beginning of one of the lines to the left and huffing it back in a quick sweep. Snorting again I closed my eyes and tilted my head up to the ceiling, letting the sweet acidity of the blow filter and drip down my nasal cavity, waking me up like a jolt to the heart. When I opened my eyes again, everything was clearer like I had been seeing things through a tunnel-lens before and now finally saw the party for what it really was.

"Cheers mate," I jeered towards Nick with a nod to the others around him who patted me on the back and shouted things I couldn't quite hear over the music. Nick leant in closer to me until I could smell the musky scent of his aftershave and feel his hot breath against my ear.

"One good turn deserves another," he whispered in a raspy voice with a sly smile, patting me on the back once more. I didn't need to be told twice and leaned over once more for round two. This line went up even easier than the last. I jolted upright after inhaling the fatty in one go and rubbed at my nostrils as the drug did its thing.

"Nice one brotha," Nick congratulated me. "Pretty bangin' fiesta my man."

I licked a finger and dabbed it in the remnants of the line on the table before running it across my gums, savouring the numbing effect on my teeth. I nodded in response to Nick's statement and gave him a wink as my hand slid back down to the bulge in his trousers and gave it a quick rub and a squeeze. He closed his eyes at the feeling, completely unphased by his entourage looking on as a gay man gropped him openly. I could feel myself begin to stiffen as well as the cocaine fueled my hormones making me feverishly horny all of a sudden.

"Let me return the favour later, hot stuff," I whispered back to him, my hand still gently touching his penis, "come find me…"

And with that I was off again. My champagne fuzz had waned, and I walked around the room with renewed energy. I let out a howl to the party putting two hands into the air and strutting across the dance floor from whence I just came. The people in the room returned my yelp as the energy of the room picked up again in turn with the music.

I needed to piss.

I crossed the room and went down the hallway towards the toilet, accepting another hug from one of neighbours in the building who thanked me for the invitation. She kissed me on both cheeks then slapped my ass before bouncing off down the hall towards the pounding music in the lounge. Our flat wasn't huge by any means, but we certainly were able to pack it to the brim with party monsters. I was riding high on the energy tonight, floating on the cloud of the evening and letting everything that was making me feel shitty the last couple of days just fade away. The thought of Everly impeding on my thing with Kyle, slowly melted as I gave in to the feeling all around me.

Just as I was about to turn the handle to the bathroom door, it opened suddenly making me stumble back slightly in surprise. There standing in the doorway, was Everly.

*Speak of the devil.*

He regarded me with a look that spoke volumes of pissiness. He immediately crossed his hands over his chest, his way of steeling himself in preparation for a fight, before chewing on his thumb nail nervously. He wasn't saying anything, but he didn't need to. I knew what he was thinking.

Even though he had confronted me before the party, saying he knew what I was planning, we fought and I thought we got it all out in the open and were cool about tonight. Well, as cool as we were gonna be. My argument was what it always was; it was my flat too, I pay half the rent and should be allowed to have a party every now and then especially when it was our birthday soon. What I didn't exactly spill to him, was how many people were going to be here...

*Which is probably why he looks so pissed at me.*

I took him by the shoulders and gently pushed him back into the bathroom and shut the door behind us. I could feel him studying my face as he continued to bite at his nail.

"You're fucked, aren't you?" he said harshly.

"Evvvvvv," I cooed, bringing him in for a hug which he didn't return. "Come, on, don't be mad, pleeease?"

He hated my cutesty voice, but it always worked. I hugged him tighter but he only seemed to stiffen further beneath my grip. He felt warm to my touch and was wearing my Jean Paul Gaultier cologne, so I knew he was sort of getting into the spirit of the night.

"You're such a shit to me Hadley, you never said there was going to be this many people here."

"I know, I know...But I didn't plan it honestly, they just sort of...showed up!" I pulled back and looked him in the face, trying my best to look innocent beneath my cocaine high.

"And the drugs!" he threw his hands up in the air for emphasis before letting them fall to his sides. "Don't even get me started. If the cops come, I'm pretending I don't even live here, you got it?"

I knew he meant it because he was pointing a finger at me now, jabbing it into my chest doing his best impersonation of a tough guy.

"Don't worry your pretty little head, seriously, nothing's going to happen. I promise."

"It better bloody not, Hadley. Seriously." He shook his head and went back to biting his nails, chewing frantically and looking towards the sink in the bathroom.

"Listen, trust me. I'm your brother, and it's our fuckin' birthday."

"Not yet it's not."

"Well soon enough, you get my drift." I assured him, rubbing his arms now and removing his hand from his mouth. "Don't do that, it's unattractive."

He shot me another look of contempt.

"Come on, what's done is done. Let's go out there and enjoy the party."

"Easy for you to say, they're all your friends," he considered something then looked me in the eye again with renewed vigour, "and don't even try and pretend you did this for *me*...Tonight was all about *you*, and you bloody well know it."

"Hey, hey, come on now. Don't be like that. I want you to loosen up. Hey, remember the club night. Remember how much fun you had?"

"Yeah, until you left me for some guy."

"He's not just *some guy*, ok? I really like him."

He just stared at me, narrowing his eyes as if trying to decide if I were serious or not.

"It's beside the point. Really. I knew you were going to be a bit mad at me for tonight, but I also know that when you let go of yourself a bit, you can have a really good time!"

"Not with *those* kind of people, Hadley," he said quietly as if they might be listening outside the doorway.

"Don't be so fuckin' judgemental, you don't even know them."

"I know they're bloody drug dealers!"

"Not...All of them..."

Another look of disbelief.

"Right, enough of this. Come on. We're going to get you a drink. I've saved all the good champers for us. Come on."

He didn't budge. I opened the door to the bathroom and grabbed hold of his left arm. Everly stood firm, as if he could reassert his control of the situation if he ignored all of my directives. Now it was my turn to shoot him a look of warning.

"Everly Stone, if you don't come with me and enjoy this birthday party you are going to seriously regret it Mister."

After a second I erupted into a fit of laughter and I could see Everly begin to falter and a smile dance across his features.

"There's my boy," I said, pinching his cheek. "Now come on, let's make a toast."

And with that I leaned in and planted a quick kiss on his lips and pulled him out of the toilet.

# Everly

I had been spending most of the time huddled in a corner with Katie from work, until Hadley found me and forced me out of hiding and into the full party scene.

"We're doing shots!" he shouted over the thud of the baseline. Katie, the only person I had time to invite, was waiting for me against the wall in the hallway. I grabbed her hand as Hadley whisked us both into the lounge, past the throngs of strangers dancing wildly and into the kitchen where Hadley was keeping his secret stash of booze and God knows what else.

"What have you gotten me into, Mister Everly?" Katie said to us as we gathered around the kitchen table, taking a seat.

"Miss Katie, I'm glad you're here, because you're about to witness something that's never happened before in our soon-to-be twenty-four years on this planet." Hadley was talking with his back to us as he bent down and was fiddling with the padlock that he had attached to the two bottom cabinets below the kitchen sink. It was his way of keeping his private stash away from prying eyes and hands when he had people over. Even I didn't have a clue what he kept in there, but I had a feeling I was about to find out.

"Uh oh," Katie mimed concern, "what do we have here?"

As Hadley opened the cabinet, we feasted our eyes on what appeared to be the inside of an off-licence; a various array of different coloured bottles all lined up perfectly like they were being prepared to be unloaded from the back of a van to replenish the shelves of a posh liquor boutique. There were easily thirty different bottles inside; as Katie and I both gawked at the contents I bent down for a closer look. There were bottles of vintage looking Dom Perignon champagne, as well as wine that looked old enough to be from the fiftys. Vodka, rhum, even exotic looking green liquores that I assumed to be Absinthe. Hadley stood back for a moment to admire his collection before starting to rummage for something in the back.

"Behold my collection lady and gent," he said proudly as he stuck his head quite far back inside, reaching blindly for something beyond vue. "Not just anyone is privileged to get a peek at what's hiding in Hadley's goody box."

Katie and I looked to each other with raised eyebrows.

"But tonight," he continued, "is a special occasion."

"Yes, I'm fully aware it's the eve of our pending birthdays, get on with it."

"No, no, no, dear brother, not just our birthdays." He pulled his head out from under the sink, his hand firmly grasping a dusty bottle containing an almost clear liquid. "Not just our birthday celebration, but the celebration of the first time my lovely twin brother does Tequila shots!"

He smiled a shit-eating grin that stretched from ear to ear as he held the bottle up into the air for us to see. It was so dusty that the label was almost hard to read. I squinted to get a better look and then stopped when I saw what appeared to be a worm floating around near the bottom.

"Is that what I think it is?" I asked making a face.

"If you think it's a vintage bottle of Don Pancho Tequila Camino Real, then yes, it is!" He said proudly not even reading from the label. "Roughly from the sixties, imported direct from Mexico, 40% and very, very delicious."

"Hadley, I'm impressed. Everly never said you were an aficionado of liquors," Katie mused.

"That's because I wasn't aware of it myself, if I'm perfectly honest." I mused in return.

"Now, we do this the old fashioned way. No wussy salt or fruit. Straight up, and down the hatch."

Hadley stood and plunked the bottle down on the kitchen table before turning and pulling out three identical shotglasses from the cabinet above. Katie and I exchanged looks of uncertainty mixed with unpleasantness.

"I, I don't know Had…" I croaked out, making a face like I had just bit into a lemon.

"Yeah, I mean the last time I had tequila shots was the night I blacked out a coupla months back," Katie piped in.

But Hadley was having none of it. He simply shook his head a few times as if to dismiss our objections and began clumsily pouring our three drinks into the shot glasses. When he was finished he took one in each hand and gave them to Katie and I, which we took begrudgingly, before picking up his own and raising it into the air triumphantly.

"To…" he thought out loud, "to Brotherly Love!" he announced a little too loudly, swaying slightly as he did.

I sniffed the shot carefully and pulled it away from my nose quickly in disgust.

"Ugh, I don't think I can…"

"Don't think, just drink," he said with eyes closed, "down in one. One, two, THREE!"

On cue the three of us tossed the shots back. The bitter liquid stung my taste buds instantly and burned as it slid down my throat. At first it didn't seem so bad after it left my mouth and continued travelling into my blood stream. That was until the afterbite kicked in.

I instantly felt blurry and had to close my eyes and hang on to the chair for a moment to catch my balance. I felt a slap on my back and I knew without opening my eyes it was Hadley, congratulating me for once again being lured down the rabbit hole.

"Thada boy!" he jeered, slapping me once more. Without missing a beat he busied his trembling hands with pouring us another drink each. I looked over to Katie who was holding her nose and squeezing her eyes shut tight.

"Oh man, that shit is funky!" she cried out, putting a hand to her chest as if to heal it from the pain it had just experienced.

Hadley was shaking so badly that he was pouring more onto the marble table top than he was into the shots. I felt giddy and couldn't help giggling to myself as I watched him fumble with the bottle of very expensive liquor.

"Shut the shit up, mate," he joked, a smile cutting up his sentence. "Another!"

He repeated the action of handing us both a shot which we took slightly more willingly this time.

"To boys!" he insisted, slightly more serious this time around. "Love to fuck 'em!"

Katie and I both burst out into hysterics before downing the shot quickly, her fingers still pinching her nose as she drank it down.

I let out a whoop of attainment as pride and excitement surged through me. Hadley was smiling at me. Not just any smile, but one of those deep smiles which you give someone when you're truly proud of them and are full of love and appreciation for them at that specific moment. He reached out a hand and rested on the back of my neck, giving it a little squeeze.

"I love you, mate," he beamed through his enormous smile.

I returned it and mouthed 'I love you, too.,' not giving him the satisfaction of actually saying the words out loud.

***

I wasn't sure how many more shots Hadley poured us in the period of the next hour. But all I know was that somewhere just before midning, with the party truly in full swing, I found myself on our little make-shift dancefloor, bumping up and down to the beat of a song with no words.

As Katie and I stood there, grooving to the music, huge smiles on our faces, I realised that at that moment I felt honestly, and truly happy. Hadley was right and at times knew exactly what I needed most to help me get out of my own head. I could get so wrapped up in trying to keep everything in my life in order and be on top of everything that happened that I ended up losing a bit of what made me, *me*. When someone did finally get me to let go of all my insecurities and just **be**, that's when I felt the most free. More often than not, that person was my brother. I could hate him at times, and at others, feel nothing but complete and utter adoration for him too. I suppose the two go hand in hand when it comes to twins.

Closing my eyes and letting my body sway of its own accord, completely unaware of anybody else in the room or of any eyes watching me, I let myself move. I may have looked utterly ridiculous to someone who didn't know me, but at that moment I didn't care. Blame it on the alcohol, or perhaps on the pending fact that I was soon to be another year older, but at that moment I wanted this. I *needed* this. I was craving release like this more than anything in the whole world. I tilted my head upwards and tried to lap up every inch of the music that was surrounding me. I opened myself up and welcomed it into my pours, absorbing as much as I could. If I continued to dance then maybe I would be able to become a part of it.

It was a few moments later that I sensed someone behind me on the dancefloor. It started out as a light brushing against my skin before it graduated into hands lightly grabbing onto my hips and moving with me as I continued to dance. I let it happen taking no real notice until whoever it was moved closer suddenly until they were practically spooning me standing up. I could feel their breath on the back of my neck and their fingers moved up slightly until they were under my shirt and gently caressing the skin around my waist. The feeling was exquisite and I dropped my own hands by my sides and slowed my dancing to take in the full effect of the feeling. The fingertips were warm and strong and danced around my back before travelling south down the front of my thighs. It seemed like the most normal thing ever at the time and it took me a moment before I ventured a glance over my shoulder to see who it actually was.

What I saw when I turned around jeered me back into sobriety like a cold splash of water on my face.

"Holy shit, Kyle!" I shouted out, surprising him and waking him too from the moment we were just sharing.

He recoiled his hands as if he had just been burned and looked at me guiltily and wide-eyed.

"Hi, shit, I'm sorry."

He looked amazing.

Casual and sexy in a white button-down shirt, untucked at the waist and open at the neck, with faded blue jeans that hugged his crotch in all the right places.

"You scared me, I…I didn't expect it to be…I mean, what are you doing here?" I asked puzzled.

*What the fuck? Was this really happening? Where was Hadley?*

"I was invited…" his voice trailed off under the music. He looked so guilty, like he had just been caught with his hands in the cookie jar. I immediately regretted pulling away as my head fantasised about what may have happened if I hadn't interrupted our dance.

"Your brother…" he added.

I shook my head in embarassment, "of course, Hadley."

"Yeah, he invited me." Kyle put his hands in his pocket sheepishly. "Happy birthday, by the way."

"Thanks. It's not until…Yeah, thank you."

"You look good, Everly."

The way he said my name made my knees weak. I looked into his big wide eyes and instantly was hypnotised again.

"Can we talk?" he asked, shifting the weight from one foot to the other.

Without waiting for an answer Kyle took me by the hand and steered me off the dancefloor and towards the hallway that led to Hadley and I's bedrooms.

As if from out of nowhere, a sudden flash of black materialised in front of us.

*Hadley.*

"There you are! I've been looking everywhere for you!" he shouted, wrapping his arms around Kyle's shoulders, who instantly dropped my hand and limply returned Kyle's embrace.

"Hi, how are you? We were just dancing."

"I just saw him a second ago. I didn't even know he was going to be here…" I looked to Hadley accusingly, narrowing my eyes in a way that narrated what I was thinking.

"We were just going to talk somewhere…Less noisy," Kyle explained.

I was sure my cheeks were growing hotter by the second. The tequila that was swilling around in my stomach was making me feel a bit off-centered and I put one hand on the wall to steady myself.

"Actually I'm glad you're both here," Hadley smiled the devious smile he always did when he was hatching a plan. "I wanted to talk to you…both…"

He stared at us from under his long dark lashes and took one of our hands in each of his and backed himself through his open bedroom door. He brought us to the bed and letting go of our hands pushed us down gently so that we were sitting, side by side on the edge. Things had begun to slow without warning and as Hadley crossed the room once more, shutting and locking the door, he seemed to be almost moving in slow motion. I blinked a couple of times, rubbing my eyes to try and refocus them, and watched as Hadley bent down and pulled out a bottle of Champagne from his mini-fridge in the corner of the room.

"I think it's time we had a little party of our own…" He waved the bottle in front of us as if it were a carrot on a stick. He had the most mischevious grin on his face that faded quickly and darkened to something I had never seen before. His lips were parted slightly and he ran his tongue over them, glistening them and making them seem somehow fuller in the dim lighting of his room. He removed the film from around the bottle and untwisted the metal coil of the cap, never removing his eyes from Kyle's face. I followed his gaze and saw that Kyle also wore the same darkened expression.

It was hungry. Carnal, as if at any moment they might pounce at each other like tigers in the wild. Kyle's hands were already grasping at the bed sheets as if they were the only thing keeping him still. He looked to me now, and the power behind his sultry stare made my insides melt. I found myself mirorring his look and I realised at that moment just how much I had been craving something to happen between us.

A loud pop of the champagne cork forced my eyes away from the beautiful man sat next to me.

"This is going to be all about us," Hadley's voice was now a raspy whisper as he took the first swig of champagne straight from the bottle before handing it to Kyle. He too wasted no time wrapping his gorgeous lips around the bottle in a slightly suggestive manner and drinking several long gulps of the fizzy liquid. When he was finished he exhaled deeply, his lips so moist it was all I could do not to lick them dry. He handed it to me and I went for it, mirroring his action and opening my mouth as wide as possible and inserting the bottle neck deep into my mouth before closing my lips around it and pulling it out until only the tip was in my mouth. I tilted it and shuddered as the ice cold drink dribbled down my throat, the bubbles burning as they assaulted my taste buds. All the while I kept my eyes on Kyle, spurring him on and keeping him engaged and focused on me and my mouth, hoping and praying that my suggestive movements were turning him on.

Music filled the air as if from out of nowhere as Hadley returned from his stereo and took the bottle from me and downed some more, wiping his mouth with the back of his hand before speaking.

"I've been thinking that this may be the best way to settle any of those wayward feelings between us three," he groaned before swigging some more champagne.

I couldn't speak, I wasn't sure this was even really happening. The bubbles were taking effect and I felt light and airy.

He set the bottle down on top of the mini-fridge and walked over to the bed. Standing up he seemed to tower over us. Hadley put a hand on each of our shoulders, his eyes skipping between us, his smile never fading.

We all knew what was going to happen. There was no turning back. The air was so thick with lust and desire you could taste it. I could feel the rise and fall of my chest as my vision continued to cloud and darken as I practically started to pant at the thought of what I was about to do.

"This is gonna be so fuckin' hot..."

I closed my eyes then, unsure as to who was speaking.

## Hadley and Everly

Hadley took Kyle's head in his hands and leaned down for a kiss. Kyle kissed him back, his hands resting casually at his sides as their mouths worked together, tongues in each other's mouths, moving together and sparring for dominance. The kiss seemed to last forever and Everly found himself unsure as to where to look. Part of him wanted to watch like the spectator at a film, but he was wrestling with the idea that it was his brother he was watching.

And yet another part of him liked the fact that it was his brother he was watching...

Either way he shifted the way he was sitting on the side of the bed, bending one leg so as to give his dick a bit more room to grow inside his trousers. He couldn't help it. He was turned on. Watching the two of them kiss was enough to make him cum right then and there. Blame it on the alcohol, but he was slowly letting himself go.

To his surprise Hadley pulled back, which judging by the look on Kyle's face, disappointed him as well. Hadley turned his head to look at his twin and the same devilish grin reappeared.

"Now I want you two to kiss," he groaned quietly. Kyle turned his head to look at Everly and then back to Hadley, uncertainty creasing his eyes. "It's okay...I know you want to..." Hadley reassured them both.

Kyle looked towards Everly again and as Hadley backed away slightly, Kyle inched his way closer to where Everly sat on the bed. His mouth was open and his tongue was ready. As his head drew in, they held it there for a moment, their mouths inches away from each other's, their breathing becoming increasingly heavy entering in through their open mouths in short gasps. Something held them apart, something almost forbidden, uncertainty hanging all around them mixed with confusion and lust. It took Hadley, who came up behind them with a hand on each of their heads, to push them together finally allowing their lips to lock.

Both men let out a deep groan as they let themselves bask in the experience of finally being able to explore each other's bodies with permission. Hadley licked his lips and let his right hand take hold of the bulge that had appeared in his jeans. He moaned as Kyle made out passionately with his brother, the sight so naughty and taboo that he felt himself getting more turned on than he ever imagined he would.

All three were rock hard now, obscene bulges pressing up against the confines of their pants. The soft music that was playing was being drowned out by the sound of their breathing which was thick and heavier now than before.

"Oh fuck yeah," Hadley groaned again. He crossed his arms,took a corner of his top in each hand and lifted it over his chest and head, letting it fall to the floor at his feet.

Kyle pulled away from Everly for a moment to look at Hadley and his thin, muscular chest. Hadley was closer to them now and Kyle reached up to run his hand over his smooth pecks, stopping to tweak a nipple between his thumb and fore finger. Hadley shut his eyes and let his head lean back at the sensation of having his nipple worshipped. Everly watched as Hadley responded to Kyle's touch, his heart beating harder than he ever thought possible. Without being able to contain it he let his own hand find his stiff member and began rubbing it slowly, enjoying the sight of his brother's naked chest and how it was making Kyle react.

"It's your turn..." Kyle whispered. Hadley opened his eyes and studied Kyle's expression.

But Kyle didn't have to say anything else, the twins knew what he meant. It was Kyle's turn to stand now and force Hadley into a seating position on the bed next to his brother. Kyle stepped back a fraction to get a better look as the two brothers, mirror images of the other, looked each other in the eye.

"Come on, it'll be so hot."

That seemed to be all the encouragement they needed as Hadley leaned his head in and started kissing Everly hard on the lips. It was like nothing Kyle had ever seen before. Ever since he first met the Stone brothers, this was all he could think about. The three of them together, semi-naked and ready to fuck. Adrenaline surged through his body as he watched the two identical twins begin to kiss.

Everly seemed unsure at first, pulling back slightly as his brother slid his tongue past his lips, but the hesitation quickly faded and he eased into it, slowly returning his kiss, massaging his tongue against Hadley's and even taking his shoulders in his hands and using them for leverage as the kiss heated up.

"Fuuuuuck yes," Kyle moaned as he frantically unbuttoned his shirt and pulled it over his broad shoulders. The material seemed to moan as it struggled to let his incredibly muscular arms free.

Everly opened his eyes for a moment and cast them over Kyle's now naked chest. He kissed his brother as his stare worshipped Kyle's flat stomach and round pecks. Reaching out he ran his fingers over Kyle's abs, desire taking over. His fingers moved up and circled Kyle's nipples, enjoying the sensation of them hardening as his fingers grazed them, circling and pinching gently until Kyle yelled out.

Then he closed his eyes again and returned to Hadley, focusing his attention on the kiss, both twins seemingly completely lost in what was happening. Their mouths were moving as one as if each knew exactly what the other wanted and how the other liked to be kissed. Everly was so gentle, planting light butterfly kisses all over Hadley's mouth and lightly lapping the tip of his tongue against his brother's. Hadley was harder; moaning and groaning as Everly worked his magic. He nibbled and bit at Everly's lower lip, pulling slightly and hungrily, their spit getting intermixed and creating a frothy film around their mouths. Hadley's hand wandered into his trousers now, slipping below the button and adjusting his hard-on. He bit Everly's lip again, harder this time causing him to moan in agreeance.

Kyle climbed up behind Everly on the bed and helping him, lifted his t-shirt up and over his head. It got caught around his face for a moment, acting like a mask and blurring his face and blinding him for a second. Hadley, who had pulled back for a moment to let Kyle start to work on Everly from behind, took the chance to dive in and begin massaging Everly's nipples with his extended tongue. Kyle stopped trying to remove the t-shirt, letting it rest around Everly's head, completely covering him from his neck upwards. Everly let out a howl of sexual frustration as his vision blurred, causing his sense of touch to heighten. He was unaware suddenly of who was doing what as Kyle moved around to the front and also began kissing and licking Everly's naked chest. Everly supported himself with his hands behind him so he was at a fourty-five degree angle with the bed. He bent his elbows and rested back on his forearms, not bothering to remove his tight t-shirt the remainder of the way, instead giving into the sensation of being blind-folded and enjoying the two men working away at his chest.

Hadley and Kyle continued kissing him all over, licking his abs and trailing their hot, wet tongues all over his naturally lean yet muscular torso. They were getting off on the power of being completely in control. Their heads were level with each other and when their mouths accidentally touched as they kissed the same spot on Everly's tight stomach they instantly began kissing each other, pulling back and sitting up on their knees, their hands moving up each other's bodies, grasping at each other's asses through the rough denim of their jeans; squeezing their buttocks and grinding their hard-ons together. Everly took the momentary gap in action to remove his t-shirt from his head, squinting at being able to see again and allowing his eyes to focus on the scene in front of him. He unbuttoned his dark jeans and slid the zipper down exposing the length of his cock through the white cotton material of his CK briefs. The head was wet with precum, moist and making a slight stain on his underwear.

"Fuck, I've wanted this," Kyle moaned through his kisses.

"Yeah?" Hadley urged, "How badly?"

"Fuck, so fuckin' badly," he groaned in response.

Their conversation was like something out of a dream. Everly steeled himself for a moment and took in the reality of the situation. He stood and quickly yanked down his jeans, struggling with them over his feet, all the while keeping his eyes on Hadley and Kyle so as not to miss a thing.

Their hands pawed and stroked and rubbed each other's backs. Everly couldn't believe the sight of their smooth chests grinding into eachother's, their nipples grazing.

"You wanna get fucked tonight?" Hadley asked, biting on Kyle's lip degradingly.

"Uhhhh, yesss baby…" was Kyle's response, which came out of his mouth as more of an animalistic growl than a human voice.

Both turned their attention to Everly who was standing in front of them in his white CK boxer briefs, his cock creating an obscene protrusion as it stretched against the confines of the tight lycra material. He let one hand slide down under the tight elastic waistband and slowly gripped the incredible length of his cock.

It wasn't the first time the Stone brothers would be naked in front of the other, but it would be the first that they saw the other's cock hard.

Hadley could do nothing but watch as his brother slid the boxer briefs slowly down over his waist line and then his cock. His mouth dropped open slightly at the sight of his brother's rock hard erection.

It was long. Longer than he had imagined. A large moist head and a hairless veiny shaft that met a trimmed patch of dark pubs which contrasted with the blondeness of the hair on his head. His nut sack hung low; two perfectly round little balls, in a tight layer of skin that were just begging to be sucked. His erection seemed to stand at a perfect ninety degree angle with his body, sticking out like a sword and cutting through the air when he moved. His hands hung at his sides, and his cock trembled with anticipation as he stood there letting the other two marvel at the sight.

Kyle licked his lips, his eyes sliding over Everly's naked body and taking in every inch of what he saw. His arms were strong; beautiful biceps and thick forearms. The skin of his chest was lightly tanned and perfectly smooth. His flat, toned stomach was tight, the result of only moderate trips to the gym and his waist was incredibly narrow compared to the fair bulk of his shoulders. Kyle marvelled as Everly's pecks seemed to inflate further as he breathed in, becoming even perkier with every inhale. Kyle looked to Hadley, as if seeking permission for what he was about to do next. Hadley nodded, his mouth open like a dog panting for water on a hot summer's day. Anticapation shook him as he stood there, semi-nude, about to watch his brother get sucked off.

Kyle quickly unzipped his tight jeans and shucked them off in a heap on the floor. He wore neon blue briefs with DIESEL emblazoned on the waist band. He kept them on as he crawled over the bed and placing his hands on Everly's hips for leverage, he opened his mouth wide and wrapped his lips around Everly's cock without hesitation. Everly let out a grunt that was half pleasure and half pain as Kyle took him into his mouth. He let his hands find Kyle's head and tangled his fingers in his hair, gently gripping his skull and leading the way by moving his head up and down on his dick. Kyle's hands moved around to Everly's ass and gripped his cheeks, kneeding them like dough.

Through his closed eyes, Everly could hear Hadley disrobing and adding his jeans to the pile of clothes on the floor. When his eyes opened he too marvelled at the sight of his twin's hard-on as he made his way closer. He came up behind Kyle who was on his knees, ass in the air and mouth expertly working away on Everly. Hadley positioned his cock perfectly so that his head rubbed up against Kyle's covered asshole. He took Kyle by the hips and let him get used to the feeling of his penis rubbing against him through the material of his underwear. Kyle moaned his approval through his dick-stuffed mouth and continued sucking Everlyoff. Sounds of sucking and spitting entwined with moans of delight hung in the air.

Hadley opened his eyes and leaned in to his brother.

"Ev," he whispered quietly to get his attention.

When Everly opened his eyes, brought back to earth from the land of pure ecstasy he had lost himself in, he leaned in to Hadley who had positioned himself for a kiss. The two twins locked lips again, as pleasure took over and nothing else seemed to matter anymore. Everly was lost, completely enveloped in the sensations that had taken over his body. He let himself go as Kyle blew him harder than he had ever been blown before. His tongue worked up and down Everly's shaft, licking and sucking, spitting and swallowing. The feeling of having Kyle's mouth wrapped around his manhood, working it up and down, appreciating and worshipping his head was almost too much. He kissed Hadley, unsure of what was right or wrong anymore. All he wanted was to feel this free forever.

Hadley knew this was what his brother wanted. He kissed and licked at his mouth to add to the pleasure his brother was feeling. He was getting off on how much his twin was getting off. Seeing his eyes roll so far back in his head as Kyle sucked his cock was bringing him closer to orgasm by the second.

Just then Kyle pulled back, letting Everly's wet cock slide out of his mouth and looked up at the two making out in front of him. He sat up instantly, lips slick with precum and suddenly all three of them were kissing. Kyle put his hands on the back of each of their heads and licked and kissed furiously, pushing their heads together until they couldn't tell who was who. Tongues acted as one, all three battling for supremacy, lapping against each other and swapping spit.

They moaned and groaned, sounds of sexual pleasure leaking from their lips as their bodies, slick with sweat, grinded and moved against one another. Hadley was the first to pull away this time, leaving Kyle and Everly to continue kissing. Their mouths pounded into each other as Everly's hands slid down Kyle's body and inched his underwear down over his ass, letting his rock hard erection bounce free. It trembled as it felt fresh air for the first time, wet and hard and ready for action. Without even thinking Everly grabbed it in his right hand and began jerking him off, to which Kyle responded by squeezing his eyes shut tightly and sucking air in through clenched teeth.

"Yeaaaaah baby, yes," he groaned, letting his head tilt back to face the ceiling and supporting himself on the bed with his hands on the mattress behind him. He gripped the sheets as if he were about to tear them to shreds as Everly stroked his cock, up and down, pulling gently on the foreskin, back and forth, his palm cupping the head.

Everly looked towards his brother who had stood and moved to a chest of drawers next to the bed. He slid one open and took out a pump bottle of cloudy liquid and a couple of what appeared to be condoms. Everly turned his attention back to Kyle and bent to nibble gently on his nipple as he continued his hand job.

"Let's do this," came Hadley's primal mumbling from the corner of the room. Everly looked over to see his brother sheathing his erection with the condom and pumping the lubricant into his palm before smoothing it all over his dick. Everly stopped working Kyle's cock and waited for his instruction.

"Kyle, I want you to lie on your back."

Hadley's voice was surprisingly calm as he whispered his instructions. Like an obedient subordinate, Kyle repositioned himself so that he was on his back, lying in front of Hadley. He pulled his knees towards his head, exposing his asshole in front of Hadley like he was putting a meal on a table.

"Yeah, just like that," Hadley acknowledged. "Now I want you to suck Ev off as I fuck you."

Hearing that come from his brother's mouth set Everly's skin on fire. He shuddered as he obeyed and crawled closer to Kyle and positioned himself so that his penis was level with Kyle's head. He looked over to Hadley who was concentrating now, one hand on Kyle's right leg which he positioned over his right shoulder and the other on his dick that he was lining up with Kyle's ass.

Kyle started licking Everly's balls and the feeling was like fireworks exploding in his chest. His body began to shiver uncontrollably as Kyle licked gently, flicking his tongue all over his ball sack, even gently sucking a ball at a time into his mouth. Everly gripped the bed for support, afraid that if he were to let go he would surely fall off. After a moment or two, there was a yelp that Everly wasn't sure who it came from, but must have been from Kyle for at that second he let go of Everly's nuts, his head shooting up to look at Hadley.

Hadley had started inserting himself into Kyle and continued slowly, inch by inch sliding his slick cock further inside him. Kyle reacted by sucking in sharp gusts of air, more and more every inch that Hadley entered him. The feeling was intense, amplified by the booze and the stimulation from all of their bodies writhing together on the bed.

"Suck his cock," Hadley instructed. Kyle obliged and took Everly's cock in his hand and slipped it in his mouth. Everly was so focused on the sight of his brother fucking Kyle that he had forgotten about his own dick. He too let out a groan as Kyle's tongue began lapping at his engorged mushroom head.

Hadley was completely inside Kyle now, his cock completely inserted and his own balls resting up against Kyle's ass cheeks. He pushed himself in further, ramming it into him as Kyle's ass continued to adjust itself to the intrusion. He seemed to respond to the feeling by sucking harder on Everly, completely lost and out of control of his own body.

He couldn't believe he was fucking identical twins; living the dream. He would have let them do anything to him at that moment; as if having an out of body experience he could do nothing but obey and let himself get fucked.

Hadley was pumping away now, in and out, each thrust being felt by all three as the bed shook and Kyle took Everly's dick deeper into his throat. Their moans were getting more frequent and intense now as the cum began to rise and build up inside all three men. Everly's eyes were wide open now, feasting away at the sight of this man he had been lusting after, being completely objectified as he lay there on the bed getting himself fucked seven ways from Sunday.

Hadley once again shook him from his thoughts as he whispered his name just loud enough for him to remember where he was.

"Ev, get a condom from the bedside table."

Kyle released Everly's cock from his mouth and turned to see what was about to happen. Everly was quick to respond and within seconds was rolling a condom down over his own cock.

"I want you to have a go while I watch."

Hadley withdrew from Kyle completely and pulling the condom off, moved to the other side of the bed. He didn't want Kyle to suck him or even to kiss him. He just wanted to watch.

What he didn't know was that Everly had never topped a guy before and suddenly was filled with uncertainty and fear. Sensing his brother's hesitation, Hadley cooed from across the room.

"Don't worry, just put it in. He's ready for you."

Everly could do nothing but obey. He beemed down at the sight of Kyle, a look of complete surrender and sexual excitement furrowing his beautiful face. His body was covered with a thin, glistening layer of sweat; every muscle in his gorgeous chest seemed to be flexed with tension as he prepared himself to get fucked again.

"Do it, fuck me Everly," Kyle encouraged.

Everly took Kyle's thighs in his hands and spread them a little bit further and without any help, guided his cock into Kyle's asshole. He slid in perfectly and without any resistance.

The feeling was like nothing he had every felt before.

Kyle and Everly let out a moan, louder than before, a moan that was made of nothing but awe and amazement. Everly's mouth was open wide, his body trembling as waves of ecstasy shook him from head to toe. He was being led by his cock, a slave to the feeling of being completely inside another human being. It felt warm and wet as the muscles of Kyle's sphincter hugged his shaft, pulling the foreskin back and letting the nerve endings of his penis head sing and dance in reaction. He wasn't sure how long he stayed like that inside of him. Still and calm but his body electric and buzzing.

"Fuck him,Ev! Fuck him till you both cum."

To Everly it was like something out of a porn movie. Completely out of his comfort zone and words he had never had spoken to him before. But he wanted to oblige. More than anything in his entire life.

So he did.

Following his directive, Everly started fucking Kyle. Hard. Harder and harder. In and out he drew himself, shaking the bed and forcing Kyle to bite down on his bottom lip as Everly fucked him senseless. He and Hadley had their hands tightly wrapped around their own cocks, jerking themselves off furiously, their brows furrowed into expressions of utter pleasure and disbelief. Hadley watched as his brother transformed before his very eyes. He watched as he became a different man before him, fucking away at the guy Hadley was dating.

Again and again Everly thrusted his hips, burying himself deeper and deeper inside Kyle. Pulling out and then forcing himself back in again. Kyle's ass was tight and like a suction cup around his dick, pulling him in and holding him for dear life.

All three were close. Their yelps could be surely heard by the others in the house as the hosts were getting closer and closer to getting off. Second by second their screams of ecstasy got louder as Kyle and Hadley fisted their cocks and jerked themselves closer and closer to exploding. Beads of sweat had formed all over Everly as he worked himself in and out of Kyle. He bit down on his bottom lip, watching the sight of Kyle jerk himself off while he pumped away at him.

"I'm coming," Kyle breathed as his hand continued working away. "I'm fucking coming!"

Everly watched as Kyle exploded cum all over himself, like a fountain being turned on for the first time. Cloudy cum sprang from his head, more and more as his hand continued to pump his cock up and down. Drops sprayed all over his tight abs, wetting himself with his own sticky mess.

Hadley was next. His ejaculation was quieter but just as intense; spraying it over himself and the bed. Thrusting his hips as he came again and again, his body shaking beneath the sheer force of his orgasm. He moaned again and again as he came, not stopping until he had sprayed every last drop, squeezing the head of his cock as if wringing out a wet towel, desperate to get every bit out, the feeling of release rocking him back and forth.

Everly was last, the sight of his brother coming and the fact that he was still inside Kyle, was the last straw for him. He fucked himself over the edge, his body bucking as he came and came and came again. His hips fucked Kyle as he sprayed himself into the condom inside Kyle's ass. It seemed to go on forever, thrusting over and over as if his life depended on it, afraid he might disappear if he stopped and if the pleasure he was sensing dissipated. He shut his eyes to better experience his orgasm, his whole frame shaking with each ejaculation he made, the aftershock sending rippling waves of pleasure through his core.

After a few moments, he stilled. The three of them continued to shudder occasionally as their heaving breaths returned to normal. The air felt wet and heavy and the music had stopped. It seemed like the last few seconds of the credits at the end of a film. The words had been displayed and the screen was fading to black as silence filled the gaps around them.

And then it was over.

# Hadley

I never got to sleep afterwards. At least I don't remember falling asleep. Everytime I tried to close my eyes and shut off they seemed to spring open like a jack-in-the-box popping up. However at some point I must have drifted off because when I turned over, Kyle was gone.

After we all came, Everly got embarassed and left. We never saw him again for the rest of the night. Kyle was quite quiet too, choosing to pass out on the bed rather than join me back at the party.

*What a night.*

After the party broke up, I spent what felt like hours cleaning our place up. Top to bottom. I even got out the Mister Muscle spray and literally scrubbed this place spotless. It helped with my comedown to keep busy and try to exhaust myself, but even afterwards, when I poured myself into bed next to Kyle, something kept me up.

I couldn't get that look on Ev's face out of my head when he was fucking Kyle. He was so into it. How could he not have been? Kyle was hot. End of. Any red blooded gay guy would be on it in a second if given half a chance.

*What have I done?*

Laying there, the sun beginning to creep in through my blinds, I thought about what this all meant. I let my brother fuck the guy I was seeing.

Part of me couldn't help but think that I had created a monster.

# Everly

Hadley was right; I was embarassed. He shouted after me, as I quickly got dressed and ran out of his room, like I was a pussy or something. But I literally couldn't have gotten out of there any faster.

What was I becoming? What had I allowed myself to get into?

When I got back to my room, completely disregarding the rest of the party, I took a long, hard look in the mirror and almost didn't recognise myself. I looked bleary-eyed and drawn, like I hadn't slept in a week. My eyes were puffy and my hair was a mess. My skin felt sticky with sweat and God knows what else from my little romp in the other room.

*What had I done?*

I quickly turned away from the reflection in the mirror, unable to look at in any longer, ashamed at who was staring back at me.

My thoughts turned to Kyle.

*I can't believe I just had sex with Kyle in front of my brother.*

I immediately feared the worst, thinking of the next time I saw him and how I would react or what I would say.

Crippled with fear I tossed myself onto the bed and buried my head in the pillow, allowing exhaustion to take over.

# Hadley

Having had enough of staring at the four walls of my bedroom I went out into the lounge and waited for him to come out. It must have been gone midday and Ev had yet to resurface.

He was definitely avoiding me. I considered knocking on his door and confronting him in his room, but then we'd be on his territory. I wanted neutral ground for what I was going to say to him.

And so I waited.

I must have waited for over an hour, making as much noise in the kitchen as humanly possible in an effort to shake him out of his little hideaway. But nothing seemed to work. After a while I gave up and went for a walk to try and clear my head.

The fresh air served me well and gave me renewed vigor, filling my lungs with cool freshness and lighting me up from the inside out. I walked with no apparent destination in mind. Hands in pockets and head down with a pair or dark sunglasses to shield my eyes, despite the overcast day.

When I turned the key in our front door I could smell him even before I saw him. He was up.

As I came in and crossed the threshold of our flat I could smell something sweet coming from the oven and heard a light sound; something classical arising from the stereo.

*Classic Everly; while the rest of the world hides when hungover, he's up baking and listening to Beethoven.*

I let the door slam shut behind me for emphasis. What I was going to say was not probably going to go down well. He jumped at the sound of the door slamming and breaking him from the trance he was in as he wandered around the room, casually watering his plants. He wore gray jogging bottoms and a loose fitting plain blue t-shirt. He was barefoot and casual looking, his hair recently washed and combed back away from his face. As he crossed the room in front of me without saying anything or even acknowledging me, I got a waft of cinnamon body wash.

"Hi," I ventured, setting my keys down in the little basket on the kitchen counter.

He didn't say anything. He simply went about refilling the watering can in the kitchen sink and returned to his plants, softly humming to himself like he didn't have a care in the world. I couldn't have felt more like another species as I stood there in the room with him. I felt dirty and unclean, dark and filthy almost compared to his freshness. He seemed to glow almost as he flitted about the lounge, obviously not feeling as shitty as I was and apparently having forgotten what happened last night.

"Hey, I said." I tried again, louder and slightly more annoyed the second time around.

"Hi," he finally returned, still not making eye contact with me like I was the bloody plague or something.

"Listen," I started, "last night was a mistake."

He breathed out something that sounded more like a sarcastic laugh than anything else.

"I mean it, I shouldn't have…I mean, we shouldn't…"

I stopped and it struck me then that I wasn't exactly sure what I wanted to say, or let alone how to say it.

Everly stared at me for the first time since I walked through the door. He stopped what he was doing and stood incredibly still, his eyes suddenly burning into me, flooding me with an iciness that I had never felt from him before. His silence was an intent to urge me onwards, teasing me and taunting me to continue.

"I think…I mean I want you to back off."

He did it again. This time it was a laugh. Short and dripping with sarcastic intent as if he couldn't believe I actually just went there.

"Oh really?"

I swallowed, suddenly full of regret and anxiety.

"Everly, I mean-"

"*You* want *me* to back off?"

When he spoke it came off more as a statement than a question.

I nodded, slightly unsure as how to proceed. I wasn't prepared for his challenging tone. It was very unlike him. He took a step towards me, putting down the watering can and keeping his eyes focused on me as if trying to put me off with his stare.

"Why's that Hadley? Had a change of heart now did you?"

I swallowed hard, blinking as if to better focus myself on the situation. I could feel my hands start to shake as uncertainty began to cloud my judgement.

"Everly last night shouldn't have happened. I'm sorry if I gave you the wrong idea..."

"The wrong idea? I'd say you certainly did."

He took another few slow steps forward.

"I'd say you gave me the wrong idea when you told me to *fuck* your boyfriend."

I blinked again. I can't remember ever hearing Everly say the word 'fuck'. Usually Everly was less confrontational. Only it wasn't what he was saying that was confrontational necessarilly, rather the way he was carrying himself. So confident all of a sudden, so sure of himself. He took another few paces closer until we were literally nose to nose and I could smell his breath as he exhaled slowly into my face. It tasted sweet, like he had been chewing on a hard candy or something.

"Everly, listen," I straightened up trying to make myself seem taller so as to take better control of the situation, "Kyle's not into you. He's into me. You need to know that last night was a one-off. It's over. Okay?"

He was nodding now, a smug look across his face.

"Oh, I get it," he started still nodding, his eyes darting from my left to my right.

"Get what?"

"You're jealous."

"Jealous? Of what? *You?*" I laughed, accentuating the absurdness of what he was implying.

But he didn't respond right away. Instead he tried to call my bluff. His silence was making me more and more nervous. Normally I could see right through him and usually bend him to my will. But today he felt different and I started to feel like I might walk away from this one a loser.

"Yeah…I think you are jealous. I think you saw something last night that you didn't like."

"What are you talking about, listen-"

"I think you saw that I can be just like you."

"What?"

"I loved it last night. It felt so fucking good to be inside him, fucking him."

My mouth opened as if it wanted to speak but my head couldn't keep up. Instead I just stared at him, slack jawed and dumbed into silence.

"He loved it too. I could tell."

"Everly, Jesus-"

"Does that make you nervous? That he loved it?"

He took another impossible step closer, closing in the distance between us until our noses touched.

"Are you scared that he's gonna choose me over you, now that he's had the other Stone dick inside him?"

"Everly! What the fuck's gotten into you?"

"Did he tell you that last night wasn't the first time we'd kissed?"

*What?*

Then the slightest smile started to play with the corners of Everly's mouth as he read my dumb-founded expression. He was enjoying this.

"Ahhh, he never told you, did he?"

"You're full of shit."

"You'd like that, wouldn't you? You'd like to think I'm shitting you, but deep down you know I'm not…"

"You're fucked up, Ev, seriously. If you think I'm gonna believe…"

"On the beach. The day after your date."

*"Fuck you."*

"My day off. He ran into me and we made out on the beach…Isn't that where you guys fucked the first time?"

I spat in his face.

"That's enough, get out of my face."

He barely even reacted as my spit accosted his face, hitting him square in the mouth. I backed away from him, turning away and going for my bedroom door.

"He's such a good kisser, Had. I can see why you're so into him…"

That was the last thing I heard before I slammed my bedroom door behind me and collapsed on my bed.

\*\*\*

I stayed in bed for the next couple of hours. I could hear him banging around in the kitchen every now and then, the smell of biscuits wafting in through the gap at the bottom of my door.

His words repeated themselves over and over again in my head like a broken record, looping and replaying themselves until they almost didn't make sense anymore.

*Was he telling the truth? Would Kyle really do that behind my back? I know we had only officially been on one date and all that…But I thought he felt it too.*

I couldn't have felt more on the outside than I did at that moment. Pushed out of my own game by the person I held closest to my heart. The tables felt turned as I began to consider things from the other perspective. It was always me who called the shots in my life. Came naturally to me. Always had. I was in control of this family and Everly was always second fiddle. But today there was something different about him, like he woke up and decided to pull the stick out of his ass and actually get in the game.

I think I always knew he had it in him.

*The fire.*

That's what our mother called it. She always said we were like opposite elements just striving to coexist. I was the firery one and Everly was the ice; cool and calm and collected.

I never really knew what she meant until now...

When I looked him in the eye earlier on, it was as if there had been a power shift over night. Like he had stolen my dominance from me somehow, like a rug that had been pulled out from underneath me. I didn't like feeling this way. So helpless and unable to stir myself from this funk. I felt aggravated and helpless and as I lay there on my bed, staring blankly at the wall and listening for sounds of movement in the house, the feelings only got stronger.

Then I heard a door slam. The noise was so loud and sudden that it caused me to sit up on the bed. Straining my ears, from the direction of the noise in the flat I guessed it was his bedroom door. Then footsteps crossing the lounge, followed by the sound of keys jangling as they were picked up. I steeled myself in an effort to listen to what was happening. As soon as I heard the dead bolt in our front door being pulled back, I instantly sprang up from the bed and threw on my shoes.

*He's on the move.*

Something wasn't right. Wherever the hell he was going, I was gonna follow.

*\*\*\**

Pulling the dark cap down over my forehead to shield my eyes and hide as much as my face as I could, I made sure to keep Everly close in my peripheral view. He was moving quickly. Faster than I had ever seen him move. He was quite a pacey walker on normal days, but today as I sped to keep up he seemed to be moving like a bat out of hell.

*Where the fuck was he going in such a hurry?*

Something about this felt all wrong. He was even dressed differently than he normally was; darker almost. From what I could make out, he was wearing dark denim jeans tucked into boots that I didn't recognise and a black bomber jacket, cropped short at the waist. As he flew down the pavement, his hands remained firmly tucked into his jacket pockets making him seem even more lithe than normal.

My lungs were beginning to ache and I began to hate myself for getting so out of it last night as my hangover only seemed to deepen as I forced myself to move. In my defense, as I was getting fucked up I didn't imagine I would be chasing after my own brother, who didn't seem to be the least bit hanging I might add, in an effort to track him down and figure out what the hell had gotten into him. I couldn't shake the feeling as I struggled to run after him, that the tables had suddenly turned and the hunted was becoming the hunter.

When he was about fifty or so feet ahead of me I pulled my mobile out of my back pocket and picked his number from my contact list. Pressing the phone tightly to my ear, I waited for it to start ringing. A moment or two later, I watched him pick his own mobile out of his pocket, glance at the name on the screen, then replace it in his back pocket.

*Cheeky shit.*

I knew he wouldn't answer, but I just had to try to see. He was heading West, away from the seafront into what seemed to be a quiet residential area. As we turned a corner, me still trailing behind him, the road suddenly opened up into a grassy square. I pulled myself back and stood with my back firmly against the brick wall of the building we had just cleared, praying that he didn't catch me as I almost strode out into the open.

Peering around the corner with one eye I watched as he pulled something small out of his jeans pocket. From where I stood it looked like a small square of paper. He only glanced at it before proceeding in the direction he was originally headed. The square was surrounded on all three sides by tall blocks of flats; Victorian style houses that had obviously been converted into separate apartments, each with beautiful columned entrances and wrought iron balconies overlooking the enormous greenery space below. The green space was well groomed and taken care of which led me to believe that the residents of the square were quite well off. Benches were scattered around the open plan field and a mother and her two children were seated on a blanket having a late-afternoon picnic of some kind.

I steered my gaze towards Everly who had climbed a set of stairs and was waiting at a doorway, his back still to the road.

This was my only chance. Tip-toeing, as if he would be able to hear me approaching, I carefully skirted the greenery and made my way up as close as I could get behind him without alerting to him that I was there. The closer I got the more my adrenaline started to pump. Slowly, with each step I took his slight figure became clearer until I caught a glimpse of something that made me stop for a second. I squinted to get a better look and confirm that I was actually seeing what I thought I was seeing. The emblem on the back of the coat he was wearing...

*He's wearing my coat. Why the fuck would he be wearing my coat?*

The sound of the door being released spurred me back into action and as he reached and pulled the door open, I sped forward, desperate to get in before it closed and locked me out. Within seconds he had disappeared inside the building. I sprinted now, not caring who was watching at this point, my arm outstretched to clutch at the handle and watching as it shut slowly, taking along with it my chances of finding out where the hell he was going and what he was up to.

I grasped at the handle a split-second too late, banging into it with such force that I was surprised it didn't collapse beneath my heaving weight.

"Fuck!" I yelled a little too loudly. My eyes scanned the doorway as if they expected to find another way in.

*Shit.*

I shielded my face and put it up to the glass of the doorway to get a better look at what was beyond. They were definitely flats. Behind the door was a long stretch of hallway leading to a lift at the far end of the corridor. To the sides were two tables, both piled high with various different coloured leaflets and other notices for tenants to read. Place looked nice. Expensive. But there didn't appear to be anyone coming in or going out in the near future by the sounds of things.

Turning around with my hands on my hips, contemplating my next move, it dawned on me to check the buzzers on the side of the building. Sure enough to my left was a panel with fifteen or so buttons, all with first initials and surnames next to each. I scanned the names quickly, hoping something would jump out at me.

Then I saw it.

*K. Bennett.* ***Kyle*** *Bennett. Fucking shit.*

My feet were recoiling from the entrance way like it was a snake about to bite. Everly was here to see Kyle. And judging by the way he was let in so quickly, it was not a surprise visit.

My skin started to crawl and the worst feeling of nausea mixed with rage surged up my spine. Looking back to the buzzer, Kyle's name was next to flat two, which meant it was hopefully on the ground floor. I was moving before I knew what I was doing, my body shutting down and my brain leading the way. Before I knew it I was walking around the side of the building, my head shifting all around, searching for anyone who might have spotted me. I couldn't have looked more like a freaking cat burglar as I traced the building, bending low as I ducked under windows and peeking over the tops of my eyes at each one I thought might be an apartment.

Shutters were closed on the first I came to. The second, which was just next to it was made of clouded glass which kept even the slightest outline of a person impossible to make out. Further around the back I crept, cursing under my breath and feeling more and more like a desperate stalker. But who was I kidding? I didn't care who saw me or how I might look. I needed to see what was going on inside that flat. At the very least to use it against Everly as ammunition if I needed it. Something happened last night with that boy and although I was probably responsible, I was not going to lose Kyle without a fight.

When I reached the next set of windows, to my surprise the drapes were open. It took only a second for me to make out the unmistakable shape of my brother, standing in the center of the room, his back to me. I saw the bomber jacket first. *My* bomber jacket, then the blonde hair, messy and pushed back off his face. It was him alright. But where was Kyle? I could hear the faint sound of voices from somewhere in another room as Everly looked around, his eyes scanning up and down the walls, obviously his first time in the flat. It occurred to me that I had never been inside the flat either.

*Cheeky git. He's gonna regret sneaking around like this behind my back.*

Then the second voice came into view. Kyle. From what I could tell he was wearing a light coloured button down shirt that was completely open over his typical faded denim jeans. Even though slightly blurred from the other side of the window, I could still make out the buff definition of his chest and abs. I could feel the muscles in my stomach tighten as he moved across the room closer to Everly.

Then I was sure my heart stopped.

He lifted his hand to cup Everly's cheek. The same way he had done to me the first time we kissed that night on the beach. He paused a moment, his eyes probably studying Everly's expression before gently leaning in and placing his mouth on my brother's. It was all I could do not to look away. But it didn't end there. The kiss continued, getting more and more intense. Everly was putting his hands inside Kyle's open shirt, running them up his torso and pushing it off his shoulders until it fell to the ground behind him. Everly ran his hands over Kyle's arms, pausing at the biceps before moving around to his back, pulling him into him to deepen their kiss.

I ducked down and away from the window. I couldn't bare it. The feeling of nausea had intensified and I was sure I could feel the bile begin to rise in my throat. Looking around at the side of the building, everything looked like it was bathed in a dark shade of red. Fury shook my hands, making them vibrate and my knees started to buckle. If it weren't for the wall that I was now leaning against, I was sure I would have passed out.

*How could he? How could Kyle? That fucking bastard thinks he can do this to me?*

For the first time in a long time I could feel my eyes start to well up, blurring my vision. Wiping at them quickly I straightened myself up and quickly darted back around the building to the front. I pulled the hat down further on my face, sniffing back my emotions and not even looking as I stepped out into the road. My ears were then assaulted by the sound of a car horn, blaring its deafening warning as I stepped right in front of it, causing it to swerve violently to avoid clipping me. I jumped back, practically coming out of my skin, my heart drumming away so hard inside my chest cavity I was sure I was having a heart attack.

I fell backwards onto the curb of the pavement and literally went ass over tit, landing hard on my ass and scraping my hands along the ground. I wasn't sure if I yelled out or not; between the sound of the car horn and the driver's shouts, everything melted into one.

Sitting on the curb in complete shock, I inspected my hands for a moment. The left was scraped and bleeding a little, but not enough to worry about. I picked myself up and this time checked the road before entering into it, then sprinted back the way I came.

I needed to get home, was all I could think as tears blinded me once more, running down my face and burning the skin beneath...

\*\*\*

The run home was one of those times where your body just goes into auto-pilot. I didn't actually remember the journey or even what roads I took, the next thing I remember after seeing Everly and Kyle together, was leaning up against the inside door of our flat.

Inside smelled like a mixture of stale cigarette smoke and booze from last night with an overlayer of cookies; thanks to Everly's afternoonbaking session. I scrunched my nose at the blending of the different aromas and quickly opened up most of the windows in the flat. Everything was making me feel sick. The smells of the house, even the sight of the pictures hanging from the walls around me. Everywhere I looked were pictures of Everly and I; looking happy; on holiday in Ibiza; with Mum at her place. My eyes fell upon one that I couldn't remember ever being taken. It was a close-up of our faces, a selfie from a couple years back when Everly and I looked more alike than ever. We were both blonde and quite tanned, indicating it was Summer time and obviously before I started dying my hair black. Everything about us was alike; the slant of our eyes, the colour around the irises, the curve of our nose and the fullness of our lips. It was a time when we both looked so innocent, before all the shit started happening in our lives and things took a turn for the worst. But now things were so different. After all the shit with our father leaving, and all the times we had to move because of all the strange stuff that kept happening and following us wherever we seemed to go.

A tear that had run down my cheek landed square on the part of the picture where both our faces met, blurring the lines that separated us and distorting the two boys staring back at me. From out of nowhere it suddenly felt like the picture was on fire. Instinct kicked in and I furiously threw the picture across the room as a surge of anger went off inside me. The picture sailed through the air before hitting the wall opposite me and shattering into a hundred tiny pieces on the floor. The noise was so loud I wasn't sure it was actually me who had caused it. I slowly walked over to the pile of broken glass at my feet and bent down to pick a piece up. My hand wiped at more tears that were flowing much freer now and my shoulders hunched as I started to cry, sniffing and whining at what was happening.

I was hurt, and angry, and furious, and aching. The feeling in the pit of my stomach, that I took to be heart ache, was so unfamiliar to me I felt it might tear me in two.

*This must be how Everly feels so often.*

There I was; a wet and snivelling heap on the floor of our apartment; hung over, coming down from a drug-induced high and utterly destroyed by what was happening. My brother had betrayed me. My flesh and blood. My twin.

I looked down at the jagged piece of glass that I was holding, then down at the picture that was buried in the rubble. The sight of our innocent and happy faces only made the hurt I was feeling deepen until it began to feel like a hollow opening that was yelling out to me, begging me to end it and make it all better.

My eyes fell on the piece of glass once more as my heart figured out what my head was thinking about. I hadn't done this in ages. Not since after Charlie disappeared. I felt like I was recoiling back into the past, back to a time when I didn't know any better and when I thought this was the only way to make the pain go away. I had come so far since those days, and yet seeing Everly…My own brother with the guy I was falling for…The only guy I had felt *anything* for in years…Was a little too much.

Then I did it. Without even thinking I brought the sharp piece of glass down against the skin on the inside of my forearm, high enough away from my wrist so as not be too noticeable, and I allowed it to pierce through. Not too deep, but enough to make it bleed. I bit my tongue to help ease the pain as the blade sliced slowly across the soft skin. As it moved across I imagined all the pain I was feeling, seeping away with the blood as it hit the air, escaping and running down my arm.

# Everly

I'm sure I must have been dreaming. I was at Mum's house and I was with Hadley. But something felt different even though I couldn't quite put my finger on it, and then I realised that I had dark hair. Not just dark, but as dark as Hadley's. I remember catching a glimpse of our reflections in the mirror on the wall in Mum's dining room. We looked exactly alike. Even more so than normal. In fact I couldn't tell us apart, that was until I got closer to Hadley and saw that his eyes had changed colour. They weren't blue anymore, instead they seemed to be darker, actually completely dark, almost black like the colour had run away and been replaced by the darkness of the iris. Then for no reason he spat on me. He turned to face me with a smile on his face, and then he spat as hard as he could directly at me. I could feel his spit as it ran down my chin and landed on my arm. Only it didn't feel like spit, instead it was hot and too runny.

That's when I woke up.

I looked around the room, expecting to see my desk and wardrobe and pictures on my desktop. Only they weren't there. Confusion seeped in and for a moment I thought I was still asleep. I wiped at my eyes with both hands and looked around again, expecting things to have changed.

Then I realised I wasn't in my room. I was at Kyle's. Outside the window the sky looked dark and the curtains billowed softly as wind through the open window fluttered them. It was then that I felt something wet on my arm. In the darkness of the room it looked like something inky was covering my forearm, like I had broken a pen and spilled the ink all over me. Standing I went over to the open window and almost screamed at what I saw.

It wasn't ink at all. It was blood. Frantically, I swung my head around and threw back the bedsheets to inspect for more. But they were clean. Kyle lay there next to the imprint I had left on the mattress, snuffling softly, an arm draped across his eyes. Sensing the shift in the blankets he rolled over onto his other side, dragging the sheet with him and covering himself like a child would when cold.

I looked down to my arm again and felt around with my other hand.

"*Fuck,*" I whispered a little too loudly. I was bleeding. Quite badly and apparently only recently. I cupped my arm and ran out of the room, flicking the bathroom light switch with my shoulder. The fluorescent light filtered quickly through the room helping me to see. I stuck my arm under the tap and ran cold water over where the blood was coming from, desperate to find the source. The cold water was like a bullet to my system, making me yank my arm back in pain. It was enough to wash away the excess and allow me to see the cut.

It was about four centimetres in length, not too deep to need stitches I didn't imagine, but deep enough to sting like a bitch. It was clean and straight, like it had been done carefully and slowly instead of accidentally.

*How the hell...*

Then I immediately thought to Hadley. The swing set. The broken arms, all those years ago. The story our mother told the neighbours and the police. The story that no one believed and that forced us out of the house we were born in. Twinship. His pain is my pain.

*What the hell did you do, dear brother?*

# Hadley

I must have fallen asleep at some point. The last thing I remember before passing out was laying down in bed, clutching a tea towel to my arm where I had cut it, regret sweeping through me the second I had seen blood. I had come so far since the last time I did that. So much therapy and money spent by our mother to get to the root of it all. And here I went, starting over and setting myself back so far with just one little relapse of bad judgement.

My pillow was wet with tears and blood had seeped through the towel just slightly; enough to make a small round stain on my beige sheets.

I had dreamt some pretty fucked up dreams. Although now they were just swimming pictures in my head, I remembered dreaming about Everly. Although he didn't look like Everly. He looked...like me. I mean, even moreso. His hair was dark, like he had dyed it black or something. So strange. I shuddered at the thought of it. It was as if he was trying to look more like me, he was even acting kind of like me. But I couldn't remember anything else.

As I sat up in bed, I thought back to yesterday and what I had seen. I was desperate to forget already, like it was all part of my bad dream. If I looked in his room, Everly would be still asleep, alone, snoring peacefully like nothing had ever happened.

But as I moved out into the hallway, I realised he wasn't snoring peacefully in his room, and what I remember seeing wasn't all a bad dream. In fact, as I stilled myself in the hall; ears straining to make out movement of any kind, I realised that Everly wasn't here at all. I was alone. Completely alone. Again.

*Had he stayed at Kyle's place? No, he couldn't have. Everly hadn't stayed over at a boy's house in his entire life.*

But the Everly I saw yesterday wasn't the Everly I remember. This Everly was different somehow. The Everly I knew would never sneak around behind his brother's back, sleeping with his boyfriend and all that shit. Something's changed. If I shut my eyes all I could see were images of him and Kyle in Kyle's apartment.

*Him and Kyle fucking the night of the party.*

What was that he had said about them being together before? Had Kyle really gone and tried something with Everly right from the beginning?

My head was swimming with possibilities and the more I let them in, the more lightheaded and dizzy I felt. Looking around the room I started to feel as if the walls had begun to tilt and spin all around me. I saw the broken glass in a pile against the wall from the picture I had broken; then the pain in my arm reminded me of what I had done to myself.

Then all at once it felt like the air had been sucked out of the room and I found myself gasping to catch my breath. I reached for the kitchen counter to steady myself and was straight away filled with the need to get out of here; out in the fresh air and away from all this.

So I grabbed my keys and was out the door before I could think again.

\*\*\*

When I left the house I didn't know where I was going. Honest. I just wanted to clear my head and get some air. But after a few blocks in a certain direction, I had a pretty good idea where my subconscious was taking me.

My feet moved of their own accord and I felt dazed and almost powerless to try and convince them differently. Although I couldn't tell you why, I knew I was headed towards Kyle's place. Something inside me, and it was killing me to admit it, wanted to see him. Maybe I was hoping that seeing him and having him see me would convince him that it was *me* he wanted, not Everly. There were a thousand reasons why I knew I shouldn't be going there, but this must be what people always describe as 'following your heart'.

*Bullshit, if you ask me.*

If this was what 'love' was, then I was already through with it. It was clouding my judgement, fucking with my head and making me act like a lunatic. I couldn't get him out of my head.

*Kyle.*

Every face I saw reminded me of him. Every smell I got wind of on the street made me think of him. If I let myself close my eyes for long enough I found myself thinking of his touch and what it was like to kiss his lips. The thought that this could all be over now was just too much to handle. I had to hear it from him.

It took about fifteen minutes to find my way back to Kyle's building. I rounded the corner that opened up onto the huge patch of greenery and immediately spotted his building. It felt like I was flying as my feet whisked me over to the front door and I willed myself to buzz his number.

*Number two. K. Bennett.*

My mouth was dry and I could hear my stomach grumbling.

*Had I even eaten today?*

There was a long pause as I waited impatiently for him to answer. It then dawned on me that Everly might still be there too…

That thought died a quick death as the door was buzzed open without him checking who it was. Maybe he could see me from his flat window, or maybe he was expecting someone else. Truth was, I didn't care. I was in and I was going to have my moment with him. By the time I was done he'd be mine and that little piss ant Everly would be yesterday's news.

Inside, the building smelled fresh, like a new car. The walls were covered with embossed ivory coloured wallpaper and there were a bunch of different types of plants scattered around the main lobby. A pretty lady in her fourties passed me as I walked down the hall, smiling and politely wishing me a good morning. I wasn't sure if I smiled back, I was too focused on reading the signs that would lead me to Kyle's place. I felt like a thing possessed as I strode down the hall quickly yet with light steps, hands balled into fists at my sides and features set in a hard line. I wasn't sure what I was going to say. Hell, I hadn't even given this whole thing much thought. Only thing I knew was that I had to see him.

*Jesus, he'd better be alone.*

There it was. Number two. My feet stopped moving and my arms suddenly felt like dead weight hanging limply from my torso.

*Should I knock? He's obviously expecting 'someone'. Maybe he'll just answer.*

Sure enough, a second or two later the heavy door squeaked open and there stood Kyle with a huge smile on his face. For a second I felt relief wash over me as I laid eyes on his smile, but as quickly as it had arrived his expression changed and the grin quickly faded. I couldn't quite put my finger on it, but he looked a mixture of surprised, angry and almost…scared.

He abruptly stopped opening the door by blocking it with his foot from the inside and put a hand up to the door frame, creating a barrier between himself and I.

"What are you doing here?"

His words hit me like a bee sting.

"Hi," I managed in a trembling, whimpy whisper.

"Hadley…What are you doing here?" he repeated, his brow setting itself into a hard line.

"I needed to see you."

"This isn't a good time."

"Is *he* here?"

"Is *who* here?"

"Don't play fucking dumb with me, Kyle."

He looked shocked as my tone suddenly shifted from innocent to angry.

"What are you talking about?"

"I know."

"You know *what?* Jesus Hadley, I don't-"

"About you and Everly."

He just stared at me, apparently not going to give anything away that he didn't have to.

"I know you two slept together."

"Yes, Hadley," he started with an eye roll, "you were there, remember?"

"Don't be so stupid," I spat, "not that time…"

"What's this all about Hadley? I don't have time for this."

He went to shut the door but I wedged my foot inside in a desperate attempt for leverage.

"I saw him come here."

Kyle was silent again, his arm still firmly holding the door closed but easing up slightly to get a better look at me. My hands were still fisted at my sides and I could feel my bottom lip begin to quiver, but I persevered.

"I saw you two together…"

"Jesus, Hadley, you followed him? What are you, *stalking* me?" He accused, trying to turn the tables to his advantage.

"I needed…I mean, I thought…"

"You thought, what?" he looked to me expectantly. "What, Hadley?"

"I thought we…I thought we had…*something.*"

Now I felt pathetic. My gaze shifted to the floor at my feet, the first time I had ever felt myself backing down from a guy in my entire life. I hated this feeling. This feeling of almost begging someone to love me. I felt like shit, absolute shit; standing there so pathetic and needy. I barely recognised myself anymore. I could feel the hot sting of tears begin to prick behind my eyes and I bit my tongue hard to stop them from coming.

Kyle sighed, seeing my state of mind and I could feel his body loosen a bit, his stance letting up a bit as he realised thatmaybe I wasn't a threat.

"Hadley…"

I looked up at him and he too was now looking at his feet.

"I thought we had something, Kyle…"

"Hadley, I don't think we should see each other anymore."

It was like a slap to my face and I was sure I reacted as though it literally were. My head snapped back as his words hit me again and again. Inside my organs seemed to liquify, and I could feel my knees start to buckle.

"I'm sorry…"

He spoke like that was an explanation or like that should make me feel even the least bit better. The silence between us was almost the worst of it all. It forced me to look away, behind me at the hallway I had just travelled up. I quickly wiped a tear away from my eye before it travelled down my cheek, suddenly desperate to get away from here before he saw me crumble.

"I didn't mean for this to happen. Everly and I…"

"Bullshit," I mumbled half under my breath.

"What's that?"

"I said, *bullshit.*"

Kyle straightened up again, his brow furrowing once more and the pathetic pity look he wore changed into something angrier.

"Hadley, I've got to go."

"How could you do this to me?" I accused, shoving a finger at him.

"To *you?*"

"How could you do this with…With my own *brother?*" I could feel myself begin to choke up again.

"Oh spare me the innocent act, Hadley. From what I hear you've been doing this kinda shit to guys all your life."

"Excuse me?" I demanded abruptly.

Kyle stood his ground, aware that he had perhaps said too much.

"What the fuck are you talking about?"

"Everly told me about all the others."

"The others. Right, that's fucking ripe," I shouted sarcastically.

"Look, I gotta go Hadley."

"Don't do this Kyle."

"Hadley, seriously…" He looked nervous, my tone obviously hitting a little too close to home.

"I wouldn't."

"Hadley, what are you…You're fucked up, you know that?"

He went to shut the door on me, like I was some door-to-door salesman when I reached out quickly with a strong arm to stop him. As my arm slammed into the door, he jumped back, surprised at my strength and his eyes going wide.

"You're going to regret this," I whispered through clenched teeth, my eyes holding his stare threateningly.

He looked frightened and he swallowed a lump in his throat.

And with that, I turned on my heel and left.

# Everly

I had to work that day when I woke up at Kyle's with the cut on my arm. I went straight to the bakery from his, doing the walk of shame and wearing yesterday's clothes and hairdo. When I left he was still asleep. I couldn't risk him seeing the gash in my arm and having him question where it came from.

*What the hell would I have told him?*

No matter what I said there was no way he would have believed me. I would have looked like the crazy one and he would have assumed I did it to myself. I scoured his bathroom and found an old First Aid kit underneath his sink. Luckily it had some gauze in it that I used to wrap around the cut, desperately trying not to get blood anywhere or wake him in the process. It hurt so badly I actually had to bite down on a t-shirt to stop from screaming out. After about an hour of sitting on the bathtub edge with my arm elevated above my heart, the bleeding finally stopped.

*Fucking basketcase Hadley. I thought you were through with all that cutting crap. Wait till I get ahold of you.*

\*\*\*

After work I checked my phone. Thirteen missed calls. All from *guess who?* Katie wouldn't stop asking me what was wrong the whole shift. Kept saying that I was unusually quiet. Thank Christ I had a long-sleeve jumper on so as to hide my bandaged arm.

Katie was plugging me for information about Kyle, but I didn't feel like chatting. I just wanted to get my shift over with so I could get the hell home. I assumed he'd be there. Waiting for me. In fact I knew he'd be. I could feel it.

As I neared the flat I stopped across the street and looked up, counting the windows from the far left of the building until I found our flat. Sure enough, it seemed from the street that every light in the flat was on. And then *he* appeared in the window as if he could sense I was there watching him. From where I stood he was just a shadow, but I would recognise that outline anywhere. After all, it was the same exact shadow I cast.

I climbed the stairs and as soon as I was about to put my key in the lock, I realised the door was open. I pushed it wide and then slammed it shut behind me, accentuating the noise as much as possible in an attempt to put Hadley off.

He was standing at the window, his back to me and his hands in his trouser pockets. I watched his frame shudder at the sudden slamming of the door before he slowly turned around to face me, his features twisted into an angry mask...

# Hadley

He came in with a smug look on his face, as if bragging like he had already won before even uttering a word. He dropped his keys in the little dish on the counter and held his hands palm up towards the ceiling before letting them drop tiredly to his sides.

"What?" he asked, his voice dripping with sarcasm and fake annoyance.

I stood my ground, my hands firmly tucked in my trouser pockets. I wanted to see how far I could push him. I wanted to see how far he'd go before he admitted to what he'd done.

But unfortunately he was having none of it.

He shucked his coat off and draped it across a dining room chair and marched over towards me, his lips set in a hard line and his eyes narrowed.

"I see you've gotten back into some old habits," he mocked accusingly as if he knew something I didn't. When he was close enough, he grabbed my arm that was cut and yanked it hard up in front of his face. He pulled my long sleeve back up to my elbow until the bandage that I had wrapped it in was exposed.

"*What the fuck?*" I shouted, trying to pull my arm away from him, but he held me tight. I was surprised by his brute strength all of a sudden as his fingers dug into my right wrist and twisted it around, yanking it up.

"I fucking knew it," he growled.

"Knew what?"

"*You're such a fucking coward.*"

He held the bandaged cut up to his eyes as if he knew all along it had been there. Then in a swift move he raised his own right arm up to mine as if for comparaison and yanked his sleeve up.

I had to do a double-take to understand what he was showing me, but truth was I knew what it was before I even looked. I tried to look away but my body seemed to have gone stiff in contrast to what my head was screaming for it to do.

There it was.

His arm was bandaged in almost the exact same spot that mine was, and when I looked up at him he was returning my stare as if daring me to deny it.

"Come on, Had. Tell us what happened?"

There was a sudden lump in my throat that was stopping me from calling out and defending myself. Something about the look in his eyes; so strange and unfamiliar. Normally when he was angry at me there was always at least a glimmer of the real Everly behind the hostility. But as I looked into his blue eyes, there was nothing there but darkness. He was waiting for me to deny it; I could feel it coming off him like a bad odour.

"I broke a glass and-" I started before being interrupted.

"*Bullshit!*" he shouted in my face, spitting on me in the mean time. "*You* did this to yourself...To us...To me..."

My head was shaking now of its own accord. "No...I didn't..."

"Don't you lie to me, Hadley. You did this to yourself. Don't you see what's happening?"

Everly's eyes were as wide as saucers and they stared into me with such force I could feel tears begin to well up in my own.

"It's just like before!"

He was grinding his teeth together so hard I could hear it, and his finger nails were still digging into my skin like razor blades.

"Stop it, Everly! I didn't...*Get off of me!*" I struggled, writhing and twisting my own arm to try and get free from his grip. But the more I tried to pull away the more he seemed to tighten his hands. "Fuck off, you're hurting me!"

"You're so pathetic, Hadley. Always playing the victim when things don't go your way, you're such an idiot why don't you bloody grow a pair and man up for a change."

I struggled further, his grip becoming hotter against my skin. But it was a battle of the wills now; who would back down first.

"Why you struggling, Had? This *hurt?*" His eyes were wild now. Possessed as if by something almost otherworldy. For whatever reason, I couldn't seem to look away. I was doomed to remember the look in his eye forever as I stood there, struggling against him. He was backing into me now, pushing me with all his might, the grip of his arm on me making me feel weak and filling me with the urge to simply give up and let go.

Suddenly I felt the wall against my back as I realised his weight had pushed me back on myself. I could feel Everly trying to crush me with all his weight, his fingers gripping the place where I had cut myself and pushing down on the wound beneath the bandage. The skin on my arm was burning now and started to feel wet. I took a quick glance down at the bandage and saw red before finally realising that he was doing this on purpose.

My body began to churn into overdrive, survival instincts kicking in and coursing adrenaline through my veins. My expression hardened, looking him in the eye I began to fight back. My free hand connected hard with his chest and pushed him off me. Everly let out a puff of air as my hand pummeled his body, causing him to fall back on himself now, releasing my arm; his own flailing for a moment as he regained his balance.

There we were. Face to face, staring each other down and adopting a warrior stance as if preparing for battle. Everly's lips twitched upwards into a patronising smile.

"Ah, ah, ah, here you go again, always thinking you can solve a problem with violence," he teased far too calmly for the situation that was at hand.

He was laughing at me; taunting me; seeing how far he could push me until I cracked. Everly had watched me get hot under the collar enough to realise how to push my buttons. He was cornering me, like you would a wild animal that you were trying to catch.

"You'll never change, Hadley. You're just like our father."

"Don't you dare say that," I warned through clenched teeth.

"Say what? That you're like Dad?"

"We barely knew our father."

"We knew he was a drunk and a user, which let's face it Had, describes you perfectly."

"Shut up Everly."

"It's no wonder you are the way you are."

"I'm warning you…"

"You know I don't think you're inherantly slutty actually, I think you just pretend to be…"

"Everly, I'm serious."

"That way you can pretend you don't actually want a relationship, when really you're only constantly single 'cause you can't keep a guy interested in you for longer than five minutes."

I could feel my hands begin to ball themselves into fists at my sides, and my breathing become increasingly more erratic as I tried desperately to remain calm.

"You've always been the black sheep of the family Hadley; fucking up every chance you got."

Listening to him talk to me like that, so inhumanly and so unlike him was almost too much to take.

"Whenever your back was turned Mum would always say 'why can't he be more like Everly'…She never loved you like she loves me."

"Shut up…"

"How could she Hadley?"

"Fuck you."

"How could she love you like she loves me? Especially when you remind her so much of her deadbeat ex husband."

"I'm warning you Everly, stop it…"

"How could I stop now, I'm having way too much fun playing you like a fuckin' fiddle."

That was enough.

He knew that if he caged me in tight enough that he could trip a switch and I'd lash out. He was right.

Without warning I swung my fist squarely towards Everly's jaw. It cut swiftly through the air and connected with his chin with the most sickening crack that I could feel the sound in my toes. Everly's head snapped back sharply, my fist hitting him so hard his feet were practically lifted off the ground causing his whole body to collapse in shock and crumble to a pile of bones on the floor. He landed hard on his back, his head impacting full on with the linoleum below and the rest of his limbs falling in succession like a sack of potatoes.

And then he was still.

# Everly

It was the pain that woke me. A seering hot feeling in my mouth that seemed to travel throughout my whole body the more I tried to open my eyes. When my head became aware of the rest of my body, it began to realise just how badly everything hurt. I felt heavy, tired and listless like I weighed a tonne and to even think about moving would be too much effort.

My eyes tried to open themselves and managed to crack everso slightly, letting in a sliver of light that made me wince all over, but it was then that the real pain showed its ugly face.

My hands felt constricted, like someone was holding them behind my back. Something was digging into them too, thin and sharp like binding of some kind. I was sitting down. On a hard wooden chair. When my eyes finally opened all the way, everything was blurred.

*Focus Everly, focus.*

My brain tried to make sense of all the feelings my nerves were sending it, but it was like nothing seemed to add up.

*What happened? Last thing I remember was…*

Hadley hitting me. We were arguing. I confronted him about the cut, and he just flipped. I was pushing him, I remembered. I was so angry at him and confused by what was happening that I let it get the better of me…

*Like I used to.*

My head rolled from side to side and I moaned at the feeling. My chin felt prickly, like I had been stung by a hundred bees. It throbbed immensely, sending little waves of white pain passing through my whole head every couple of seconds. I wanted to cry out from the pain, but it was then that I realised that something was stopping me.

*I've been gagged.*

Things were starting to focus now; objects starting to take shape as my eyes focused on the room I was in. The colours were all off, dulled somehow probably by the pain I was feeling. I was still in the flat. Sitting on a chair with my hands being held behind my back and with a gag in my mouth. I closed my eyes once more as pain laced with the reality of the situation hit me like a tonne of bricks. When I reopened them they caught sight of something they hadn't been able to see before.

There, on a chair in front of me on the other side of the room, sat Hadley.

And he didn't look happy.

\*\*\*

Something hit me again. Something hard and warm, like a slap across my face, stinging my cheek and forcing me out of the dream I was just having. I was dreaming of Kyle; we were alone in his flat, lying together naked in his bed. His fingers were running themselves gently over my skin, caressing me lovingly and softly. I felt warm and safe, happy and calm knowing he was near like nothing in the world could ever harm me or take away the feeling I was feeling at that very moment.

My eyes snapped themselves open and were instantly accosted by a bright, blinding light. I squinted beneath the harshness of it and instantly felt the same pain coursing through my face and head as before.

"Wakey-wakey," came a voice I almost didn't recognise from directly in front of me. When my eyes decided to focus themselves again they fell upon the dark shadowy-figure who stood in front of me. Their face was hidden behind the light from overhead as they loomed in front of me, studying me and my reaction as reality crept in.

*I must have passed out.*

I turned my head in the opposite direction of the blinding light above me, letting my blurred gaze fall to the floor at my side. I didn't have to see their face to know who it was who stood before me. It was the same person who attacked me in the first place and who had tied me to the chair and put a gag in my mouth.

*My twin brother.*

"I didn't think you'd ever wake up. Didn't think I hit you that hard…" His voice was deep and raspy and his breath reeked of liquor. It was Hadley alright and from the smell emanating off of him, he'd been hitting the booze since I passed out.

"But then I remembered how you bruise like a peach and got worried that maybe I had knocked your nose into your brain or some shit."

He let out a deep laugh from somewhere dark inside him, obviously amused by his own little joke. The sound made me wince as the volume of his voice hit my head like an anvil. His hand was on my chin, pulling my face to look into his. White pain shot up from my chin as he gripped me hard before yanking down the gag so I could speak. I yelped at the feeling and spat what must have been blood onto the floor around me.

I felt out of breath, sucking in as much air as I could now that my mouth was free. As freshness filtered though my open lips, the cool air burned as it travelled deep down into my lungs.

"Hadley…" I breathed, my voice dripping with fear even though I tried to conceal it.

"Oh dear brother, you knew this was going to happen."

"Hadley, what the hell are you doing? Untie me, this is ridiculous."

I could feel the panic starting to rise in my voice. A thousand thoughts were racing through my head.

*What was he going to do? Hadley has a dark streak, always has. This is all my fault.*

"Isn't this what you wanted? You wanted to push me to see how far I'd unravel, just like you always do."

"What are you talking about?"

"You're always playing the 'high and mighty' card with me, flaunting how much better you think you are than me."

"Hadley, stop this. Now. Untie me, please," I pleaded, my voice cracking slightly.

"Ever since we were younger, you always thought you were better than me; smarter, better at school...You even said it yourself, you were always everyone's favourite." He was pacing now, his body trembling and quivering with anger. I could feel the heat radiating off of him; blind, white fury. I hadn't seen him like this since...

"But I was always better with guys."

"Hadley, please..."

"You may have been smarter but I was always more confident and got all the blokes. You hated that, didn't you..."

"I never hated you, and I never thought I was better than you."

"*Liar*," he spat.

"It's true. Hadley you may think that, but-"

"You always hated that I got all the attention from guys. Even though we look identical, they always chose me over you."

I swallowed hard, staring him in the eye.

"You just needed to take that away from me, didn't you? You needed to have it all."

"Hadley, this is insane. I never wanted to take anything from you. Seriously."

"What about with Charlie?"

"Charlie?"

"Don't pretend you don't know what I mean."

"Hadley, Charlie...I had nothing to do-"

"It was you who told me he was cheating."

I opened my mouth to speak, then reconsidered.

"But, I...Well yes, but-"

"I bet you just *loved* finding that out. I bet you couldn't wait to spill that news to me."

"Hadley, I had to tell you, you needed to know."

"I remember when you showed me that picture of him and that other guy, you were so smug about it, like you were throwing it in my face. Don't think I didn't know."

"Know what?"

"That you were in love with him."

"In love with who?"

"*Charlie.*"

"Don't be ridiculous."

As we were talking back and forth I was desperately trying to wriggle free of the restraints, the sharp plastic digging into the soft skin of my wrists.

"You were always jealous of him and me, always staring at us when you thought I wasn't looking…And then you took him away from me…"

"How can you say that?"

"If it wasn't for *you*, we would have been happy…I loved him so much."

"Hadley, he was *cheating* on you."

"And then you did it again with Kyle."

"But-"

And then I stopped. As I studied his face, my vision clouding over with tears, the anger I had seen before was slowly being replaced with something softer.

Pain.

I wanted to reach out and hug him, hold him close to me and tell him this was all going to be alright. But he must have sensed something in my eyes for the softness was gone as quickly as it had appeared.

"I'm not going to let you take Kyle from me too, Everly. He's the first man I have felt this way towards since Charlie, and there's no way in hell I'm going to sit here and let you take him from me too."

He had grown serious again. His face was set and his eyes seemed darker than before. I struggled harder now, pain shooting up my arms as the plastic dug deeper into my skin.

It was no use, there was no way I was going to be able to get free.

"What are you going to do?"

It was the words of a victim. Someone who had lost and was slowly accepting his fate. After what happened with Charlie I quickly realised that my brother was capable of bad things. Very bad things, and something in the pit of my stomach was telling me that I was about to find out just how bad.

Hadley crossed over to me and squatted down so he was lower than me and looked up into my tear stained face. Every time he moved I flinched as paranoia and fear took hold of my nervous system. He stared into my eyes, and for the first time in my whole life, I actually felt scared of my own brother.

He pulled out his mobile phone from his back pocket and taking his eyes off me for only a second, punched in a number before holding the phone to his ear. His eyes narrowed as he studied my face trying to gage just how frightened I might actually be. I squeezed my lips together in an attempt to stop them from quivering and forced air deep down into my lungs.

Just as I was about to make another plea to him, I heard someone on the line pick up. I strained my ears to listen, afraid to even breathe. There was noise on the other end, like someone repeating something over and over again. I listened harder, my breath caught in my throat and fresh waves of terror rippling through me. More noise from whoever Hadley had dialed, and yet Hadley was quiet.

He was enjoying this.

He pulled the phone away from his ear and pressed a button before holding the phone out flat in front of him.

"*Hadley? Hadley, what the hell's going on?*" came the voice from the other end of the phone.

It was Kyle.

Instantly I shouted out for dear life, "KYLE!" My voice cracking as the word left my lips, "KYLE, HELP!"

Then Hadley just laughed before taking the phone off speaker and replacing it to his ear. He stood and walked across the room, his voice becoming muffled as he moved away from me. I struggled more feverishly now, rocking the chair back and forth in an attempt to loosen the ties. What was he doing? Why was he calling Kyle? If I could just get a hand free I could put an end to all this.

"This is all your fault," he said into the phone, recommencing his pacing once more all the while keeping an eye fixated on me. "I want you Kyle. I love you, we can still be together…"

I screamed out again, to Kyle, to our neighbours, to anyone who could hear me. As my voice echoed out around the walls of our flat, Hadley crossed over to me once more and delivered a swift slap across my cheek for the second time, silencing me with its force and causing me to cry out as I bit down on the inside of my cheek.

"You hear that Kyle? It's your precious little Everly. If you ever want to see him again you'll get your ass over here."

I wasn't sure what happened next, but the next thing I heard was silence.

# Kyle

As the line went dead, my feet steered me out the door and onto the street. I didn't have time to catch my breath or to even make sense of what was happening. All I knew was that something was wrong and Everly was in trouble.

He sounded wild, feral almost like an animal locked in a cage.

*What the fuck happened? What have I gotten myself into? Could Hadley hurt his own brother?*

I wasn't sure of anything anymore except for that he was angry and that I was the only one who could do something about it. As I sped down the road and along the seafront I scanned the passing cars for a taxi to get me there faster, but there were none in sight. The roads were surprisingly deserted for this time of night. I thought about ringing the police but thought better of it.

*What if I do and they get there first...He wouldn't do anything rash...Would he?*

I rounded a corner and without looking almost crashed full on into an oncoming car. The air was suddenly filled with the sound of a blaring car horn as I pulled myself back onto the pavement, my heart leaping up into my throat.

*Focus, Kyle. Before you get yourself fucking killed.*

I leapt back into action, pushing myself to go faster. This was all my fault. I should never have gotten myself so deep into all this shit. I had no idea what to expect when I got to their flat, but I just prayed I wasn't too late.

\*\*\*

The main door to their building was on the latch when I finally reached it, obviously not having been closed properly by whoever last entered. I climbed the stairs two at a time, taking light swift footsteps and trying to keep the noise down to a minimum. My ears were listening intently for any strange noises, but as I rounded the corner and the door to their flat came into view, all was surprisingly quiet. I stopped for a second and caught my breath. My heart was beating so loudly in my ears I thought I might go deaf from the sound.

Their door was open. Just a crack, and it seemed as though it was dark on the inside. I stilled myself for a moment, unsure as to how to proceed. There wasn't any time to waste, so I carefully inched the door open, hearing it squeel its protest as the wood worked against the hinges. I let it open all the way before I proceeded inside.

Once through the threshold, my eyes adjusted to the darkness of the room. All the lights were off and there were about a dozen little candles lit and spread out all over the room. The flickering light danced wildly as air from the hallway blew through the room gently, making the shadows stretch and shift along the walls.

I immediately thought to the last time I was in this house. Images of that night burned through my mind as I recalled what had happened. My eyes squinted as they adjusted to the dimness of the flat and scanned the room for any sign of movement. At first glance everything appeared normal; the furniture seemed in the proper place and there didn't seem to be anything upturned or out of sorts. Unsure of what I was expecting I began to feel around the room for a light switch to illuminate the scene. Blindly I searched, my fingers feeling around in the dark. When they finally found it, I flicked it up and down a couple of times before realising that the power had obviously been cut.

*For fuck's sake.*

I swallowed the lump in my throat and forced myself to continue deeper into the flat. My skin crawled and my hands shook as I felt like I had entered into a bear cave, constantly feeling like there was something or someone behind me, lurking in the shadows and just waiting to pounce. I should have had a better plan but I didn't think as I left my place. All I could do was think of Everly and how I needed to help. It never occurred to me to have brought something to defend myself. I felt so stupid, so powerless as I felt my way awkwardly into the flat. I wanted to cry and to call out but was terrified that if I did I might give myself away.

Turning the corner from the main hall and into the lounge I stopped myself quickly as my eyes fell upon something in the middle of the room.

There was someone in front of me. Squinting through the candlelight shadows I realised it was Everly. Without thinking I shot over to him. He was sitting in a chair with his hands behind his back. Something was in his mouth, a gag, and I quickly went about untying it.

"Jesus, Everly, what the fuck? Are you alright?"

My hands struggled in the darkness of the room, fumbling at the knotted piece of material that was stuffed in his mouth and tied behind his head.

"Oh Christ, Everly. I came as soon as I could...What the hell happened?"

I couldn't get it undone. The more and more I tried to loosen it, it felt like it was somehow getting tighter. Frustration surged through me, making me fumble further. "I can't...I can't get it untied." I could feel sweat begin to bead itself on my forehead as panic took hold of me. Everly mumbled something incessantly as I worked away at the gag. His muffled cries rising octives as the seconds ticked away.

"I'm hurrying Everly. I can't understand you."

He struggled manicly beneath me, trying to help loosen it from his mouth so he could speak. It felt like minutes passed as I struggled with the knot. My eyes darted around the room, searching the shadows for any movement and watching my back.

Then as if by a miracle, the knot finally loosened and Everly spat the gag from his mouth. Drawing in a huge breath he screamed out.

"BEHIND YOU, watch out!"

But it was too late. I felt it before I saw him. Something metal against the back of my head, hitting my crown with a resounding cracking sound that echoed through my whole body. I swore I saw stars for a second as I fell to my knees like someone had pulled a rug out from beneath me. I wasn't sure if I was standing or even awake at that moment. I was nothing but pain. Seering hot pain from my head to my toes.

Then it happened again, only this time I felt it on my back. Straight across my spine, the same thwacking sound of metal hitting bone. More white heat blurring the world around me and deafening me with its feverishness. Then I could feel coldness on my cheek and after a few seconds my hearing returned and I detected the sound of screams filling the air. High pitched shrieks like from a banshee, screaming my name then someone else's.

It took a few moments before my body delivered the message to my brain that I was on the ground. The coolness of my cheek was the hard linoleum floor against my face. I was face down on the ground.

*Am I dead?*

I couldn't feel my body. I couldn't tell if I was bleeding or if I even had all my limbs attached. My eyes felt closed but even that I couldn't be positive. I kept waiting for something to happen, for the world to start turning again or for some sign that I was still in my own body. But nothing seemed to come. After a while I started to feel like I might actually be dead and I waited for the bright white light to come and take me away. Sadness filled my head as I began to give in to the realisation that I had failed. This was all my fault. If I was dead then Everly soon would be too. How could I have let this happen? I prayed for it all to be over.

But then from out of nowhere I felt something. Hands on my shoulders, yanking me upwards. I could feel my head again, and although I couldn't control it, I could feel it flop forwards, my neck craning against the feeling of being forced upwards. Then there was moaning. Anguished cries of pain filled my ears and it took me another moment to realise that they were coming from me. My eyes were the next thing to focus.

I wasn't dead. I was alive. Pain coursed through my body as the numbness subsided slowly and feeling returned. I bit down on my tongue so hard that I immediately felt the metalic taste of blood fill my mouth. I heard Everly screaming. Rocking back and forth in the chair to which he was tied. Screaming over and over again for Hadley to stop.

It was Hadley who had hit me. His face came into focus in front of my eyes, wild with fury and demonic almost as he yanked me forward so that we were nose to nose. His jaw was clenched so tightly it looked as thought it might break off. We made eye contact for only a split second before he rammed his forehead into my own, cracking himself against my skull and sending me jerking backwards so swiftly I was sure my whole head had snapped clean off. I stumbled backwards again, arms flailing out to the sides desperate for something to break my fall. My vision clouding once more I fell against the hard floor again.

This time I prayed to die as my body screamed out in pain. I couldn't think anymore, my brain felt liquidised from his head bunt and I let it rest on the ground. Inside I felt the rush of surrender take over as my hands and legs let go of all tension and prepared themselves for what was coming. I opened my eyes, just a sliver, enough to see Hadley standing over me. He was holding something in his hands. Something long and slender that caught the light from the candles for a moment making it shine and illuminating its metallic surface.

This was it. I was going to die.

*I'm sorry Everly.*

That was all I could think as I prepared myself for death. All tension disappeared from my body and I welcomed what was coming. It would be an end to the pain that was currently tearing its way through my body. Why wouldn't I just pass out from it? I prayed for it. Wished for it as I watched Hadley, bathed in shadow, raise the metallic object high above his head. He held it there as I watched the expression on his face shift from demonic to calm. Seconds passed and still my whole frame shook with the pain that had taken hold of me.

*Please. Please make it go away.*

I urged him to do it in my mind as time seemed to stand still and images of my life flicked through my mind.

Then something happened. Not the impact I was expecting followed by the relief I was praying for. Instead, in the blink of my eyes, suddenly Hadley was gone. Everything was silent as I opened my eyes again, wider this time, my brain trying to make sense of what I was seeing. There was no one standing above me anymore. Then I heard something drop to the ground just a tiny way off from where I was laying. The ground shook with the thud of the impact, followed by the metallic clanging of something hard being dropped.

Then more silence.

I waited. I listened, straining my ears for anything. Anything at all that might explain what had just happened.

*Get up.*

I willed myself to move. Tried to move my head; lift it off the ground, even turn it sideways to inspect my surroundings. But then I didn't have to. A figure appeared in front of me, leaning over this time, so close to me that I could feel their warm breath upon my face. They were saying something. Something I couldn't quite make out. The words were repeated, over and over again. I listened as my brain tried to make sense of them and translate them into a language I could understand. Slowly they got louder as my ears adjusted and my body came alive again.

Was it Hadley?

Then I saw the blonde hair. Warm and bright, like the sunrise.

*Everly.*

I focused in finally on the beautiful blue hue of his eyes and saw that they were filled with sadness and concern. They searched my face, darting all around it. Then I felt his hands on my skin, running themselves through my hair and cupping my cheek. He was crying. Then I made sense of what he was saying.

"It's over...It's over..." he repeated again and again.

I felt my lips curl up into a smile as he leaned forward and pressed his mouth to mine.

# Hadley

"Do you know where you are?"

The voice came from out of nowhere but seemed like it was all around me. With my eyes so firmly shut, each word muttered created spasms of strange neon colours to dance behind my lids. The silence that followed was deathly.

Each muscle in my body was tensed so tightly that a fire was beginning to snake its way through my veins. Somewhere in my head lay the thought that if I remained perfectly still, then I wouldn't feel. To let myself *feel* right now would be suicide, for I was sure my insides would simply cave in from the pain and no one would ever be able to hear my truth.

The long inhale I heard was a prelude to the words that would follow, and when they came they were louder than before as if spoken through a loudspeaker.

"Do you know who you are?"

Each question was more ridiculous than the last; the answer so obscenely obvious and trite that these questions still did not deserve an acknowledged response. So I remained still and unmoving. The fire in my limbs was growing hotter with each sound and my head was trying so desperately to block it out. If I were to open my eyes right now I was sure I would see that the hairs on my arms had been singed off by the pure white heat coming out of my pores. My body tightened even further, if that were possible, as if trying to fold itself away from this situation.

It was then that I noticed the beating of my heart. It was quieter than I would have expected, but I noticed it anyway. Perhaps it was *because* it was so faint that it drew my attention. After that I couldn't hear anything else. My hearing registered nothing but the slow, faint beating of my heart. In my head I counted the beats as it vibrated delicately against my chest cavity. So slow, it felt like a valley separated them.

1…2..3..4…

"You're in the hospital."

My thoughts were spurred from their trance-like state as the deep voice came once more, his words no more twinged with enquiry, but rather the cold harsh truth.

Two dark pools that were once my eyes finally revealed themselves as my head tilted upwards to face the man before me.

"Hospital?" I asked, my voice a husky whisper. "How'd I get here…"

# Sometime after...

He paused for a moment outside the tall, white-washed building. Shielding his eyes from the blaring sunshine with his hand, he studied the outside structure carefully, taking in the frame and letting his mind imagine what the inside looked like. He wore a long, dark trench coat despite the unusually warm temperatures for the time of year. His blonde hair was slicked back and the collar of his coat flipped up so as to hide his face as much as possible. He watched as smart, business type people came and went, their heads low as if deliberately trying to avoid making eye contact. The revolving door seemed to move constantly with the passing traffic, allowing muffled voices to escape every time it was opened to the outside world.

He stole a glance behind him and inspected the car park he had just crossed, but nothing seemed out of the ordinary. With a deep breath to steady his nerves he crossed through the threshold.

Inside, it smelled appropriately of hospital. Nurses and orderlies rushed past without taking much notice of the beautiful stranger who had just entered the building. Empty gurnies lined the hallways beyond the double doors to his left and the beeping sound of life support systems echoed loudly all around him.

Approaching the nurse's station, the young nurse seated at the computer raised her head and did a double-take as she took in his appearance. She was ginger haired with a plump face full of freckles that were speckled around her nose and cheek bones. Her navy blue uniform was a little too snug, hugging her in all the wrong places and making her seem perhaps more overweight than she was. When he piled his hands neatly on the counter, she opened her mouth to speak but then hesitated, suddenly looking full of nerves.

All he had to do was flash her that million dollar smile and she seemed to instantly relax.

"Hadley Stone's room, please?" he asked in a milky tone that seemed to wash over the young nurse causing her eyes to flutter.

She seemed caught up in his icy blue gaze as if she could see her own reflection in the irises of his eyes. She gave a quick shake of her ginger curls to steel herself out of her little dream world before responding.

"Hi, yes…Of course, I'm sorry…You just…"

She didn't need to finish her sentence, he knew what she was going to say and simply smiled politely as a response. She tapped something into computer before her, her eyes moving slowly down the screen and her lips mouthing something he couldn't understand.

"Right, let's see…Hadley Stone is in room…315. Shall I get someone to show you up?"

But he was already on his way to the lift as she finished her sentence, waving a hand dismissively behind him as he went.

\*\*\*

Everly stared at room 315 expectantly from down the hall. A rent-a-cop guard was sat in a fold-up chair outside the room, reading a magazine and looking bored as he flipped carelessly through the pages. As he approached the guard, his hands tucked neatly into the pockets of his trench, the guard looked up with wide eyes. Everly stopped and held the guard's stare in his own, a polite smile upon his lips.

"Uhh, I'm afraid visiting hours are over, sir," the guard stuttered nervously as he stood letting the magazine fall to the chair.

"I'm family," he replied curtly.

The guard studied his face, obviously caught by surprise.

"Yes, but he's resting…Doctor's told me-"

"I'm family," he said again reaching for the doorknob without waiting for him to move away, "and he's requested to see me anyway."

Inside the room the scent of bleach was intense and burned his nostrils as he shut the door behind him, leaving the guard powerless and gaping outside the room. Everly paused once inside and took in the pitiful sight of his identical twin lying on the bed in the center of the room.

The sight was almost too sad to look at.

"How the mighty have fallen," he breathed as he crossed the room unbuttoning his coat in a series of swift, easy movements. Hadley's black hair was a tangled mess upon his head. His usually tanned skin looked pale and blotchy in the fluorescent lighting from above. His eyes looked sunken and the skin on his face, drawn as if he hadn't eaten or drank anything in days. Around the better part of his head was wrapped a white bandage, fastened with surgical tape and a hospital band branded his right wrist.

His stare was vacant as he focused on the visitor who had just entered his room, but his lips parted and formed a word that came out a choked whisper, lingering in the air for a moment before disappearing forever.

"Everly," he whispered.

Hadley appeared too weak or perhaps not bothered enough to try moving. Instead he simply stared straight ahead, his expression screaming defeat as his brother crossed the room and lowered himself into the chair by the bed. He let out a deep sigh and allowed his eyes to flicker from Hadley to the open window to the right.

"At least you've got a nice view," he said, laughing at his own little joke. Hadley didn't stir, but his eyes never left his brother's. "Oh Hadley, Hadley...Look what's become of you."

He let his eyes wash over him, a look of pity and loathing on his face.

"I really, really want to say 'I told you so', but I feel that if I did I wouldn't get the reaction I'm so desperate for."

He was grinning ear to ear deviously as if he knew something Hadley didn't. "You always hated hospitals…I guess we both did. For me it was always the smell. What about you?"

Everly waited for the response he knew would never come.

"Kind of ironic, I suppose isn't it? Considering that at the rate you're going, you'll probably never *leave* the hospital now."

Everly stood again and crossed to the window, folding his arms and surveying the traffic below as he spoke.

"I wanted to come and say 'goodbye'," he flicked his head back to his brother to gage his reaction. And even in his sedated state, Everly could see his brother's eyes enlargen at this news.

"Kyle and I are moving away. To London. He's got a new job there and I thought it was time for a fresh start, you know? Somewhere where the infamous Stone family isn't so well known. Don't get me wrong, I'll miss Brighton, but after this…I just feel like I need to start over."

Everly looked up at the sky, inspecting the clouds as they passed.

"I'm so sorry Hadley…For everything. I'm so sorry that it all had to end this way. You see, you were right after all…You were right about everything."

Hadley turned his head imploringly. He was definitely listening now.

"I *was* jealous of you. Always have been. You see, I may have had the brains out of the two of us, but growing up…You were right, I was always jealous of your…Your *charisma*. After all, you were the popular one of the two of us. You always had the most friends…The most boyfriends…"

He paused for a moment, reflecting on his own words.

"You know what's funny? I used to go to bed at night wishing that I could be more like you; popular, confident, sexy…And what do you know? Now I am!"

Everly threw his hands up in an exaggerated gesture.

"All it took was to get you out of the picture…And now…It's my turn to shine."

His voice got quieter as he turned back to the window, shifting his weight from one foot to the other.

"You know who I was thinking of just this morning?" he paused expectantly, looking over his shoulder at his brother. "James…You remember him?"

Hadley's whole body twitched at the mention of the name.

"James, James, James…poor thing, eh? That feels like a million years ago, doesn't it? Do you remember that time when you guys caught me playing in my room with a doll? He was so fucking mean to me about the whole thing…And you…You never did a thing to help me…"

He swallowed in an attempt to compose himself.

"I was so jealous of what you two had. You guys used to leave me out of everything, you were always off doing your own thing. It was the first time in our lives that you chose someone else over me."

Hadley was rigid now, lucid yet completely tense as he listened to his brother speak.

"It's such a shitty feeling being an outsider. That day on the cliff top…I remember that like it was yesterday. Why the fuck would he want to climb down the cliff?"

Everly wiped his eyes with the back of his hand.

"I remember so vividly watching James climb over the fence, getting ready to climb down…I remember thinking about it before it happened. I saw myself do it before it actually happened. I was so angry at him…and at you. I felt so on the outside…And then you turned your head for a second and it was like I couldn't stop myself from pushing him off…"

A single tear slipped down Hadley's own face as he listened helplessly to his brother's revelations.

"Everyone believed me when I told them that he fell. Why wouldn't they?"

Hadley felt like there was a vice gripping his chest making it almost impossible for him to draw a breath in as he listened.

"You see Hadley? It was your fault James died. I may have pushed him, but if you hadn't been such a shit to me…Then…"

His voice trailed off, as he turned back to face his brother, his back resting against the far wall of the room.

"I've been covering for you my whole life…And you never seem to get that, do you? I mean all throughout school…Everytime you fucked up…Who was there to help you pick up the pieces?" he asked rhetorically. "You never thanked me. Not once. Always too wrapped up in your own life to see that I was always there for you," he started biting his nail, like he was having a casual conversation with a girlfriend. "Nothing ever changes with you does it? It's just like what happened with Charlie…"

Hadley was willing himself to move now. Thousands of thoughts running through his head; if he could move he was afraid that he might kill his brother right then and there as he anticipated what was about to come next.

"When Charlie cheated, who was there to help?" He asked again, patting himself on the chest for emphasis. "Once again…when you were hurt, I was there. I helped you. I took care of that little cheating piece of shit. When I saw him with that little fucker Dale, that day in the coffee shop, I knew I had to protect you. I knew it was my job to make sure that he didn't get away with it."

Hadley mouthed something that looked like '*you*' to his brother, to which Everly just smiled and nodded.

"I mean come on, no one was gonna miss that piece of shit 'Dale.' I knew I had to do something to make sure he never hurt someone else again like he hurt you."

Hadley coughed, desperation creeping in. He choked out another cough and spoke for the first time, his words coming out a woozy slur. "What did you do…" he whispered.

Everly looked surprised that his brother could actually speak for a moment. "I took care of it Had…Just like I always do. How could I just sit back and let someone hurt you like that? But you never even thanked me…I got rid of him and you never even thanked me…" He said shaking his head.

"Everly…" Hadley muttered, his eyes squeezing themselves shut as the sheer weight of his words came crashing down on him.

"I've been taking care of this family since the day I was born…Dale was simply a pawn that needed to be eliminated for us to continue to thrive."

Everly's voice was as steady as ever. Stern and direct, stating facts matter-of-factly. His stance was dripping with authority as he delivered truth after truth, shedding light on mysteries that had haunted their family for years. Hadley could do nothing but let the meaning of his words sink in, hitting him in wave after wave and causing his heart to cry out in mournful tones.

For so many years he had blamed himself. James. Charlie. All of this was because of Everly. And now there was nothing he could do about it.

Everly pushed himself off of the wall and sat down on the edge of the hospital bed, crossing his legs as if meeting a friend for tea.

"You see Hadley…I was always destined to be in the limelight…And now I can finally stop fighting for it," he breathed a sigh of contempt, obviously happy with himself. "I used to think that we could share it. You and me. Identical in so many ways, yet polar opposites in others. You're so predictable; I knew that you'd snap if I pushed you far enough…After the night of the party, it all became clear…How I'd finally get you out of the picture, that is. It was so fucking perfect. All you needed was a little push and then you did all the work for me. And I'm going to finally get my happy ending. Me and Kyle. The way it was meant to be. There was no way I'd let you win this one."

He smiled down at his brother, but there was nothing warm about his smile. It was dark and full of malicious intent. The sort of smile that Hadley himself was known for. The kind he was used to giving right before he shattered an innocent's dreams. And now it was being mirrored right back at him by the one person in the world who he never thought would betray him.

His twin.

"I am sorry it had to happen this way, though. I really do hope you can find it in your heart...Some day...Some how...To forgive me...After all, Kyle really is too good for you anyway."

And with that he leaned down towards his brother, pausing when their faces were a mere inch apart, lips lined up perfectly and each's eyes burning into the others. Then as if it were the most natural thing in the world, he lowered his head and placed his lips ever so gently on Hadley's.

It was a kiss that was weighted with goodbye and ripe with deceit.

Everly lifted his head, keeping his eyes firmly focused on Hadley's. Brother to brother. Born of the same life. Identical, and just as cold, destructive and twisted as the other. He stood and turned his back on his other half and strode towards the doorway, leaving Hadley seething and powerless.

But just before he opened the door to leave, he turned his head to face his twin one last time.

"Goodbye Hadley," he taunted condescendingly, "you're over."

And with that, he turned and left.

# About the Author

Joey Jameson lives in Brighton, UK; a world of decadence, glamour and intrigue. He believes life is better when drizzled with naughtiness and drenched in layer upon layer of sparkling glitter. His work is best appreciated with a hard drink and the lights down low and will leave you wondering just what goes on in his twisted little mind.

He is the author of "Candy from Strangers", "Blackout" and the recently released short "Interview with the Porn Star." Keep your eyes peeled for more titilating adventures that are yet to come.

For more on Joey, please visit www.chancespress.com or visit his Facebook page at https://www.facebook.com/joeyjamesonauthor.